REMEMBER TO BREATHE

A NOVEL BY

SIMON PONT

www.u1_____.com

First published in Great Britain in 2012
by Urbane Publications Ltd
20 St Nicholas Gardens, Rochester
Kent ME2 3NT

A CIP catalogue record for this book
is available from the British Library.

ISBN 978-1-909273-00-9

Typeset at Chandler Book Design, King's Lynn, Norfolk
Printed in Great Britain by Ashford Colour Press Ltd.

www.urbanepublications.com

To Marjorie, with love.

ACKNOWLEDGEMENTS

To all of the following, without whom, no book and no me.

To the authors, personal favourites, massive influences: Norman Mailer, Ian Fleming, Len Deighton, Robert Ludlum, Carl Hiassen, Stephen King, Martin Amis, Bret Easton Ellis, Jay McInerney, Hunter S. Thompson, George Orwell, Graham Greene, S.E Hinton, William Goldman, Alex Garland, Douglas Coupland, Iain Banks, Frank O'Connor, Anthony Burgess. If you want to learn how to write, keep reading, and read all of the above.

To the archetypes, who capture our imagination, channel their time, and feel as real as anyone I've ever met; to the likes of Bridget Jones, Adrian Mole, John Self, Sherman McCoy, Patrick Bateman, Walter Mitty, Arthur Seaton and Alfie, thank-you. Samuel Grant owes you a whole heap.

To Matthew Smith of **Urbane Publications**, for buying into me, and figuring *Remember to Breathe* was a leap of faith worth taking.

To Andy Day, for acing the cover, because you should be able to tell a book at least a little bit by its cover.

To Spotify and LoveFilm, for granting Samuel a genius playlist, and damn fine movie collection.

To Alison, for her cast-iron belief in me.

To GP & TP, for everything.

REMEMBER TO BREATHE

A Novel

Simon Pont

"*Operationally, God is beginning to resemble not a ruler but the last fading smile of a cosmic Cheshire cat.*"

Sir Julian Huxley

"*The more you scream, the faster we go.*"

**Toilet Cubicle, the Gents,
Ground Floor Bar, Notting Hill**

PROLOGUE

EVERY STORY that you could ever tell has already been told. At least, that's what they say. Some go further, suggest whether rattling away at a keyboard, sitting round a campfire or up-lighting your face with a torch from inside a tent, there are only a certain number of stories you ever could tell. Some say 4, others 8. A Russian by the name Vladimir Propp (hell of a good name) weighed in with 31. 31 story units (*Naratemes*, as they're called), and there's nothing beyond that, except repetition.

Well, I never said I was going to be original. Though I will say, when you live it, it surely feels original enough; like you're the one leaving that first set of boot prints on the moon. 4, 8, 31, I say: whatever, they're just numbers. Numbers aside, these are the words, which is all else we have to go on.

Samuel Grant, London

OCTOBER

Friday, October 15th, 1999

Not a great place to start

My name is Samuel Grant and today is my birthday. My friends call me Sam and this birthday of mine is my 27th, though I have not been spending it in the company of friends. The majority of the day has been spent under two duvets, in the company of a hot water bottle and my mother bringing me glass tumblers of water and aspirin to keep down my temperature.

I have flu.

My doctor, where I rose from my deathbed to pay a visit earlier this morning, rewarded my efforts by defining the symptoms of my current suffering as "flu-like". Symptoms… *like* flu. This spells flu in my medical book, but obviously not my GP's, and besides, I didn't spend 5 years studying medicine and terrible penmanship. (I got a degree in psychology, which equipped me with an understanding of nothing. My handwriting remains however quite neat.)

But what is all this business of *like* flu? Like, learn a little exactitude, stop being so goddamn non-committal; tell it like it is. Birthday Flu, that's what I've got.

While Birthday Flu is, in my unqualified opinion, a touch unlucky, I didn't visit my doc for sympathy, or to confirm my flu-like symptoms.

Oh yes, it gets better.

I woke up this morning, shivering in a t-shirt and bed-linen-wrap, flushed with flu-like sweat, but not too distracted to discover what medically can be very *exactly* described as a boil (unless a third, non-scrotally located testicle?) growing on the inside of my left thigh. To go with my 27th birthday: my first boil, and a belter at that.

Fast forward to the doctor's surgery, I dropped my trousers at the appropriate invitation, brandishing my boil and earning the comment: "Around the groin." This, "Around the groin," my GP, Dr Jane Walker then proceeded to write in my file. Dropping my slacks had been a point of issue, but the matter of demarcation was of considerably greater concern. This was, after all, my permanent medical record.

"Quite high up the thigh," I gladly conceded. "Not really… groinal, do you think?"

It was too late. The ink was dry. "Groinal boil." That's what she'd written.

"So, antibiotics, or can we just stab it here and now?," I asked, trying to sound brave and decisive.

"It's not come to a head yet," the good doctor informed me.

Ironic; it was practically the size of a person's head in its own right.

"It may well just go down with antibiotics, or just come to a head and pop."

"No Third Scenario then?" I prompted. "It might not decide to make friends, then turn nasty and later try and take over the Earth?"

I was smiling; I was trying to be charming. Inside: I grimaced, feeling wave after wave of self-loathing crash into me.

Dr Walker said nothing.

"In the event of a Pompeii," I asked, "can you prescribe something that allows me to be in a different postcode?"

"Sam, if that boil gets any bigger, you will be."

*

Why the boil? Fate, chance, divine intervention? In truth: none of the above. The truth is much less metaphysical. The Boil is self-inflicted. You see, of late, I've run myself down. A diet worth shit, a metabolism and body-clock shot to pieces, late nights and early mornings drinking gin and or scotch (never in the same glass at least) in Soho bars, sweating, dancing, and fast-sucking on cigarettes like they were the candy kind you used to get as a kid for a penny a time, back in the days before political correctness, when tooth decay and lung cancer weren't such a big drama.

And why such behaviour? Well, just over 3 months ago, 3 months, 3 weeks, 1 day, if you want the kind of specifics in which my GP doesn't trade, my girlfriend and I broke up.

If I was aggressively and expertly cross-examined by the finest barrister in the land, at the peak of his game, I may just concede that my girlfriend dumped me. Move on, 3 months, 3 weeks, and 1 day (let's not forget that 1 day now!), and I'm celebrating my birthday, shivering, cold from some Crazy Jazzman Sweats, and while I remain Single & Alone, I now keep the company of a Not-Quite-Groinal Boil.

Not Fair

So…

…this doesn't feel fair, and nor is it much fun.

I'm no longer talking about the boil.

I'm talking about the Other Thing, and the thing of it is, no one tells you about it, shares any knowledge, gives any prior warning.

Then it happens to you.

And when it's happened you're on the inside, part of this Secret Society. Only it's Not So Secret. Every other fucker of a certain age is pretty much a member. Everyone's part of the Broken Hearts Club. And it's… "No Biggie". Everyone's all, *"No, it's not very nice is it? Bit of a bummer, that's a fact. But, it'll get better. It won't feel this bad again. You don't let it. And anyway, what about that Earthquake in Sao Paulo? How many hundred thousand dead? You see, it could be worse."*

My girlfriend and I, we finished. We're over. Fini. Kaput, nada, pick one, or take 'em all. I don't care. Shouldn't be a big deal, because I know it happens all the time, to all sorts of people, but… Well, for one: it's *not nice.* For two: it's a slowly inhaled world of misery, pain, blame, recrimination and gnawing, stomach-heaving sadness. I've dealt with other life experiences better; better than this.

My head is a rage. Every waking moment, thinking about just one person, the *Why's?* and *If only's!*, then the brief sleeping moments, dreamtime showing little sympathy, even my dreams annoyed that maybe they don't have my full attention, me being tired and all. I have no escape, no chicken-switch. Get drunk, smoke fags like it's The Last Night on Earth, and briefly, the edge is off, but not for long. Not for long enough. Not unless you completely break down, give in to it, try and erase yourself. And to establish what? That you hurt? That you feel "bad"? Bit indulgent, don't you think?

No one explains "relationships," not really. There's lots of talk, lots of words used, spoken, books written, songs sung, but no one really *explains* it through, the inexactness and fragility of it all. Maybe I just haven't been listening? Though I'm pretty sure no one explained the *feelings* bit: the how you will "feel," how you should feel, what and when you'll feel it, in the Before, During and oh yes there will be an After of it.

Am I making sense, or am I sounding like a loon? I put it down to my temperature of 104; or maybe it's the boil talking?

My Mum & Dad

My Mother is presently In Conflict.

My Mother doesn't like to see me unhappy (whose Mother does?), BUT she also hated Sarah, meaning Mum is unhappy in that I am unhappy, but she's quite openly delighted at the circumstances which have prompted my current unhappiness.

Mum hated Sarah; hated her in what can only be fairly described as a really deep-seated way. We're talking fundamental, ancient civilisation born, ideological clash kind of hatred.

It's always going to be easier when *the rents*, your parents, back the lass you're seeing, the relationship you're having. With Sarah, there was No Backing. I'm talking zero endorsement from the Matriarchal Corner. I always thought it better Sarah didn't turn her back on Mum, just in case Mum saw an opportunity and went in with a blade.

My Mum made it abundantly obvious (without events ever culminating in a knife fight) how she felt about Sarah.

Sarah "was not good enough". According to my Ma, I could do so much better. Sarah was not supportive enough; would always be a bane, a drain, a pain, keep the rhyme going if you like.

My Mum thinks I should be going out with a Movie Star; a Movie Star who, should I request it, be willing to sacrifice everything for me. You know, that self-sacrificing Movie Star-type you meet in bars all the time? And Miss Oh-so-Right would obviously have to be smart, compassionate, tender, and very funny; ideally a sex kitten but demure on command Movie Star-type. No run-of-the-Mill Movie Star for my boy, that's what my Mum would say. And you know what? I could be stepping out with all of that on my arm, and my Mum would worry that I'd be seeing someone who just couldn't be all-perfect. She'd worry about the imperfections she didn't see but suspiciously feared must exist: "She seems so perfect. Do you think she smokes crack??"

My favourite line? My Mum once described Sarah as "a defect". Believe it!

"Mum," I said, "You can't call my girlfriend of the last 2 and a half years a *defect*!" Mum simply added: "Sarah was a defect we all just overlooked, so that everyone else could carry on happily and nothing was too affected".

You can't answer thinking like that. There's no recourse, just stunned silence.

To be fair, my Dad was never a problem when it came to Sarah and I. For one, he never suggested Sarah was a walking, breathing problem that everyone was working hard to overlook.

Sure, Dad was not a raving fan of Sarah's, but with the wisdom of Yoda, he sat back and let events play themselves out. I asked Dad what he thought about Sarah and I breaking up. Dad said it really wasn't his business who I went out with, but in truth, he wasn't surprised that events had culminated the way they had. "People have to pull together," he'd said.

About 2 years earlier, when Sarah and I were about to move in together, he asked if he could have a "quick word".

"Sam, can I have a quick word?" Dad asked.

"Sure," I'd said.

Mum had been spinning out to him, wigging out over my flat-sharing plans. Dad had said: "Your Mother tells me you're thinking of letting Sarah move into your place in London?"

"Yes, Dad," I'd said at the time.

"Now it's none of my business who you do and don't live with, okay?"

"Okay," I'd agreed.

"All I'd like to say on it is this…"

There had followed a pause, I don't think because my old Man is a natural dramatist, but maybe he is, because the result was much the same.

Post-pause, my Dad then said: "The further you go down a road, the further you have to walk back."

Then: another pause, following which I expected more, much more, but then Dad just smiled, kindly, lovingly, fatherly, and finished with, "That's all I want to say."

That's it?, I thought. *The further you go down a road, the further you have to walk back?* Was my Dad having sessions with the Dalai Lama or something?

But you know what? My old Man, he knew what he was saying. My walk back's proving a walk and a half, a real true blue bastard of a hike, a goddamn odyssey no less.

My Dad: fucking Yoda sometimes.

Back to London

My temperature appears to be dipping, though I have no encouraging news on the boil. Either way, I realise I have to rally myself, call a halt to this regressive back-to-the-parents behaviour and return to my flat in London. I have no car, having always used Sarah's, so I'm bizarrely forced to take a train into Paddington. The journey will take an hour without delays, but delays are inevitable.

The entire experience is miserable, but was only ever going to be. Public transport sucks: in the train carriage, multiple and some quite Hypnotically Extreme Body Odours, students, the elderly, discarded chewing gum and all manner of general grime.

The October weather has created the ultimate amplification. The kind of severe grey-wet day when the very thought of Summer, of fluffy white clouds and dreamy powder-blue skies feels like a surrealist's peevish joke.

Tonight, TV weather men will no doubt don cheerful smiles and garish ties to compensate for their delivery of dismal forecasts, of how Mother Earth will tomorrow be again dressing in her dullest, drabbest frock.

The sky has spat ceaselessly since breakfast and I wonder just where all the colour has gone? I wonder whether anyone else has bothered to ask? As the train rolls by, platforms, people, buildings, streets, fields, all the same it seems: all the texture and hue of well-worn and over-washed bed linen. There is no clarity to anything.

Once at Paddington station, I join the taxi rank then take my cab to Notting Hill. I pass a hand over the condensation and grime on the inside of the cab's window, only to realise there's nothing to rub away.

The weather is nearly as bleak as my mood and I realise, this has to change, I have to break this downward spiral.

In My Sitting Room

Four turned keys and a standard 4 sequence pin to deactivate the burglar alarm later, and I'm in the flat. It's 5.30pm on a Saturday and there is silence. The silence is of a kind that is sometimes punctuated in films by a dripping tap, though none of my taps drip, so I'm not granted the distraction. The silence is all-embracing.

My back to the front door, I look around the sitting room.

I have an *Arco* light, very dramatic, very much an acquired taste, too Bold- 60's for some. The Arco's a floor light, designed in 1962 by Achille Castiglioni, and makes for a kind of off-centre centre piece. Journeying across a good portion of the room, the light's metal arm arcs (yep, hence the name) down to a solid Carrara marble base, which stands in the corner. The head of the light casts a high-visibility pool for reading when I sit in my *Barcelona chair*.

The Barcelona chair (as designed by Modernist Big Daddy Ludwig Mies van der Rohe for the World Exhibition in Barcelona in 1929) came in a choice of aniline leathers and left me torn between black or white. I finally went with white, succumbing to the full Porn King Den effect.

The chair is accompanied by a matching footstool, which was irritatingly sold separately, but which I bought at the same time. The footstool cost me an extra £600, which upset me greatly then, but the upset has thinned with time. With or without footstool, it is impossible to slouch in, which is why Sarah disliked it so much.

For an Alternative Seating Experience, there's my *Hobby* two-seat sofa. Also "Contentiously Comfortable', but more importantly designed by Paolo Passerini, it is ideal for "The Modern Home". In the literature that accompanied the sofa (lifestyle-identification bullshit), there was some speculation as to whether the sofa's minimalist design was inspired by the fashion houses on Via Montenapoleone (the fashion district of Milan). On this point, I wouldn't care to comment. While the sofa (like the chair) was "available in a variety of leathers," I chose grey leather, which tonally matches the grey casing of my 32" *Sony Wega* Widescreen TV.

For me, the real centre-point of the room is the *Konx* coffee table, by Ron Arad. In any description you may care to read of it, "stunning" is used. Only the legs are metal (satin-finished) but the top looks like it's made of manipulated mercury. It is in fact glass, with a kind of silver effect infusion.

I look around the sitting room of my flat and I feel Utterly Isolated and Growingly Nauseous. My sitting room is a tour in branded acquisition, certainly revealing that the occupant has read The Right Magazines. The possible inference is "Style-Brand Lifestyle," but ultimately I think, the whole look screams: Wanker.

Her Stuff

I hated her chattels. You know, her *Stuff*: the things she had around her, that I guess were representative of her. I know that sounds harsh. But honestly, the vast majority, it was… *Really Shit Kit*. I wanted to surround us with… *Good Gear*. Good Gear, as I saw it at least. You know, stuff in chrome? Branded stuff. The *right* brands, the *right look*. Materials, just materials, but it all seemed so important at the time. While I ask myself now, *Was it important?*, I already know the answer.

It was just a preference (to have a Super-Cool Pad) but not an important one. It was a preference that just got carried away with itself, becoming enough to make a big difference and help cause a very big rift. It was all actually very immaterial, stressing about all those materials, but boy, how we'd row about bathroom cabinets crammed with make-up, a wardrobe chocker with discarded clothes, dresser drawers full of "bits," odds, sods, broken CD cases, candles burnt down to a millimeter of wick. This I would have found acceptable a decade ago, say the chattels of a schoolgirl, but I found it absolutely turd a decade on. Infuriating. And now it's all gone, all that stuff of hers, and the flat is bare, and now I ask myself: How is it better?

Solitude, I Say No

I turn on the TV, go to MTV, Madonna in a full yester-decade moment, telling the world she's at least *like* a virgin. Madonna is no company; it's just noise *within* the vacuum.

I don't like being on my own. I'm no Robinson Crusoe. Me, myself, a desert island and just my own sand tracks, I'd go stir crazy. I'm a private person, and I'm selective over who I'll let be my friend, but I'm more comfortable "in-company". It's not that I don't like myself – be silent in your chair all you armchair psychologists! – just that I like to chat. I find chatting with myself just a bit self-defeating. I know myself well enough to know what my response is to any given question I may ask. I always find the joy of asking a question is because you don't know the answer.

My point of view: A moment is only truly great if it's a moment shared. The whole Meditation-thing may say otherwise, but I reckon meditation is for the birds. Go find that higher plain, cool with me, but if it is so great, why feel the need to come back down from it and tell me how great you feel because you managed to sit quiet long enough to get there? Solitude can afford great moments of clarity and insight – the word here is introspection, I guess – but ultimately, even after such inspections, you still want to tell others about them. Hey, it's just my opinion, but it's why I'm telling you. My opinion is: People don't keep things to themselves. They like to talk about it.

As If On Cue

Still Saturday night, still in the flat, I turn off Madonna, and again, silence all around me, circling me, ready for the kill. My mobile rings and I jump, actually jump, startled by my own ring tone. It's Sean, he's down the road on Portobello market, wondered if I was back in town, suggests a pint. Salvation.

Inside of ten minutes later: pint in hand, a comfortable slouch on shot-through chesterfields, Sean, and whatever the aggregated noun would be for a fair size gathering of Trustafarian-come-Boho-types warming up for a Saturday night in W11.

Tuna

"How was last night?"

"OK," Sean replies, then sips at his pint.

"OK?"

"Yes Sam, it was OK."

"Just OK?" I'm curious already. There's more to Sean's two OK's than just "OK".

"How OK?" I persist, suggesting: "She was OK, it was OK, what – by commonly used descriptors – about your Friday Night Date was just OK?"

"Jesus – a fucking inquisition! The evening was fine, pleasant, agreeable, OK?"

"Oh, I see, that kind of OK. Sounds like a fucking riot."

"No Sam, it was not a riot. It was just, as I have tried to explain, OK. *OK?*"

There is a pause. I look at Sean, Sean looks back at me.

For the mental picture, Sean is 26, good looking, has premature flecks of silver (as he calls them) or premature grey (as the rest of the world would describe them) at his temples. The hair gives him a certain Captain Fantastic look which girls seem to find attractive. If I was a girl, I'd find him a bit short.

"So what went wrong?" I finally ask, eyebrow raising, smirk forming.

Another beat passes then Sean returns the smirk, but furrows the brow.

"She tasted of fish," he explains.

An unexpected explanation, I have to admit. "I'm sorry? What? Fish?"

"What can I say? Hardly my fault, but impossible to overlook: The girl, she tasted of tuna."

"*Tuna?*," I repeat.

"Tuna," he repeats.

"Are you just being cruel?"

"No, neither cruel nor fishy, I'm being absolutely serious. The evening went well, and when we got to her doorstep I was feeling quite affectionate towards her."

"Affectionate in the *Do I or don't I have a condom in my wallet sense* of the word?"

"Yes – I had after all just treated her to dinner; turned out to be a shocking investment."

"So, what happened?"

Sean gives it shape: "I'm at the doorstep. We both remark what a lovely evening we've just had, yardy-yardy-yar, I move in to kiss her, she reciprocates, a classic 6-former end-of-date kind of scene, and then – WHAM – Welcome to Mr Fishy's Fantastic World of TUNA!"

"So the girl tasted of tuna?" I manage in monotone, still not really getting this whole tuna thing.

"That's right," Sean confirms.

"Well, you did take her out to eat, you had been sitting across from her when she ordered or at least ate? The introduction of tuna at the doorstep point of the evening must have been kind of expected?"

"I don't think you quite grasp the magnitude of what I'm trying to say. Yes, we went out. For *pizza*. Pizza without so much as a *Friends of the Sea* topping in sight; she ordered goats cheese and jalapeno peppers, said it was the first thing she'd eaten all day. So, do you see?"

"OhMyGod!" Light dawns – it's more than just a case of rookie ordering.

"God," Sean suggests, "may have a lot to answer for on this one. The girl, *by design*, tasted of tuna. Perhaps I'd entertain phoning her again if I had fewer date-options than JoJo the Dog-faced Boy, but as it is, I'm going to be screening my calls for the next few weeks.

"Anyway Sam, on a different tact, you look like shit; dare I ask how you're holding up?"

Heart on a Stick

How am I holding up?

"Let's just say the Girl–Boy dichotomy deal continues to trouble me," I say. "I'm no clearer to understanding why girls are the way they are."

"I'm surprised you're even trying," replies Sean. "I take it you haven't heard from her?"

"Absolutely not."

"Well, Sarah's moved on, which is what you should be doing."

"Which is exactly my point: How the hell is it that they're made that way? Girls, how come, so much fucking stronger, hearts of fucking wrought fucking iron?"

"Fuck knows?," is Sean's reply.

"You'll have to do better than *"Fuck knows"* if you want me to get the next round."

"Well maybe they've made an evolutionary step blokes haven't yet sussed? They live longer after all."

"Like they don't have enough of a head start!," I appeal. "The fact women have breasts already slopes the playing field ever so in their favour! I tell you, once my flux capacitor's up-and-running, I fancy burning some back-in-time rubber and introducing some suffragettes to a little De Lorean grill."

"You must be running a fever if you're referencing *Back to the Future*. Shall I continue?"

"Please do, it was just the boil talking."

Sean returns to his point: "And if not evolutionary, the whole hearts of iron thing could be genetically imprinted, programmed in from the very beginning?"

Me: "You're saying, take it right back – blokes on the one hand, good-natured, supportive hunter-gatherers;

women on the other, cold-hearted, manipulative, closed-minded bitches?"

"But not at least averse to being dragged into the occasional cave and shown some etchings. I think though Sam that you're present thinking could be a little clouded?"

"Duly influenced more like: let's just say it feels like Sarah has ripped out my heart and taken to touring it round the country on a big stick."

"Curious role reversal; how very hunter-gatherer of her," Sean suggests, "but also possibly a bit melodramatic Sam? Sarah is hardly William Wallace."

"Better legs," I concur, "but I hear she's just submitted 'Bloody Heart on Big Stick' as a coming attraction to the Saatchi Gallery."

"Did I read something about that in *Time Out*? Anyway, enough of this; Dude, I think we should get very drunk now."

Not So Easy Sunday Morning

Oh bugger. Oh bugger-blast-buggeration. Water turmoil - and unsurprisingly, self-induced water turmoil.

"Morning Afters" are seldom pleasant. The pressing urgency to pee and the really rather desperate urgency to re-hydrate are as consistent as they are cause for alarm. Efforts to down a pint of water have met with even less success than those to urinate accurately. In each case, direction has been a Great Disappointment; the first gulp of water triggering what need only be described as a cough-come-splutter, forcing the contents of my mouth to exit through my nose (impressive, I think) and bringing about a never-before-experienced torso-twist (unpleasant) which re-distributed a good half pint of what may be detailed as "icy tap water" over my groin. Hence: water turmoil.

I'm charting out whole new frontiers of fuck-wittery. My slouch pants now have a second unpleasantly sodden patch – the water at the groin lacking immediate distinction from the smattered urine zone down the left leg.

Classy.

Okay, not classy. Added to which, something has broken in my head. Whether a temporary feature or a disability now to blight me for all and any life I have yet to come, I neither know nor care to consider. I don't want to think about it, because in truth, my lager-marinated brain-pan is too clogged to demonstrate capacity for thought. What a malicious little fucker of a quite titanic hangover this is.

Bloody Mr-Saturday-Night-Sean; Bloody-Lets-Get-Drunk-You'll-Feel-Better-What-Flu? Sean. Sean's fault.

In truth, it was the tequila that did it.

Tequila can be like that. Correction, tequila is always like that. Tequila is spiteful; tequila is two-faced – sweet as pie when you're saying hi, paying your monies and throwing 'em back, but nasty in a metal fangs kind of way when last night's fun-lovin' fast-forwards into next day's buggering regret. I tell you now, Tequila is unwise.

I managed to vomit four times, equal(ish) amounts at evenly spaced intervals on the 15-minute return walk to my front door.

At what I believe was around three o'clock this Sunday morning, I must have formed a rather crumpled silhouette, weaving homeward, vomiting in measured amounts, not a scary shadow in the city night, just an oblivious piss artist relying on auto-pilot to re-unite him with his bed.

To my neighbours, and anyone who may have witnessed

the aforementioned: My Apologies.

Like I said, it was the Tequila. All 8 of them.

When I build sufficient courage to confront day-light, and find my shades, I may examine the vomit trail as I take a little walk to the newsagent's. I suspect last night's (more accurately "this morning's") Chicken Jalfrezi will still be in much undigested evidence. (*"Hey, let's go for a curry?"* Bloody Sean). Portions of hardly digested Peshawari Naan will lead me to the newsagent's, the presence of sultana confirming my ownership.

I don't think it clever to share this vomitous episode with you. You probably think I should be more embarrassed. Truth is, I am embarrassed, but too hung-over to presently care. I will join up with my embarrassment later, most likely around early evening.

And I absolutely hate being sick, but I am finding myself compelled to drink. Yes, maybe I am losing myself in alcohol? Yes, I am being self-destructive. But you see, I am unhappy.

The Female Mind

The Female Mind: it Doesn't Add Up, it Doesn't Make Sense, and though I am Mingingly Hung-Over, I Remain Confused.

The Female Mind makes sense like a murder mystery, but where the detective, the clue-finder, the one investigating the murder also turns out to also be the killer. You see? A neat twist perhaps, but the conflict is obvious. It's like the Female Mind: so twisted, conflicted, unable to add up or make anything remotely approximating good sense. This is how I figure:

Someone cannot tell you they want to spend the rest of their life with you, that you are inseparably linked to everything that is *their* life, their *being*, their *purpose*, and then the next minute, all bets are off, and if you were then to be, right then, knocked down by a great big red bus, or eaten by a lion, then you, the Dead You, the Splattered or Eaten You would just be a sad unlucky chapter in *their* past.

"I once had a boyfriend who went under the number 220 to Hammersmith, only a single Decker, but heavy enough to make him road kill. Ho hum, anyway must dash, I've got my own bus to catch."

How can Sarah be able to just switch off like that, just flick a switch, and everything changes, all past feelings wiped? How, to be certain of one thing one minute, then indifferent, and convinced of an absolute opposite dogma the minute after?

The Female Mind: fucked.

That Was Mother

By now, mid-Sunday afternoon. I don't know how it happened? Time just dribbled away.

Mum phones, to ask me how I am. In truth, her question is a little more closed.

"How bad are you feeling today?," Mother asks

Just what I don't need.

"OK," I offer by way of reply, hangover compounding, me feeling displeased that the only person to call me all day is My Mother.

You know, it's as if the phone has changed its ring tone. This one is definitely different to before, somehow more "mocking". My landline phone, which cost a lot, looks aesthetic as hell, but has the acoustic clarity of a wind tunnel. Ironically, the actual ring tone is crystal clear, and strangely "implicit". I swear it has this, *"Loser, yeah Looooser, yeah you, who's got no girlfriend"* melody to it.

"Why didn't you ask how well I was, Mum?"

"I thought I'd indulge you," she replies.

"Very kind of you."

"Oh, I'm joking," Mother "jokes". "I don't mean anything by it. I just finished on the phone with your grandmother, and she's also very depressed. It's snowing in Durham…" – Durham incidentally, is where my grandmother lives – "…and with the exception of the postman and milkman, she's had no visitors all week. If you get a moment, you could give her a ring?"

"I'll try Mum, but it's a particularly busy Sunday. I'm on video conference with the PM at 4, then a telephone interview with *The New Yorker* at 4:30, something to do with my thoughts on the candidates running for Mayor, then Jamie Oliver is popping round early evening for a lesson in how to marinate blow fish. I told Zoë Ball not to say anything to him, but she just couldn't help blurt that she thought the diversity of flavours I'd achieved at my last dinner party were, and I quote: To die for."

"Well, if you do get a free moment, call your Granny."

"OK, will do," I concede. "I'll enquire after her junk mail and about next week's milk order. Should be fun!"

Mother asks after a moment, "For how much longer do you plan contriving this wounded, young angry man persona?"

In the background I can hear the rustling of cellophane.

"What's that you're rustling?," I ask, knowing damned well.

"Cattle," comes the reply. "Don't change the subject."

I persist: "Not the cellophane to a virgin-fresh packet of cigarettes? How many are you smoking at the moment?"

Mother counters, "How many are you smoking at the moment?"

"Don't worry, you're up on me and I doubt I'll catch up."

"Well, keep it that way. Obviously you haven't seen much of anyone today; obviously you're looking for a good argument. Just like your Gran."

Talk about making someone happy with a phone call. I'm just like my 86 year old Grandmother. At least, according to my Mother I am, and she could even have a point.

Gran's lifestyle and mine have started to assume Worrying Parallels.

Maybe my compulsion to have a good row is why I find myself single? Maybe it's why Gran finds herself widowed? Maybe Granddad just bailed, hollered "Seeya in the Afterlife, this is one barny too many," and ran at the Big Exit?

Okay, enough with the nasty thoughts, I tell myself.

"Mum, why've you called?," I ask.

"Just to chat," she explains, "To make sure you're okay. Worry, pester, make phone calls, they're all functions of motherhood."

"Well, consider the boxes ticked, I'm fine, just heading off to the gym in fact, to counter all those recent cigarettes I've been eating - I mean smoking. See, I really am a novice. So, let's speak another time, at my 30th birthday party say, or maybe my 40th?"

"And how's the boil?"

I just sigh. "That's why I'm off to the gym. The boil needs to be enrolled on a separate membership."

"Okay, love. Remember there's chilli in the freezer left over from when I visited last month. And call you're Gran."

"Sure thing Mum. Bye."

I re-cradle the handset and look around the sitting room. Silence again. I'm tempted to scream at the inanity of it all. Instead I pack my gym kit while considering Gym Avoidance

Strategies. Once packed, I call my Gran. In Durham, it's still snowing.

★

There's chilli in the freezer.

I'd had it easy. Sarah had been a great cook. I presume she still is, unless she's had some kind of Culinary-Lobe lobotomy?

Like I said, Sarah was a great cook, just awesome. She could take the scraggy, dejected contents of a bachelor's fridge and whip up a 3-course feast in under an hour. It was inspiring, like the A-team building a tank out of discarded Lego bricks while under lock-up in the bad guys garden shed.

It helped that Sarah enjoyed cooking so much. She liked the contribution it made to our lives. For females, this is not untypical, I think. In a very obvious way, food actually is love.

In the end, I resented Sarah for her cooking, the way she'd ask what I wanted to eat that night, whether I wanted to eat with her? "I'm making a Fusilli Carbonara, would you like some?" My mature response, as we ascended the relationship DEFCONS was usually to scowl and say, "No thanks" (without meaning the "thanks"), feeling as if *Me* eating *her* Fusilli Carbonara was like giving in to her, admitting to *needing* her, to my life being *better* because of her carbonara-sauce making presence in it.

So, in all the time I'd been seeing Sarah, I'd never had to cook. She cooked, or we ate out, or I ate out in other company. Either way, the dynamic suited me rather well.

At university, I'd once sliced my finger open when my intention had been to open a small tin of *Toast Toppers*. Toast Toppers were – are they still around? – a processed mush that came in various "flavours" – mushroom, chicken, I won't continue the list – but the outcome that was smeared over (read: topped) the bread and then slipped under the grill was consistently unpleasant and triggered a degree of self-loathing that lingered considerably longer than the topper did in the digestive system. Whatever the Toast Topper flavour, it always looked and tasted the same. Yellow, with fine grained "bits" that could have been gristle, or just really resilient carrot. The time I sliced my finger open had produced sufficient blood to remove any appetite, even for gristly carrot. Bloodletting was an extreme diet plan that I'd prayed was forever in my past.

Now, the very thought of Toast Toppers and exposed index finger bone was enough to abandon any thoughts of chilli-warming.

I didn't feel hungry but knew I had to eat. I'm losing weight, and I'm bored of batting off semi-concerned remarks from friends of a more attentive eye.

Current fridge contents boasts processed cheese slices, and there's a pre-sliced loaf in the cupboard. Excellent. A pre-sliced snack that much like a Toast Topper, can fit snugly under the grill. The bread, I discover, is complimented with tiny specks of mould - not ideal – but an abandoned pair of Sarah's tweezers from the bathroom cabinet are equal to the surgical task. Moments later, the smell of burnt toast alerts me that my feast must be ready. One bite alerts me to the fact that I didn't take the cheese slice out of its plastic wallet.

With a rising sense of panic and the knocking of self-hatred from years gone by, I grab my gym kit, scattering plucked crumbs of mould to the four corners of the kitchen and race for the front door.

Bad Idea

The gym was a disaster. When I arrived, everyone but Me looked healthy; by the time I left, I looked green and pretty unsteady on my feet. In some strange moment of self-persecution, I tried to make myself sick doing abdominal crunches (there was a time when they were just called sit-ups). After curling dumbbells that I should have left well alone, I did actually retch (but in a quiet corner on my own where nothing came up and no one witnessed my display).

On the running machine, I nearly fell off. I took myself off to the sauna and nearly passed out. Then I took myself home and crawled into bed.

I am now in bed staring at the ceiling, just thinking and feeling wan, of which neither is good for me.

What I'm thinking about:

The Way Girls Think

Girls, women, birds, title 'em as you wish – *The Female of the Species*, they are *different*. And I'm not just talking morphology here, not just remarking that bloke's bodies look like, well, blokes bodies, and a naked girl can look more yummy than a Ben & Jerry's ice cream sundae. With extra cream.

Also: Girls *think* differently.

A sweeping generalisation? Like I care? It's still true. I had it confirmed by a friend, who's a girl, so this is proven, legitimate, even scientific. *"Girls are different,"* that's what Tam admitted to me. So this is not Theory, but Fact.

My friend Tam (you haven't met her yet, but you will), she confirmed it; she confirmed that girls *think* differently.

Emotional make-up, coping skills, decision making, in these matters you're either in the Boy camp or the Girl camp, and there's a canyon of space in between.

A girl, Tam explained to me, will take ages when she is thinking something through. She will deliberate, agonise, devote every due process imaginable (intuitive, psychic, occasionally even empirical) in the pursuit of a decision. But once she's reached that decision…

… that's it.

BAM.

No more thinking.

No ever looking back.

Her mind is made up.

She moves forward.

Only forward.

Like a shark maybe?

(The shark thing is my analogy, not Tam's.)

So, to recap: a girl arrives at her decision and then, like stepping through a door, she locks it. Granted, this particular behaviour is less shark-like (sharks not wearing clothes and therefore having no pockets for keys), but the forward-only motion remains valid. And then, once through the door, that is now locked, she throws away the key. But that's not enough, not for girls. Oh no.

Then she bricks over the door (with the fastest acting cement available from her local B&Q), lines the top of her new wall with the sharpest, meanest looking barbed wire to be found either side of Christendom, and proceeds to side-wind slowly forward, dropping land mines like a modern day *Shake-and-Vac* housewife. Decision made, with no U-turn available or wanted.

There's strength in it, the way girls decide, that's for sure… *but it's not how guys are.* By comparison, we're cowardly - or maybe just never so convinced? We wouldn't bother with the bricks, barbed wire, or pressure sensitive bombs. We may lock a door or two, but we'd hold on to the key. Just in case; because blokes find commitment difficult, and that includes committing to a decision. Blokes tend to wonder about the *"What if?"*

Remember those role-playing books, you might have read one or two as a kid? You had to work your way through the story, reading paragraphs here and there, then jumping about the place, confronted with a situation and having to decide what to do and where to read on: *"Offer the hooded fellow a drink from your hip flask, and turn to page 50,* or *You don't like the look of this hooded freak and think it best to brandish your axe. Turn to page 93"* I'd always read both pages, then progress with the better outcome. And on this, I haven't changed any.

Pillow Talk

It's 11:50, in the pm.

I'm not asleep, just drifting, thinking that girls are too much like sharks, and allegedly, worryingly, that some of them even taste like tuna.

Ringing. I hear ringing.

My arm leaves the duvet enough for me to grab my mobile phone from the side table. The side table is a Pop Art effort designed, somewhat curiously, by the *Generation X* novelist Douglas Coupland.

"Not dead then?"

It's Tam.

"Actually, yes, but my phone network extends into the afterlife, and the cloud I live on comes with its own booster signal. How's life with you?"

"Fighting the good fight, as ever. Actually I'm just finishing off an article, thought I'd call to see whether you'd done with your flu melodrama and fancied a belated birthday supper, now that you're back in town?"

"Such sympathy, but supper sounds lovely; when?"

"Tomorrow night? I'll spin out the suspense and drop you an e-mail with details. Are you going into work tomorrow?"

"I thought I might try it; humour them."

"And how are you sleeping?"

"Great, just great," I lie, making no attempt to hide the lie.

"That bad, eh?"

"Y'know, probably no worse than anyone else who's ever wintered in the nuclear fallout of a break up."

(Ego-centrism aside, I appreciate I'm really not the only person on the planet to live through break-up woe.)

"Still sticking to your side of the bed?," asks Tam.

"Balls to that!" Such defiance in my voice. "Sure, the first few nights I stayed up smoking fags for the duration, didn't even go near the bedroom; spent the whole time feeling like I'd participated in some Nazi sponsored sleep deprivation programme."

"The beginning's always a bit of a misery," Tam confirms.

"Then it became a sleeping bag on the sofa. It's a sofa bed, as you know, but I didn't pull it out once. It was more *uncomfortable*; I liked it that way. Bit of self-inflicted suffering, you know? Then I completely changed the bedroom around, now *my* bedroom, boil washed the bed linen and slept upside down or diagonally across the bed for a fortnight. Belligerence, I think.

"After all that, I'm now back to *my side*."

Tam details, "The side nearest the door."

"Of course. But why is that?," I ask, now very awake.

"Why is it that blokes always default to the side nearest the door? I'd like to think it's the intuitive need to make a sharp exit, but I suspect that there's a pinch of truth in it being down to some bullshit 'protect your mate' coding in the Male DNA. I reckon it's time to re-write that fucking acid string!"

"But you are sleeping?"

"Yes, I am sleeping. I wake up occasionally hugging a pillow – absolutely contemptible – but at least the fact that I'm waking up proves I've been asleep."

"As long as you're just *hugging* the pillow."

"Not humping, I assure you - that would leave me feeling something other than just contempt. But it's still a helluva proxy. And you know what's weirdest?"

"What's weirdest?"

"What's weird is the way it went from her with her arm always around me as we slept, to me with my arm always around her.

"At some point, there was a *shift*. I was this contained, self-sufficient sleeping machine, a slumber-good unit of one, then something *changed*, and I suddenly needed to hold on, to fall asleep *holding* her. Sleep wasn't properly sleep without her."

"And now it's a pillow," Tam reminds me.

"Yes, now it's a pillow… but at least it's goose down."

"And on that note, I'll leave you to your pillow love."

"Until tomorrow then."

"Until then. Night night."

What I Do For a Living

*"If you work in marketing, two words, kill yourself.
No, seriously, kill yourself."*

Bill Hicks

I don't work in marketing. I work in *advertising,* which Bill
and much everyone else if they knew the score would agree
is even more contemptible. Advertising is a rarefied strain
of marketing, and it's arguably more pointless (if that were
possible) than marketing straight.

Of course, I imagine that my white-collar moments
are much like the majorities. I put in the hours, I talk on
the phone, I schmooze, occasionally skulk and sulk, sit at a
desk, attend meetings, delegate, follow orders, get bored, feel
frustrated/underpaid/undervalued, crave greater creativity,
contempt others, and accept that working life can be a real
bum deal.

So what's my complaint? Well, to begin with, I didn't even
have one.

Once I'd got over the fact I wasn't in the Noble Cause
Game, I used to think advertising wasn't too terrible. After
all, it's just One Big Blag and the money isn't too insulting.
Advertising doesn't pay Big City Bucks, but salaries go the
right way quickly, and the lifestyle *enhancements* are numerous.
To use work-speak, I'm talking "Bolt-On-Spin-Offs," stuff like
Coutts card expense accounts, long lunches in flash restaurants
where the menu is corporate-costed and everyone indulges
in heady 80's excess flash-backs, exclusive invites to a steady-
stream of over-blown parties where the "theme" is realised
at a cost comparable to buying a bungalow in the North
of England.

Yes, it all seemed bearable once upon a time.

In advertising, everyone gets to float down agency corridors on their own little cloud of self-importance, talk nonsense and make decisions that never amount to anything. Advertising produces more advertising, no one ever dies, and everyone gets to go to lunch. I used to think all that sounded pretty good.

These days, it's all I can do switch off and zone out for fear of killing someone.

Somewhere along the line, I grew Very Tired. I guess I was just treading water in this vast sea of triviality and finally just got so bored, so numb, that I just opened my mouth and let myself sink?

You see, advertising equals meetings; Endless Endless Meetings. These meetings are So Inane, So Remarkably Trivial, I can't help but sink. They say that, in the final moments, death by drowning is quite serene? Every meeting, I drown, and it's a kind of escape. Internal worlds, Fantasy Islands, in meetings entering some Theatre of the Mind is the only safe exit strategy, otherwise I'd have to come to work armed with an Uzi.

Where am I at the moment? It's 4pm, we've just broken the first hour in Meeting Room 3, and Kim Wam Poe plays a mean game of poker…

The Demon Queen

It comes down to this. A single, defining point; the length of a heartbeat; time for temple sweat to hit the floor. Welcome to the crossroads, son. Tell me, do you regret jamming with the Devil?

Two figures remain, seated. Across a round table, a battle has been fought, but not between Knights. The table is covered in green felt. Two figures seated. You, and another.

A game of cards; just a game of cards. But, no. Not *just* a game. Not by the longest shot

And now this, this angle-point, in time, the face-off, the trade-off. A *soul* trade. *"How do you shoot the Devil in the back?,"* Kevin Spacey once asked. Easy. You aim and squeeze. But the real toughie: How do you look pure evil square in the eyes, and not let on you're bluffing? How do you look the Devil in the face and say, *Come get me?*

You refuse to sweat. If you sweat, it'll be over, end game.

Your gaze doesn't falter, it couldn't if you wanted it to, and you don't want. The eyes are where it's at. The eyes across from you. Cruel, narrow eyes. The whites are a dirty pink, the pupils the size of silver dollars. And behind, a frightening intelligence; the witness to a lifetime of horror, and pleasure in those many horrors.

Kim Wam Poe, Triad Queen of Northern Kowloon sits across from you. A game of poker has been played. The stakes have been… exceptional.

Each player has staked their life. Each player that is, bar Kim Wam Poe. And now there are two. The most feared matriarch in all China, and you, just a guy in the wrong place at the wrong time.

But now, your luck has to change. Otherwise, you'll soon have little need for luck, or anything else.

"So, Meeser Grant. Now shall we see the fear enter your eyes? You have played well. You are a good man, a brave man, and because of it, you will die. You should not have meddled in our affairs. Affairs that did not concern you."

"What are you wanting from me? An apology?"

You're surprised by your own voice, the strength and insolence still there.

"Your English sarcasm is lost on me, Meeser Grant. Your efforts to save the orphanage have failed. I hold your life, and the lives of all those orphans in my hand, and the cards are with me."

"We shall see, Kim Wam Poe. If I lose, there's no way I suppose you'll consider sparing the orphanage?"

"Ha!"

The laugh is like exploding glass, the kind that then hits you full in the face.

"You make me laugh, Meeser Grant. Do you think the Demon Queen knows compassion?"

You can't help but scoff. In the Adventure Business, people who refer to themselves in the Third Person have always spelt trouble.

"The orphanage will burn," she declares. "Its contents can either burn, or fall under my employ. I care little either way. But those children will serve my sweat shops well."

"And the Nunnery?

"You mean my new opium den, ready populated with fresh virgin flesh?"

"And the donkey sanctuary?"

"You would have my minions starve? Really Meeser Grant, do you think I am a women of *any* mercy."

"Then I guess we have nothing left to discuss."

You feel the room rocking, but remind yourself that it's just the waters of Hong Kong harbour chopping against the sides of the Junk. You are in the Demon Queen's floating lair, a ring of artillery-packing Chinese heavies for company, the bodies of four other poker playing chancers out of their chairs, weeping blood and brain matter onto the cabin's floor.

The Demon Queen licks at her cracked lips, and you feel surprised that it is not the scaly tongue of a serpent you see.

"You think yourself, some kinda hero, Meeser Grant? I tell you now, martyrdom, is over-rated."

"Since Christ, I'd have to agree."

"But why then? Why risk your life for nothing, for people who would never risk themselves for you?"

"What can I say, I'm a people person."

"So very pithy, but how can you believe that the strength of one may halt the momentum of so many? "

You've had your fill of this whole Mr Miagi moment. Hong Kong was never meant to be like this. You just want to settle your slate, whatever the cost. "Enough's enough, Kim Wam Poe. Save me the fortune cookie crap and let's see your hand."

The room stirs. Simultaneous, fearful intakes of breath. Never has this audience heard such disrespect.

Over the table, just a sickly wet chuckle. "You will see my hand, yes indeed Meeser Grant, and it will cost you your life."

A talon of a hand plants down a fan of five cards, face up. A suit, to the hearts. Almost ironic, considering the rumours that Kim Wam Poe has been known to eat the hearts of her enemies; medium rare.

"The world is full of dead heroes, Meeser Grant. Soon your corpse will be among them, and oh how I will enjoy dining on your heart. I think I shall have it with hollandaise."

"I've always been more a béarnaise man, myself."

You look down at your fan of cards. They haven't changed. To win, as you know, is to walk away. The orphanage, the nunnery, and yes, even the Donkey sanctuary, all saved. For all its vice, the Triad way is at least true to its word. Even in Kowloon, thieves have honour.

And even now, your face shows nothing. Even now. Again, Kim Wam Poe fixes you with that cracked smile; again she reveals that saliva-white tongue of hers. Oh, how she's lapping-up the moment.

But now it's your turn to smile, and you know she senses the game turning.

"Stomach this."

You drop the cards, one at a time. Another suit. But these guys carry spades.

Like a Flashover. All air feels to leave the room; Poe's ring of henchman contract around the table, disbelieving what they see, but sensing the power drain from their Queen. *She has lost?*

"It cannot be!," she screams. The room's air returns in a welling back-draft, quartered by her incredulous wails.

You stand to leave, then pause, your safety - and those of the orphans, Nuns, and donkeys - assured.

"A word of advice Kim Wam Poe: Don't just talk a good game, play a good game."

And then you leave.

*

Proceedings in Meeting Room 3 wound up at 5. Just the 2 hours. I couldn't tell you one word of what was discussed. Other than taking on Kim Wam Poe, the only other highlight of my day:

From: tamsin.flint@londonlights.co.uk

To: sam.grant@sdb.com

Sent: 18 October, 1999 16:18

Re: Birthday scoff

Ce soir: table 4 2 at 7.45. Marco Pierre White's doing

kitchen duties. Toast Toppers unlikely to feature.

Taking you to Mirabelle must mean I love you a little,

Tx

Monday Night Mirabelle

Tam's just texted to say she's ten minutes away, her cab stuck in traffic. I'm striking a pose in an armchair, drinking a margarita while I wait. I look pretty casual, but it requires a little effort. *Affected?* Me? Hell, no more than the French, or their cuisine, which is what Mirabelle is all about.

Ties are currently So Out I'm thinking they actually could be Back In, so tonight's piece of neck fabric is a block-copper coloured number bought from the *Paul Smith* on Westbourne Grove. Sarah *originally* bought me this tie. When she left, I cut it up, a symbolic gesture suggestive of severing the link between us. Okay, I was pretty pissed at the time. Then I went back to the store the next day, with a hangover, and spent £50 on an identical replacement. And some say I'm a smart guy?

While I wait, I drink my margarita and flick through the West End final edition of the *Evening Standard*. At the vendor stand, the headline ran: *Big Turk Death Quake – Latest Pictures.* I scan over the *Latest Pictures,* sensing the colour of tie I'm wearing is probably down there on the totem pole of global importance.

Tam comes down the stairs and into the bar. She looks drop-dead and every guy's looking, even those guys politely pretending not.

"You look as effortlessly glam as ever," I smile at her.

"Thanks, nice tie," she smiles back. "I'm famished; shall we go through birthday boy?"

★

The table is excellent. Intimate but not isolated. Hugh Grant sits two tables away with a very pretty blonde who certainly isn't Liz Hurley in a wig. The blonde has perfect eyebrows.

Our sommelier looks like he's been overly impressed by the whole Keanu Reeves/Matrix thing and has dressed accordingly, all in black and wearing a coat down to the floor. When he comes over to the table it's anyone's guess whether he'll talk wine or firepower.

"And how was your day, dear?," Tam asks.

"You know, same old same old," I offer. "Attended a meeting, played cards, saved an orphanage, nunnery, even a donkey sanctuary."

"In your dreams," Tam laughs

"Actually, yes, that's exactly where it was. And how's David? Still the same Porsche?"

"And still the same Chelsea duplex," Tam confirms.

"And I assume still the same smug-fuck attitude, so that completes the trinity. The world is as it should be."

"I detect a too-heavy hint of sarcasm. Is David something you'd like to talk about," Tam asks evenly.

"No," I back down, palms out. "I'd like to order, then I'd like to talk about you."

Fifty-Two

"God, I just want my life back."

"What do you mean?," I ask.

"My life is not my own," Tam explains, then takes a healthy sip of just-poured Sancerre. Our sommelier didn't say a thing about high-calibre weaponry.

Tam continues: "I just wish I'd never got it into my head to buy a place. But once you start, that's it, you can't think of *anything* else. It's an all consuming mental..." Tam pauses, finding her words, "... skull-fuck."

Of all the words to find? "That's colourful," I tell her.

"But Sam, it really is. You want to stop, eat, sleep, try and think about something different, but it's impossible. Every waking moment is geared towards viewing the next property and reviewing the previous one: *Was that last place big enough, could I really see myself living above a shop? This next place sounds really great...etc etc.*

"And with each *next* place, you start getting hopeful, desperately hopeful, and then - WHAM - it's another shit pit. And so it goes on. A vicious never ending round of misery, set-back, false optimism, and clawing despair."

"Thrown against the rocks of life, collected in the backwash, then dashed again... and again?," I suggest.

"Ship-wreck analogies, that's all I need?," she asks, giving me a mock scowl.

"You don't think you're becoming a little obsessive?"

"That's rich, coming from you. Sarah-obsessive is practically a new disease. But it's true, I'm becoming a *lot* obsessive. But Sam, it's not that I *want* to obsess like this. I have no choice in it. It's like a mental disorder, like yours about Sarah. Once you register with your first estate agent, that's it, you're hooked."

"So you're saying you're a bit mental? Like most if not all girls?"

"And like some boys too," she suggests, pointedly.

I don't want the focus. "How many places have you seen now?," I ask.

"52."

"Fuck off! 52? Seriously?"

"52," she assures, and she certainly looks serious enough.

"That's ridiculous," I tell her.

"I know."

"And you haven't liked *any* of them?"

"I'm picky, OK?"

"Discerning is one thing, but 50-fucking-2!"

She defends, "I made an offer on 1, but I was out-bid. The housing market seems to be an evolved form of Monopoly, but I'm the only one playing with real money."

"Certainly doesn't allow much time for anything else."

"That's my point. I have *no* other time. *All* my time is being spent in the company of estate agents, visiting the homes of strangers – some of which are very strange."

"The strangers, or their homes?"

"Both. One tends to be a natural extension of the other."

"But you must be getting a few ideas on decoration. Most people are wallpaper voyeurs at heart."

"Let's say I've reached saturation. There's only so much Laura Ashley I can take. I really need to detox after all the recent chintz."

I advise, "Just don't do anything rash and buy the next place you see, just because you've seen 52 others. The right one will come along – much like the right girl, or the right guy."

"And in the meantime?"

"Keep the faith Hon, keep the faith."

"I don't think listening to Bon Jovi's going to help."

"Well, how 'bout for starters a cassoulet of clams & mussels?"

Over Tam's shoulder I spy our plates arriving.

"Yeah, that might help a lot."

"In that case you're in luck, grub's up."

My starter is a steak tartar with black truffle. For main I'm having grilled sea bass with salsa verde. Tam has gone for the white haddock on crushed artichokes.

At one point, Hugh-that's-my-surname-Grant checks out Tam when he passes our table on the way to the gents. I can't help but think: Yeah, unlucky Hugh. Your date's okay, mine's better. Of course, I know it's not a competition, but it's amusing how the Alpha Male takes over sometimes.

Tam

A little background on Tam:

Tam and I were at university together, which is where we met. She didn't exactly join The Beautiful Crowd when she arrived at university. More so, they joined her. Tam is very attractive and very sassy; tall, blonde hair, confident, borderline fearless and invariably out-spoken. She's a kind of Hitchcock Blonde for the Cyberpunk Generation, though beyond sounding "cool" I can't say what I mean by that, other than she sometimes wears pink extensions in her hair. Tam is also a journalist, writes a weekly column and contributes occasional features to *London Lights*, a kind of wannabee but needs-to-try-less-hard *New Yorker* for Londoners. You may even have read Tam's column, *A Girl's Eye View*?

Any guy would want Tam for a gal pal. Why Tam and I

are friends I'm not exactly sure. For one reason or another, whenever I mean to ask her, something else just comes up.

Clapham

"Have you thought about Clapham?," I ask Tam, somewhere into the second bottle of white. "People speak very fondly of the area around the Common."

"The only people speaking fondly are those who don't have to live there. With the possible exception of the wino's living on the Common, but rumour has it, even they'd prefer to drink their Special Brew someplace else."

"Clapham's the *New Fulham* apparently."

"Making Brixton the *New Clapham* I suppose?"

"So the chain goes. You've obviously been reading the same things I have."

"The same bollocks, yes; and who the hell would want to live in the Old Fulham anyway?"

"But Clapham's pretty good; some good bars and restaurants. Clubs, a cinema, all that. There's a buzz; lots of young people, the implication of dynamism and style-trending; funky looking "hair studios" where you get to sit in torn leather club chairs and the cutters have perpetual bed-head and wear clothes that make them look undernourished."

"Perhaps if I was an aspiring hairdresser, then Clapham would appear very chic to me, but I'm not, so it doesn't. Life's too short to live south of the river, and Clapham in particular is shabby, over-priced, over-rated, over-hyped, and probably most concerning of all, over-weird."

"Over-weird?"

"I was there last week for a viewing."

"In Clapham?"

"Yes, in Clapham."

"But I was getting the distinct impression that you weren't too… impressed with Clapham?"

"Well I didn't realise just how unimpressed until last Saturday. The actual property sounded like it might really have been something."

"But it wasn't?"

"No idea; I didn't keep the appointment."

"Because…?"

"I came out of the Tube station – a really crisp, fresh Saturday morning when anywhere is capable of looking at least pleasant, and Clapham instantly struck as being really *unpleasant*.

"I was walking down the high street, and one in roughly every five people I passed was talking to themselves. People walking along, talking into *space*, some having arguments, others just making small talk. Faces knitted in heated debate, others genteel from exchanged pleasantries, and the entire time only one person present in a conversation that clearly required two."

"Are you sure that these people weren't talking on hands-free mobiles?"

"Very sure. They were nutters, plain and simple, and seeing as I'm not planning on making any invisible friends anytime soon, Clapham is not for me."

"I think you're being unfair. I think you're a victim of urban paranoia."

"Do you now?," she says dryly.

Nutters Everywhere

"Okay," I say, "you see some bloke walking down a London street, doesn't matter whether it's in Chelsea or Camberwell, or indeed Clapham. This bloke's not the best dressed of cats, has an odd walk, maybe talking to himself, muttering under his breath, only you can't make out whether he's mouthing a happy rap, talking on a hands free, or admitting mass-murder to his invisible mate.

"Alarm bells ring. All you hear in your head is: *Danger Will Robinson!* You can't cross over the road quick enough."

"That," Tam simply explains, "is because there are nutters everywhere, not just in Clapham."

"But it is," I suggest, "hardly fair or rational? Take my For Example Guy. Just because this Weird-Walking Bloke isn't sporting a wing collar or double cuff, because he like's giving himself little pep talks, and most importantly, because he's in a Big City setting, people leap to one conclusion: *Psycho*. At best, he's an axe murderer on his day off, at worst he's packing a machete, walking the streets with a chronic case of blood lust, and you fear you've just found yourself in the wrong place at the wrong time."

Tam's having none of it: "Big City suspicion is perfectly healthy. It's why girls when they're walking around on their own, most especially at night, adopt those don't-fuck-with-me expressions, and never make eye contact, and always walk in a way that suggests they're about to step into a war zone; a war zone that they're looking forward to more than a 2-week holiday in Mauritius."

"I see," I say.

She adds: "It's why I love my long black leather coat: because it makes me look hard - and because it's Gucci.

I think our Sommelier might be wearing the same one?"

"Quite possibly, but forget our wine guy for now. Take my For Example Guy again, still a club-footed Verbal Kint…"

"Who?"

"*The Usual Suspects;* it doesn't matter. Same guy as before, but a different environment: now in a quaint little village somewhere. Now you pass him on the pavement and at most extreme, you think: Little bit weird but hey, maybe he's the village idiot? How awfully charming!

"You're probably no more inclined to spark up a conversation, but you sure as hell don't feel life-threatened. Instead you're imagining the locals saying, *'Don't mind Ole Joe, he's kinda soft in the head, eats wild berries, chases cows, talks to himself for sure, may molest a small child now and again, but he's very endearing and wouldn't harm a fly – 'cept the ones he likes to eat.'*"

"Ole Joe sounds a lot like your Dad."

"What I'm saying is, cities breed suspicion and misgiving. City equals: home to vicious psychopaths; Village equals: home to cuddly dopes. Dependent on setting, Ole Joe's either a pudding-headed lug or The Machete Maniac."

"Thing is, Ole Joe could be both. Again, much like your Dad."

"Well, with my Dad, you have every reason to be suspicious. I think it's time for the bill."

The Secret to My Future Success

Out on Curzon Street, we get lucky, two cabs bumper to bumper, roof lights ablaze turn into view. I kiss Tam lightly on each cheek, post her into the backseat of the front cab and hand the driver twenty quid. I then jump into my cab and my driver greets with: "That's not the sort of girl you want to part company with at the end of a night?"

"It is if she's your sister," I lie. To this the driver becomes all business, asks where he's heading, then turns on the radio, some talk piece debating whether mobile phones should come with health warnings. My mind drifts as we drive through the street-lit night.

★

You know, the ego hit stings. We might add up to a greater sum than just our egos, but ego is a part, and mine smarts like a bastard right now; smarts the way it would if I'd just been body-slammed by a mankind-threatening meteor. My ego is not the size of a planet exactly – well, not in my more humble moments - but I do feel an altogether extreme sense of impact.

For someone to leave you, they're effectively saying, *I'm going elsewhere. I'm backing a different pony, getting better odds on a better bet - a bet that isn't you.* What they're simply saying is, *Fuck you, and fuck off.* This is what Sarah's saying, what Sarah's doing - *I back another human being, over you. So long Sam. I choose A. N. Other.*

Fuck.

That's what I think.

And now? Now I have to prove Sarah wrong. I have to be an INCREDIBLE SUCCESS. Just to make a point. I have to live to 100, be doubly driven, all the way, then even a little further, become nothing short, not even half a yard short of a NINE YARD REMARKABLE SUCCESS.

I might even have to sample success across many fields of human endeavour, illustrating a bewildering level of specialism and expertise, all to show Sarah what bad judgement she has, show her the most royal 2-fingers or flipped bird, establishing without question what a mistaken bet she's placed.

To be driven by bitterness, anger and purple-bruised ego does not seem healthy – I realise this – but when I accept my Pulitzer, my Oscar, my Knighthood (I appreciate that all in the same year might prove unrealistic), I may feel indifferent to my motivating force. I may concern more with dusting my crowded, gong-heavy mantelpiece. I shall dust away, possibly not truly happy, but certainly successful, my point made and argument won, and I shall toast Sarah, *The Bitch,* The Bitch who places bad bets!

And I'm driven to keep in shape. If Sarah goes for a fully-fledged body builder (say, of the Austrian oak variety), I may struggle to compete, but I'll be damned if I won't be in better shape, and stay in better shape for longer than anyone she's likely to go out with, and/or marry. (God, *marry*! What a thought!)

I might even do some ab crunching when I get back to the flat, work on that washboard, and possibly do some curls, work those guns, get those Action Hero Arms going.

I hope Sarah spends the rest of her life with someone who has a very hairy back. Like a fucking baboon's, or a yeti, assuming yetis exist and their backs are even hairier? While I, free of back hair, but with a well-bedded year-round tan, will at 60, casually slip in a quick thousand stomach crunches each morning before breakfast, notch up 50 lengths in my very big pool, and finish by slipping into my devastatingly attractive, obviously glamorous, and now retired movie star wife (of 30 years joyous and sex-ravaged marriage). That will be my breakfast time. Every day.

I don't exactly wish on Sarah a series of ugly and financially ruinous divorces, that leave her with endless nights sobbing into her one and only pillow, but part of me would not be too disappointed if events approximating this become her fate.

But how to let Sarah know, how for her to learn of me and my Super Nova Successes? I'll need spokespeople. I'll need media attention.

I'm thinking, *Esquire Man of the Year*, a big front-page splash – of ME, my face. Accompanied by another big full-length pull out – of ME. Me, then radiating a humble smile, a smile like I'm hardly sure I know what all the fuss is about, but if I can make a difference in some small way, then hey, what the heck, put me on the cover if it helps. Yep, that's the kind of smile I'll be going for in *Esquire*.

I'm also thinking of Me on the front cover of *Vogue*. I don't believe in over exposure, and it would ram my message home, make my point to Sarah doubly loud. Hell, why end there, only the 2 titles?

Again, cover of *Rolling Stone*, Me, perhaps with two supermodels of the day, one on each arm, looking like they've just been satisfied in a quite marathon way, if you get my meaning. We'll get Annie Leibovitz to shoot it; it'll be cool. And if Annie does a good job, I'll use her again for my front cover in *Vanity Fair*, maybe *just* Me in the frame this time, but if Annie prefers to go with supermodel or Hollywood Siren garnish, I won't complain.

I probably won't bother much with *Fortune Magazine* – could be a bit vulgar, but mainly, it's not part of Sarah's reading list. Lastly, I'm reckoning on a front cover pose for *Men's Health* (now don't laugh), with the main feature proclaiming, *Six Pack like Sam's? How inside!*

I appreciate *Men's Health* is unlikely to be part of Sarah's reading list, but her fuckface boyfriend may just be a reader, and any extra mile I can go in stirring feelings of inadequacy, well that's just swell with me.

Oh yeah, vengeance will be mine, baby! Vengeance in

spades, when I'm a Big Fucking Star! The Biggest Swinging Dick, even when I walk into a room full of big swinging dicks. Fucking pendulous, that'll be me, everyone forced to take cover, everyone potentially in my arc. And yet as dangerous as that may be for their more mortal souls, they'll *want* to be in my arc. So they can feel my *heat*. Maybe get touched by my radiance, like some of it just may rub off on them, just a little gold dust, a little sense of that Midas touch. Oh yeah, that'll show her. That'll show Sarah.

The Boil – An Update

I wake with a hangover and a slowly reducing boil. The boil could have gone one of two ways, as the good doctor Walker had outlined. Vesuvian, then all over, all out, or bowing out slowly, over time, everyday getting a little smaller and smaller. The Boil has chosen the second way, ultimately keeping me company for longer, but not exposing its inner workings, which I can only be thankful of. If only my head was improving, and I'm not just talking the long-shadow of last night's expensive grape. I do not want to go into work today, though from somewhere I discover strength enough to wrestle off the duvet and head towards the bathroom.

Routines, Spectres & Rock Stars

My emotional wiring's gone screwy. It's on a 24-hour loop, aided and abetted by routines which serve to trigger or parallel my thought patterns. In greater clarity: I think the same things, go through the same thoughts, day after day, at the same points in time. Like a kind of hell maybe? Hell is an eternal rerun; just ask Sisyphus, the boulder man.

My pattern goes something like…

Wake up… aware that it's *over*, that it's not all just a really crap dream, but all very real, all very over. This is Thought 1 for the day, every day.

Then:

Gawp into the toilet bowl as I give it some half-hearted piss-artistry and think, BLOODY HELL!, over and out. Thought 2: Sarah will be getting up now too, but somewhere else, in some other world that is *her life*; a place where I don't have an invite.

Then:

Brush my teeth, wondering how in the name of Eric and Ernie did I get to this place, *my place*, a place *sans Sarah*? Thought 3.

Then:

Caution myself for being a self-suffering melodramatic fuck, and chuckle. Emptily. (This chuckle has become part of my teeth brushing routine, it even helps me get to the back molars.)

Then:

Shower, and as I'm pelted by thunderous (really very stinging indeed) jets of water, I wonder where she's showering, and hope petulantly that my power shower is the more monsoonal. Thought 4.

And then the day begins, same after same after same; then repeat.

★

It's ironic. I said I never want to see her again, but mentally, she's permanently at my side. Sarah lives in the vast majority of my head-space. When I'm asleep, it's just the same, she is there in all my dreams, and while she's rarely dressed as Freddie Kruger, the effect is similar. I wake up from dream after dream, Sarah having always been the main lead, her name above the title. Invariably my T-shirt is soaking. My ex-girlfriend: the Nightly Invader of my dreams, the Daily Spectre at my shoulder. Think about her every day, dream about her every night. At least there's balance to it.

I don't want to ever see her again. That's the place I'm in right now. I asked her to stay, she said sayonara, so I said, well sod off forever then. A mature exchange, I know.

To never see her again – ever - it's such a crazy thought, so abstract; just Too Bizarre. And while I'd admit it's also a hideous thought, I'm shitting myself at the random possibility of simply bumping into her.

I keep thinking I see her in the street, the back of her head, an out-of-focus figure at the end of the block, a face through the window of a passing bus, so many times, and I just freeze and stare. Those "sightings," it's never been her, but one day it's bound to be, and that'll sure be one fissured moment in the time-space continuum. For me at least, London isn't a big enough place when it comes to avoiding ex-girlfriends. 12 million people don't provide enough cover. No number is safe enough when the Law of Sod decides to enter the play.

Now I get anxious whenever I'm doing the South West London thing, her old stomping ground, and one that she will have returned to. A District Line tube train, a leisurely lunch on the Fulham road, but two experiences I chose to now avoid for the sake of a life path overlap. The Kings Road has become a complete no-go zone.

I play out the moment of that chance encounter, that future place yet to happen, thinking on how I'll act, how I'll keep my shit together, whether I'll play the Nice Guy, the

Indifferent Arsehole, or the Cocky Fuckhead? Whether I'll pretend like there's a joke only I'm in on, but a joke that's very much on her? Maybe I'd do that smile, and knowing head-shake thing? Blow a little air down my nose even. A snort that says our parting was like a lottery win for me, so liberating and life-giving. It would be a very articulate snort, for sure. Yep, I'd play it cool all right, so long as the power of speech didn't leave me.

I foresee of one scenario where I just bump into her, and a second where it's her AND this new boyfriend of hers. If it's the latter, then boy had I better be looking ever so AWESOME! Like a goddamn Rock Star! With a West Coast tan, my eyes somehow a laser-piercing green (rather than their normal everyday green), and giving off the kind of Big Bang aura that's capable of seeding whole new worlds. Unless of course the Law of Sod dictates that it is to be a day-after-the-night-before? Me then, nursing a hangover that leaves my brain feeling cleaved and my stomach like a bucket of frozen sick. I hope it's more the Rock Star situation, less the turd in the bottom of the rock pool, but I know I'm unlikely to have any say in this episode of fate. Like any other episode to date.

Tuesday

Ultimately, though not inevitably, I make it into the office, this Tuesday morning, and now in Meeting Room 5, 4 of us spend 30 minutes confusing ourselves over whether we are talking "Brand Position" or "Brand Proposition". It amounts to no more than 3 letters, p, r, and o, but everyone is getting in such a pickle. With a heavy head, I leave the others to deliberate away in the dark, as if hunting the heavens looking for a black hole that was never there.

My favourite quote of the meeting: *"Hopefully, we all know what I'm trying to say, without understanding the language I'm using to say it."*

Back at my desk:

> To: tamsin.flint@londonlights.co.uk
>
> From: sam.grant@sdb.com
>
> Re: My question is this…
>
> Sent: 19 October, 1999 12:28
>
> Just to say, Thanks for last night, Mirabel is My New Favourite Restaurant. And, I have a ponderable for you. Please feel free to take your time:
>
> Is it simply the case that boys like girls and girls like cars and money?

Two minutes later, a reply:

> To: sam.grant@sdb.com
>
> From: tamsin.flint@londonlights.co.uk
>
> Re: My answer is this…
>
> Sent: 19 October, 1999 12:30
>
> "There are a number of mechanical devices which increase sexual arousal, particularly in women. Chief among these is the Mercedes-Benz 380SL convertible." Source: Lynn Lavner
>
> Tx
>
> PS: Supper was my pleasure.

In the Afternoon Meeting everyone Goes Nuts (in a Positive Way). We have biscuits (jaffa cakes and hob nobs) and charts. Everyone eats lots of Jaffa cakes. I have five myself. On most of the charts, there is a Red Line and a Blue Line. The Blue Line goes predominantly one way, the Red mostly another. Some brows furrow, then smiles follow. The Blue Line is apparently behaving as hoped and that's making everyone really happy. We all talk of lag times, up-turns, the need for more regressional analysis to prove causal links and inform future-scaping, and then we all scoff more jaffa cakes, before returning to our e-mails.

Fighting Talk

From: jamie.sykes@gs.com

To: sam.grant@sdb.com

Sent: 19 October, 1999 17:18

Re: Old Man

If your October's feeling like a month of Mondays, getting those endorphin's racin' has got to be the answer!

Sam, I say you're getting older and you're getting slower.

Prove me wrong.

Proposed this Thursday evening: 2 hours, 2-dots and a serious can-opening of whoop ass for the main plate of one Mr. S. Grant.

And if you're really lucky, I'll shout supper afterwards,

somewhere marvelous to toast your 28th year.

The Cross-Court King

To: jamie.sykes@gs.com

To: sam.grant@sdb.com

Re: 2-Dot Challenge Accepted

Sent: 19 October, 1999 17:28

Jamie my Man!

Funnily enough, you just sprang to mind. Moments ago, post meeting, was flicking through a new mag which, trust me, is Very You. Called, "Bling," it calls itself "The Magazine of Luxury". Inside, a good article on bidding for the Right Watch at auction, a test drive of the newly-sooped Aston Martin DB7, a feature on the Better Bars in Monaco, and some top tips for hosting the Perfect Soiree in Marrakech. I shall retain my copy and pass it on.

In regards to squash, are we talking Big Boy Squash, or would you prefer I spot you, say, 5 points a game?

Sam "Feel the T" Grant

PS: Belated Birthday Quaffing and Posh Nosh sounds extremely palatable.

To: sam.grant@sdb.com

From: jamie.sykes@gs.com

Re: Good luck Old Man

Sent: 19 October, 1999 17:40

And drop... and scuttle.

And to the back wall... and scamper...

And careful of the shoulder..!

And drop...

(You)

... to the floor in defeat.

Such a harsh world of on-court pain awaits you, but some say it'll be character building.

However, medics will be standing by, and assuming you're not dead by the end, I've booked Lombard Street Brasserie for 8.

See you court-side, 5:00pm.

Sincerely,

J. Sykes, aka. Lord & Master

PS: The new Aston does drive like a dream (I test drove 2-weeks ago), but I'm thinking of something more timeless. A chap here's thinking of parting with his DB4 GT. You don't want to know how much cash I would have to part with by way of exchange.

Supper in the City

Squash proved the usual Battle of Titans, the same as ever gladiatorial affair with Jamie, Competitive Little Bastard he is, refusing to lay down and die, throwing himself at everything, never giving in. All. Quite. Exhausting. I took the final game, settling matters with a 3–2 win. I nearly coughed up a lung or what felt at least like a lung fragment in that final game, but the prospect of a decadently rich supper makes me feel instantly more at ease. My current cigarette is also helping.

The venue: 1 Lombard Street Brasserie, on Lombard Street, which makes it easy to remember. An earlier incarnation saw the place as a banking hall. Now it houses hungry/thirsty after-work bankers who have a hungry need to spend their money. The décor: linen covered tables, off white walls, and a big round skylight above a big round bar where big round bankers sit eating pretzels and drinking double digit priced G&T's.

I have ordered foie gras in a *toasted sandwich*, with saddle of rabbit on tagliatelle in a basil cream sauce to follow. In my choice, I'm being *ironic*. Jamie's trying for *irreverent*, having chosen caeser salad, followed by roast beef with Yorkshire puddings. The vino is obviously red, specifically a Rioja, even more specifically, a Marquis de Riscal 1997 which we are informed is drinking very well at the moment.

Get Over It, Get On It

"Don't you think it's about time you got over this?," Jamie asks as our starters arrive. "It's been 4 months!"

"Thanks for the time check." I'm fully aware how long it's been.

"It's not that I'm not trying," I try and explain. "It's just that I seem to have spent the last 4 months *not* getting over her. Some days it's a little better, some days a little worse again. I'm trying to identify a pattern - wondering if it could outline a formula to the meaning of life or something? I keep trying to remind myself of all the things I hated about her, but instead I keep coming back to breasts, and those I liked. Both of them. A lot."

"You need to get out there," Jamie suggests with all the compassion of a Nazi. "Get amongst some serious tit-and-arse action. One-night stands, meaningless, base, throw-away encounters with numerous examples of the opposite sex. Get into some filth, more gratuitous the better, really devalue women, turn 'em into statues with pulses."

"Sounds healthy," I remark.

"As opposed to what you're doing?" I get a sense Jamie's taking to his soapbox. "Here Sam you are, trying to find some kind of rhyme and reason, indulging in all these romantic fucking pretensions: true love, star-crossed love, paradise fucking lost, even when you never beach-combed paradise with Sarah in the first place!"

"Jamie, you look like you're overheating."

"No, that was at 2-2, but really, " he appeals, "all your Shakespearean *oh-what-a-cruel-world* delusions of tragedy and loss just sound ridiculous. This shit happens; happens all the fucking time. Time to move on; *get over it*. The only tragedy in this whole sorry business is you Sam. Ditch the self-suffering. Get some balls. Don't have to be brass. In your case, ping pong will do."

I don't say anything, so Jamie does: "So, enough of the indulgence, enough screwing with your own head, enough not being fully with it, enough not being all there. Just. Stop! And move on."

Jamie forks up some lettuce and parmesan, while still managing to shake his head in frustration and scan an eye along the bar.

"Just look over there".

"Where?," I ask, but seeing him stare indiscreetly over my left shoulder.

"At the bar."

I turn, then turn back, asking flatly, "The blonde?"

"Yes Sam," Jamie sighs, again doing his little bewildered head-shake.

"She's not my type."

"Fuck-off," snorts Jamie, "that girl's anyone's type. Great looking pair of tits, *Hello Boys!* cleavage, an obviously quality cut of ass, compliant, potentially very comely pair of thighs. It's an oh-so-there-if-you-want-it invitation to get up to your balls in it!"

"Jamie, she looks like a hooker."

"Best way to get over the last one," reasons Jamie, "is get on to the next one… even if it costs a couple of quid."

"Jamie, you're a beautiful man. What would Jane say if she heard you talk like this?"

"Jane would get turned on, trust me. But sadly, Jane's a yesterday girl."

"Oh, sorry to hear it." I'd met Jane a couple of times; she was not especially pretty.

"Sorry? Why?," Jamie asks. "Jane wasn't that fit. I only went out with her because she'd take it up the arse. She wasn't even a very bouncy girl."

"Well Jamie, I suspect you had a lot to do with that. I imagine she was a bit tender most of the time? So, you're on the market again?"

"Well, yes, but depending on the audience, no. I've been seeing this bird called Chloe for the last 3 weeks. It's nothing serious," he explains. "She's very much recreational."

"She's your fuck-buddy?"

"She's a dancer, got great abs, so yeah; but she absolutely isn't Einstein."

"Well, when it comes to a fuck-buddy, it's not meant to be rocket science. Hell, if you find the act that much of a struggle, you're lucky to be with her!"

"OK, Jamie concedes, "but try this: we were having lunch last Saturday in Holland Park. A fly landed on her forehead. She didn't flinch, couldn't feel it. I looked at the fly for a second, then brushed it away with my hand. She said: *What?* I said: *A fly, on your forehead, its proboscis was starting to feed off your skin.* She said: *Proboscis? You do use long words sometimes.*

"So you see?" Jamie appeals.

A hollow tongue would be a girl's definition of heaven, I muse, but don't see Jamie's point at all. "No Jamie, in truth, I don't see? Who the hell uses the word proboscis in any form of conversation, whether when mentioning a fly or not?"

Jamie doesn't answer, just rolls his eyes. "She's doing an Open University course; Sociology. I do her homework, in exchange for sex."

"What kind of grades are you getting?"

"B's mostly."

"I'd say Chloe's brighter than you think."

Jamie

A little background on Jamie:

Jamie works for Goldman Saks (aka. Goldmine Sacks). He is a banker-wanker, a high-net worth individual, a man of little good sense but much money. Specifically, he runs a hedge fund (which does not mean he invests in topiary), and is not an interesting job as far as dinner party conversation's concerned. Afforded by his job, Jamie's interests include: (1) fine cheeses, (2) good wine, (3) anything that is expensive. "Anything expensive" includes: (1) Italian sports cars that brandish the pony and (2) pretty girls that require frequent gifts but little commitment.

Jamie and I were at school together. We are friends because we *were* friends, when we were 15. The fact that we are still friends is Borderline Baffling, seeing as Jamie is an unquestionable fascist, sexist, sometime racist dickhead. However, there is something often quite amusing and vicarious about spending short periods of time with him, like tasting a sweet little cup of evil.

He is short enough to have a Little Man Complex and to everyone's delight other than his own, Jamie is losing his hair. He is Man Most Likely: To have hair plugs before he is 35; order a bottle of '66 Margaux at Petrus and not mind (too much) paying £800 for the privilege. I see Jamie retiring at 35 (assuming hair plugs don't become extortionately expensive), then start hanging out with 19 and 20 year old girls, a sad man ravenous for young flesh and lost youth.

Czech Out Prague

It's 11pm and this third amaretto (with crushed ice, *only ever* crushed ice) is definitely my last. Epic Squash, followed my Epic Scoff can take it out of a man. We ask for the bill, giving Jamie opportunity to show-off his new Black Amex card.

"They give them to pretty much anyone these days," I tell him of his new plastic.

"Then where's yours?," he asks.

I just make a face, which isn't much of a retort.

The night is cold and crisp when we leave the restaurant.

"Thanks for that, mate."

"Pleasure," he says. "Share a cab?"

In the cab, aiming west, "You should go check out the

women in Prague," Jamie offers. "Now that's a good plan."

I know I shouldn't, but I ask anyway: "Why in the name of Jehovah would I want to do that?"

"Sam, tell me you're not going gay on me?"

"No Jamie, I'm not going gay on you."

"Then go to Prague," he suggests again, "because the girls in Prague are fit."

"The girls in London are fit."

"Not like the girls in Prague, they're not."

"*Really* fit, perhaps?"

"More than that." Jamie is absolute.

"Really?"

"Controversial theory, but limit women in the best patriarchal sense, keep 'em down, give 'em the lowest possible glass ceiling, and they'll instinctively fall on their obvious assets; their most transferable skills."

"Their obvious assets…?"

"All women are prostitutes by default. And by design."

"Yes, I can see how you'd think this theory of yours could err on the controversial."

Jamie feels clear need to expand. "The only kind of self-enterprise I want to see from a chick is when I'm in bed with her, or when she's in the kitchen. And while the collective sisterhood has burned too many bra's and kicked up too much gender liberation bullshit to admit otherwise, most birds are happiest being kept. They're happiest baking cookies, cooking pot-roast, and getting a good hard length inside them. For most birds, contentment is over a stove or in the sack. And it's where their contribution is most appreciated. It's where they can do the most good."

I have to wonder how deliberately provocative Jamie's being. I have to point out: "Certain circles would, I think, take umbrage at your theory. They may even like to castrate you for it."

"Well, balls to them."

"They may like to liberate you of those too."

"Well, they can have 'em slappin against their chin for a whiles, but that's as far as I'm willing."

"Lovely image. And charitable too."

"Sam, my point is this, a little bit of female oppression is good all round. I'm not suggesting slavery for Christ's sake!"

"You sure?" I'm not so sure he's sure.

"Just take Prague." Jamie is back to Prague. "As you know, I just spent the weekend there, and all the birds - excluding a mixed bag of tourists and hen do's - were just... *fine looking*. Even the Czech Chick's with slightly dodgy boat-races had made every effort to be tidy and trim everywhere else, lift their game as much as possible, where possible, all things pointing North as much as possible."

Jamie is now quite fuelled: "And why do they do this? To be attractive to us Menfolk; to be *desirable*; to bag a man; to find a *provider*. And how? By providing the kind of playtime kit that a bloke will find appealing. Sweet lookin' tits, ripe lookin' ass, a yummy-scrummy tummy, the kind of pins you'd happily wear round your hips."

I look out the cab window at a succession of passing street-lights, imagining that it's we who are stationary and the scenery that's moving, a carousel backdrop in a 20's silent movie. Only, Jamie's chatter insists that we're very much in a talkie.

"In Prague, capitalism's only just stepping out of the blocks," Jamie continues. "It's not evolved to the stage where women are getting the chance to become captains of industry, learn to play golf, and participate in all other manner of Man's World activities. And I say... Fucking Great, because that kind of opportunity is a distraction. It can put women off their form. And I say, *Honey, don't neglect your form!* Let us guys worry about playing off scratch and having the perfect swing. Ladeez, they're better off worrying about their skin, fine lines, the cruelties of gravity, cooking for us men and doing lots of sit-ups for themselves. Give chicks equality and they stop being chicks. Just look at Margaret Thatcher.

"I say, let women be good at what they're good at."

"Fucking and cooking?," I conclude dryly.

"Sam, you're hearing me... and you get out here."

I step out the cab, handing Jamie a tenner as I go. As the cab pulls away from the curb, Jamie winds down the window and winking, throws my crumpled tenner back at me. I catch it, which is preferable to fishing it out of a puddle.

Like a Plan B

OK, I admit it. I treated Sarah like a back-up plan (but there was more to it than just fucking-and-cooking, I swear.)

I think guys, those lacking a certain emotional depth (so, maybe the majority I'm talking about?), those guys lacking a certain level of compassion, they think of girls like plans, contingencies, best or worst case scenarios. Maybe it's the influence of watching too many War movies? It's not that I thought I was "settling" for Sarah, just that I wanted to weigh up my options, like any good soldier in the theatre of gender battle.

I *had* Sarah, but I wanted to keep my options open, play it like a spread bet. Girls bring out the gambler in guys.

Us guys, we calculate the odds, the level of risk, the potential winnings. The thing is, it's difficult to leave the table when you've just won the last hand. You still wonder if that "one more hand" will leave you that bit better off. Sarah was a winning hand. Was she THE winning hand? I don't know, but I do know the deck had been kind. At the time I wondered: Nice hand, but is there a better one coming up? I'll hold my cards, set 'em to one side, now deal me another 5, and let me play those too. That was me, not strictly by the rules, I know.

You see, Sarah was so sure, or seemed so sure at the time, that we were "meant for each other," that THIS was IT, the Real Thing, no fear of a Pepsi Challenge. Sarah seemed *convinced,* and that conviction freed me up to behave like an asshole – because I figured I couldn't lose.

In a way, it was Sarah that dealt me that second hand, telling me my keepsie hand was a Sure Thing, a banked asset; that I was always going to be Quids In. Do you see?

The thing is, I wasn't ready to settle down and I wasn't convinced, not equivocally, that I couldn't bag something better: a little taller or cuter, blonder or darker, more bouncy and even riper, more together, shrewder, who maybe earned more or knew more, perhaps someone sexier, filthier and yet also more demure? I wasn't really sure what "better" really was, and I never once thought about all the sexy-shrewd, filthy-demure, ripe and bouncy, tall and sultry assets I'd be trading in if I was to meet my apparent "up-grade"?

I blame her a lot.

Yes, because it makes me *feel better*, but also because she shouldn't have expressed such certainty about "Us". The tightest reign requires the lightest touch; you can quote me. Girls are *taught* to be teases, for God sake! Us guys, we like the kiss-chase, the thrill, the being told what we can't have. Makes us hungrier. We relish the electric "possibility". The first glance is the best glance. The first kiss is the best kiss, the one you have to work for, the one you have to steal.

Fact is, guys covet. We live life most richly when in a frenzied state of anticipation. Ownership, possession, even if they bring some hard earned sense of contentment, they're still not a patch on the excitement of being In The Chase. Sarah should have kept me motivated. She should have made it clear: the chase is still on. In a chase, there is No Sure Thing. But she didn't, Sarah did not do that, so I got complacent, fucked it all up by fucking someone else, and now, well, now the chase is over.

The Avenue

Friday's "Working Lunch" is at The Avenue on St James's Street. It's a bit like eating in an art installation, a White-Out affair that tries for a So-Serious NYC feel, but is occupied by Daddy's Girls wearing pashmina's and too many Pin Stripes worn by too many people called Hugo.

Lunch is courtesy of a rep from one of the Conde Nast magazine titles. I can't remember which mag, they have a few. I can't even remember the girl's name. I can't remember her name, but for days after, I tell you now, I will effortlessly remember what she ordered off the menu, and I ask myself: How can that be right?

We go straight to mains: I eat a lamb tagine which is actually quite pedestrian, while she's opted for the roast Lincolnshire duckling which she tells me is very tasty and would I like to try some?

We talk about possible partnership deals, mutual wins for her magazine title and my client's Brand & Business. She's very attractive but somehow rather unsexy to me, maybe *because* she is flirting with me? "Treat 'em mean…," and all that, but I'm also thinking about what Jamie said on Lombard Street, about new flesh, and so when we leave, I say, Perhaps we should meet for a drink next week and talk some more? I leave the interpretation of "drink" to her conclusion. She says, Out of work? I say, Why not? She then says she has a boyfriend and so I don't say anything, just stare passively at her. She pauses, then says, You know the name, you have my number. Not strictly true, I think, but don't share.

And it's That Easy, and that makes me feel incredibly depressed all of a sudden, so I phone into work, tell my PA Charlotte that I have a meeting off-site for the rest of the day, but also, who did I just have lunch with? Answer: Jenny, from Vogue magazine. Then I get a cab home and go to bed. It's 3 in the afternoon.

Mr. Third Party

I haven't mentioned it until now, but there is a "Third Party". An Added Variable in the Dynamic, if you like? As in: an 'orrible little fly in the ointment.

I've come to realise that I don't want to play any kind of triangular tournament, but I contrived it so there was a trois in the ménage.

I felt it was time you knew; I'd better explain.

The Third Party is a bloke Sarah met at work. Just some guy, who she'd mentioned to me in passing, on a few occasions actually, while hostilities between she and I were hotting-up. It wasn't long after she'd started The New Job, and I, thinking myself some kind of puppet master (while actually being some kind of prick), had thought, GREAT, I see a way out. This bloke became my escape route. To give it my best Charlie

Bronson, to tunnel through the dirt like butter, I'd just start behaving like a complete shit, and I'd make my great escape. Genius Thinking, I thought. Lunatic Thinking, I now know.

You see, Sarah would never leave me unless she had somewhere to go, namely *someone* to go to. I decided to give Sarah scope to entertain the possibility of an alternative life, an alternative *someone*, with me slackening the rope enough to let her get close enough to thinking, *Hey I got options here!*

"Would you like to come out with my work for drinks this Friday?," she'd ask, and I'd say "Nah, I got work stuff on too." And off I'd let her go. And then when we did spend time together, it was a waste of time – degenerative, breaking down, always getting worse, less fun, more hostile. Friday night prior, I'd already know my reply to a following Monday morning, *What did you do at the weekend?*

"Me? I had a miserable time, thanks very much. Bickered, rowed, verbally sniped at my girlfriend, then went out on my own leaving her in the flat to sulk and whine down the phone to her Mum and friends."

It took a good few weekends worth, a real war of attrition, but I got there in the end, got to the death throes of the relationship. And why did I want it that way? Why couldn't I have just said, "I want to end this, I want it over, I want out?" Cowardice, I think that is why.

*

At first my ego wasn't even bothered about her leaving, whatever the circumstances of departure, Third Party or not.

"Third Party" wouldn't have even gotten in the frame if I hadn't let him in, wouldn't have been a consideration for her if I hadn't started behaving like a monster, becoming the walking breathing antithesis of love. This was my reasoning, and I know what you're thinking. *My God, does he ever back himself!* You're thinking, *What an asshole, she's better shut of ole Sambo!* Well listen, I'm not making myself out to be the sympathetic character here, but I do know what I know.

I know, I know: Be careful what you wish for. I know that well enough now, because I wanted Sarah to leave me. And I also know she was in love with me and I Killed It very consciously, making repeated lusty stabs with my most pointy stabbing stick. I mean, I didn't return home from work of an evening, slip on my wife-beating string vest, shotgun a quick few cans of *Stella*, then go about my bare-knuckle business. All I did was very consciously stop behaving like a boyfriend.

I just stopped showing I cared.

Now Third Party is Sarah's "Other Half," and I'm a Past Chapter. And truth be told, it fucks me right off. Royally so. You might have gathered this already?

Those snippets she'd mentioned about "Him" (while she and I were doing our death throes thing) now keep scratching at my brain, whereas before, I just kept thinking: Excellent, aren't I the smart one! Wiggle my thumb and pulls tight the string.

I remember his name, his christian name at least. It's Hans. Can you believe it? What kind of a fucking name is that?

I remember her saying one time that *He* drives a sports car. Well, fucking Hans fucking wouldn't he! Well, so fucking what?, I think (but knowing it annoys the hell out of me). Now I've book-marked *autotrader.com* and am too often checking the prices of German engineered pocket rockets I can't afford.

Sarah mentioned that *Hans* is a Board Director, the youngest in The Company, and that when he was younger still, he'd modelled t-shirts. Apparently *Hans* has Big Arms. I doubt Big Arms had anything to do with securing a Directorship, but perhaps it helped?

I bet the photocopying machine operator at Sarah's company is also a board director - for ambidextrous stapling skills perhaps? While this fancy comforts me, I still found myself going out to buy a rather too-heavy set of dumbbells very recently. And they have become something of an appendage - though I draw the line to taking them on the tube (the commute is grizzly enough).

In conclusion, this bloke, *Fucking Hans*, "Mr. Third Party," is a complete TWAT. And boy, Han's is a *great* Hate Figure. Irony is, I put him on the podium. I gave him Sarah.

No Coffee

It's 4am, Saturday morning. I've just slept 12 hours straight. My t-shirt is covered in sweat and I am utterly awake. I reach out from my bed for the nearby remote and zap the radio. Early morning airwaves bounce round the room. *The Beatles,* John Lennon singing, *"I'd rather see you dead little girl than to be with another man. I'd rather see you dead little girl 'cos I don't know where I am…"*

I grin. I hear you John.

Radio Pathos. How is it that the airwaves are always at hand to play the real-time soundtrack to the movie of your life?

I punch the remote, changing the stations. John "I am the Walrus" Lennon is replaced with Brian Adams, accompanied by Sporty Spice. Sporty's giving it full throat-throttle, explaining herself, *"Got the TV on cuz the radio's playing songs that remind me of you.* Then Bri chimes in: *Baby when you're gone - I realize*

I'm in love... The days go on and on - and the nights just seem so long". Yeah Sporty, yeah Bri, I feel your pain.

I zap off the radio and go make coffee, only the kitchen cupboard reports that there is no coffee to go and make. What fucking time does Starbuck's open? Plan B; I grab my running shoes from under the bed, throw on some Tracky-B's and figure I'll jog into the dawn. I've got nothing better to do than add to my t-shirt sweat.

Time Passes

Time, more specifically 6 days have passed, and I couldn't tell you where they've gone, only that they are never coming back. There will be no refund.

6 days on, I still remember my name, what I do for a living, that I have slept a lot of sleep, that I've visited the gym every evening for the last 5 days, pounding the treadmill like a running fool and trying to hurt myself in the weights room, trying hard to keep my auto pilot switch permanently lit.

Today is a Friday, tonight is a Halloween party (perhaps a touch premature but the 31st falls on a Sunday this year); venue is the Bluebird restaurant on the Kings Road. The host is Conde Nast publications. There is a Charity Excuse for the pomp, ego show, and posh canapés, but the healing hands and arms-for-hugging sentiment is thinly veiled. The reality will be: grinning B & C list celebs, an excuse for pretty girls to get noticed and for guys to letch and maybe get laid. I consider blowing the whole thing out and continuing my auto pilot ways, but Tam's going, and I'm dragging Sean along, so the evening poses to be less insufferable than a night on the treadmill.

Happy Halloween

The scene: Bluebird, 350 King's Road, SW3. The time: 8:20pm.

A steady queue of party goers form and their names are duly checked off. Next up: Samuel Grant and Sean Wahab. We're on the list and we're in, climbing the stairs, checking our coats (no hats) and making our way through the gathering party throng to the bar at the far end of the large first floor space. At the bar we elbow Edmund Conran (son of Sir Terrance), who one could argue has only got an invite because his Dad owns the place.

"This party better not cost me as much as the last do you and I attended," says Sean, looking just a little ashamed.

"Yes, that was a little bit awkward," I tell him, then to the bar man, "Two gin and tonics, preferably Tanquery."

Back in late June, we'd attended a Summer party at Kensington Roof Gardens. Just off Kensington High Street, some 8 floors up, sits a mini Kew gardens, like a fauna/flora icing atop a brownstone slab. The host was Channel 4, it was a strikingly hot evening for early Summer, there was a lot of bubbly flowing, Sean had done more coke than is even wise at a media party, and there were flamingos. Of course, the lack of reason or responsibility that follows the aforementioned details is no excuse.

I grant that Florida pink flamingos (aka, Genus: *Phoenicopterus ruber rubber*) are not a typical sight in W8, but for whatever reason known only to Sean, he was of the late night opinion that he should set one free. "To Tampa with you my pink feathered friend," announced Sean as he manhandled then threw the bird into the air and (sadly) off the building. The wing-clipped bird dropped all 8 floors without a sound. Fortunately there had been no one passing on the pavement directly below.

The management were far from impressed, and those present to witness found the episode quite upsetting and left even before we did. Sean too was quite upset, became quickly sober, profusely apologetic and wrote a cheque there and then for £4,000. The matter was closed, with Sean paying for an expensive lesson that we should all heed: in London the flamingos can't fly.

"To Tampa with you my pink feathered friend," I tell Sean as our drinks arrive.

"I think we should change the subject," he suggests without much mirth, before more cheerfully asking: "Did you know that our generation's a head cancer time bomb waiting to go off?"

"Is this the: should mobiles come with health warnings debate?"

"Might be - but it's not an endearing prospect, your pituitary gland being pushed out your ear by a fast growing tumour that matures to the size of a steroidal cumquat."

"No, not particularly," I concede, "but we all need something to worry about. My PA, Charlotte, has a radio on her desk. Whenever her mobile rings, three seconds prior, her radio stops with its phat beats and assumes a very good impression of a Geiger counter."

"Three egg heads in Norway," Sean continues, "just cooked an egg using the microwaves emitted from their three mobile phones. Their conclusion: mobile phone users are microwaving their heads and this is not healthy, or any healthier than using plutonium rods as ear rings."

"Y'know," I offer, "the test market for the first consumer mobile phones was New Zealand? The phone was attached to a battery pack of similar dimensions to a *Smart Car*. You had to be a weight lifter to get the handset to your ear, and I understand it leaked radiation on a par with Chernobyl.

The phone would ring, and after you'd said "Hello," you'd only have time to hear the caller tell you "You're dead" before your head started melting into your neck."

From the back pocket of his jeans, Sean retrieves his phone, his New Phone. "We've come a long way since New Zealand," he offers. "I give you, the very latest, ultra light-weight, super-sleek, silver-cased telephonic accessory, the *Nokia X21*."

"Phone pride is an ugly thing," I tell him.

"Perhaps, but this is not an ugly phone."

"Meaning that while head or earlobe cancer is a concern, having The Wrong Phone is even more concerning?"

"Precisely."

Sean

A little background on Sean (beyond the one-time manslaughter of an exotic bird):

I've always felt that Sean will amount to a lot, or very little. He's the kind of guy for whom it could go either way, that despite being intelligent, aspiring, and quite possibly talented, he could ultimately amount to little more than an Icon of Underachievement. He aspires to being The Great Director, or just some kind of film writer/director type, has a number of writing projects (TV screenplays, adaptations, feature film originals) forever on the go, but in my opinion should just finish one properly, then get the thing out there. The Great Auteur, or the Great Amateur, both are within his grasp.

Sean doesn't have to do a regular job-type-job, and never will, but such luxury came through grisly circumstances.

Sean and I graduated university the same year, moved up to London, and began the job interview circuit at the same time.

On Sean's first interview, he left the offices of a leading-light production company in Golden Square, feeling he'd done well and perhaps dreaming that one day he would make that leap from Dogs-Bodying to Running The Show. Spring still in his step and future greatness still on his mind, Sean made his way towards Regent Street, where he then attempted to cross the road but failed to see the Very Large Red Bus.

Sean should have been killed, and yes, that is Pretty Horrific, but there was a juicy pay-off. Sean should have watched where he was stepping, but the bus driver was two days from retirement and subsequent investigations established he was too myopic to be behind the wheel without a near half inch of prescribed glass in front of each eye. Sean endured more broken bones than Evil Kenevil, spent a calendar month in a coma, and when he woke up, was greeted with the kind of out of court settlement that made his permanent limp really rather bearable. Sean doesn't even mind the limp thing, believing it offers him a certain "mystery".

Ever since The Big Bus Episode, Sean has tended to be something of a Live For The Moment Guy. The fact that Sean lived to kill a flamingo could be defined as a certain kind of irony.

★

By quarter to ten, Tam hasn't yet materialised, and I've already had too many gin and tonics, or just enough to start feeling quite pissed and on the verge of being truly offensive to someone. I wonder whether Tam will show, and if she does, whether her idiot boyfriend David will be accompanying. I don't want to see David, but I would quite embrace an opportunity to be rude and hostile towards him. Sean is talking, but it feels more At Me than To Me because I'm not properly listening, just looking at girls and who I like the look of. I'm about to tell Sean that I think his latest film script idea sucks – "A Spy-Horror. Think: Dracula with a double 00 status. Think: a supernatural assassination bureau." – when Tam suddenly appears in front of us, saving Sean from my criticism and looking Balls-Out Awesome in a Stetson, frilly dinner shirt and denim skirt. On anyone else, it might look like fancy dress.

"Hey Cow Girl!," I say, kissing her lightly on each cheek (David nowhere to be seen) before accepting the flute of champagne she offers. Sean then does the same.

Girl Kiss

"Boys, I have to tell you, I've ticked another life-experience box."

"Oh yes," I answer, a little curious, happy to be reeled in by Tam's excitement.

"You've finally raided Larry Hagman's wardrobe?," suggests Sean, who is ignored.

"Of course, I shouldn't tell you this… but I can be so indiscreet."

Tam smiles, maybe enjoying the fact that she's about to tell us something that she believes we'll enjoy, teasing.

"I was out last night with some of the girls – Nina, Sophie, and Helen. Late afternoon shopping with Nina, a few pink drinks at Harvey Nick's where we lorded it up like regular high class prozzies, as favours the fifth floor…"

"I hope this was all done with a strong sense of irony?," I interrupt.

"Absolutely - completely self-aware, a massive parody."

"That's fine then," approves Sean. "Please continue."

"Then after Harvey Nicks, Nina and I cabbed it down to Oriel's in Sloane Square to meet Sophie and Helen."

"I know where Oriel's is," Sean adds.

"Well done," I tell him, before Tam continues.

"But did you know that they do a fantastic Belini?"

"As in peach schnapps and champagne?" I ask, just making sure everyone lives on the same planet.

"Yes," she confirms, "as in Krug and Archers when done the Oriel's way."

"Sounds like an atrocity. Girls will be girls, but why you'd want perfectly good Krug to taste of peach is beyond the understanding of ordinary decent champagne lovers."

"Champagne lovers such as yourself?"

"Champagne tends to give me heartburn," Sean comments obliquely, then adds: "Irrespective, peach flavoured Krug surely doesn't merit its own life-experience box? I'm sure a straw poll would prove me right?"

"It does if it's been passed from mouth-to-mouth; specifically girl-mouth-to-girl-mouth."

Blimey.

Sean: "I'm sorry Tam, but you might have to explain what I hope you're about to explain."

"Not that I'm a lesbian…," she starts.

"Good start," I encourage.

Then continues, "…or have ever excited at the prospect of myself in a girl-with-girl moment of intimacy."

"Are you serious?" Sean looks genuinely excited. "This Tam, promises to be exactly the sort of explanation I was hoping for."

"Seriously guys, I've never been with another girl, nor wanted to."

"Until now?," I ask bemused, "until last night?"

"Last night," Tam verifies, "I happened to kiss a girl. Important to state: *Just* kiss."

"Who? Nina, Sophie, or Helen? I think the mental image works best if it's Helen."

"Sam! Nina, Sophie, Helen and I are good friends, not lipstick lesbians!"

"Hey, this is your confession, and you do admit to being *good* friends."

"But not Just Good Friends the way people sometimes mean Just Good Friends."

"Well, if it wasn't one of your good *platonic* friends, are you telling me you, er, pulled in Oriel's?"

"More she pulled me."

Sean: "Bloody hell! Who's *she?*"

"Some girl called Sally."

"Does David know about Sally?," I ask.

"No Sam, he does not. I may be capable of indiscretion, but you two…"

"Unlike some, our lips are sealed," I assure.

Sean: "Fucking brilliant! Mustang fucking Sally! Was she fit!"

"Hey, it was just a kiss. I was more than a bit tipsy."

"I'd say, but was she fit?," I echo.

"Yes, of course she was fit! You think I would kiss a minger?"

Sean, eagerly: "Are you going to see her again? Perhaps move in with her, start web-casting episodes of live lesbian action? I don't reckon your parents would be that delighted at first, but it would, I think, be a very selfless contribution to the greater good."

"Listen, it was very much a one off."

"You didn't like kissing another girl?" I ask. "I'm normally quite a fan of it."

"I didn't mind it. I was curious, which is why I let it happen, though it was a bit of a shock when I discovered she wanted me to sample her mouthful of Belini."

"I bet. What a gal! This is incredible! And you're absolutely right, this deserves its own life-experience box. Helluva tick! Other than the peach aspect, did you find it very different?"

"Not really, it was much like kissing a guy." Tam pauses, "Only with less stubble involved."

"One would hope so."

"But I prefer kissing guys, being as guys are what I fancy, and girls are who I shop with. So it was as a I say, a one off."

"Well, that's a shame, but you might not be as sure as you sound - you should never say *never*. I think Sean's live webcast idea could be a real goer, and even less ambitiously, this kissing girls thing could be a real party trick for you. Just so long as I'm always invited to the party."

"Sam, Sean, you're such boys."

★

My Very Nice Watch says 20 past 11, and I accept that it's time to go, to leave this place. *Never be the last one leaving.* I do however want one more drink – just one – so with Tam departed and Sean getting the coats, I zero in on the bar.

Before even placing my order, a tap on my shoulder. I turn to face a face I vaguely recognise but can't immediately place. Female, very cute, a bit short, a bit too blonde, wearing an almost diaphanous silk blouse over a not-hard-to-be-sexy black bra. The blouse is a wee slip of a thing, but looks like it cost a large amount of somebody's salary.

Black Bra Girl smiles: "So, how 'bout that drink?".

I'm about to brush her off, black bra or no black bra, but then: Memory returns! It's the Vogue bird from the previous Friday at the Avenue. And her name was…?

"Jemma, hi," I say.

"Jenny," Jenny corrects, her slight scowl understandable.

"Yes, sorry," then add, "The roast Lincolnshire duckling, right?"

"Pardon?"

"It's what you ordered, at the Avenue, as a main."

"Oh." Well, what else was she going to say?

I smile: "Jenny, tell me what I can get you to drink, then tell me how you are. You know, I've been thinking about you all week."

Morning Has Broken

Touch.

Touch at my lips; the touch of another.

"Sarah," I murmur. Then, as I pull myself out of the darkness, I think: Sarah? Err, No. Then: The girl, last night, Gemma, no Jenny?

I open my eyes, knowing despite the growing understanding of a Hangover In The Making that circumstances will become clearer. In reality, I couldn't become more confused.

Sean?

What the…?

Okay, this is highly odd and irregular.

I am not dreaming, though in a way I wish I was.

I place a firm hand on the corners of Sean's shoulders, create an arm's length of space between us and ask quite squarely and evenly: "Sean, mate, what the fuck are you doing?"

Then: the doorbell.

"Saved by the bell," says Sean, avoiding eye contact.

The first thing I think is the first thing I say: "Get the fuck out my bedroom." The doorbell rings again. God only knows what kind of expression I'm pulling? I throw the duvet off me; brush by Sean in his state of semi-blush, then turn back to him, just sitting on the corner on my bed, and announce: "Sean, this is Highly Gay."

Bleary eyed, of serious bed-head, and feeling oh-so-very-very-confused, I step out of the flat and into the hallway, taking the stairs three steps at a time, pulling on a sweatshirt as I go. I look at my watch. It's 10:52am and I already don't know how much more Saturday morning I can take.

I open the front door, happily showing my boxer shorts to the world at large, and standing directly in front of me:

Sarah.

It's Sarah.

I am truly speechless. My legs very nearly buckle.

"Hi Sam," she says, evenly, calmly, in control.

Silence; the silence you get where everything just stops, the planet no longer turning.

"Hi" is as much as I can muster in return.

I feel hot and cold and very distant from the whole tableau of events. I might break into song, I might start crying.

"Hi," I say again.

★

NOVEMBER

Friday, November 1st, 1996

How I Met Sarah

I'd lined my stomach well. Solids, made simple: *Marmite,* definitely my mate, spread generously over numerous thick-grained carbohydrate slabs. Toast x8. That should do it; that should soak it.

The night, This Night, I knew, was likely to be Large; the ticket's back-pocketed, fever building, the path there to walk, later stagger.

It was a night for beer, Big Beer, consumed in Big Quantities, thus making a Big Beer Night Out; so worked the Formula. I was as prepared as preparation allowed. I was ready. Though I may wobble through the valley of imbibed carnage, I shall fear no flagon, for I am not the lightest beer swillin' girlie at the festival. Well, I hoped, not quite.

The *Holsten Beer Festival,* location: Battersea was an act that struck just the faintest semi-quaver of fear. I was face-offing a Friday Night Commitment that could right-off a good deal of my weekend. It didn't take a crystal ball to know what Saturday morning was going to be about: the suspicion that someone had detonated a large, crudely made bomb in the lower part of my brainpan, 24 hours of stomach tumble and skin the uglier shade of ashtray yellow. Great prospects, none of them.

It was a Three Man Mission, the 3 of "Us" being, Sean, Jamie, Me, us blokes, buddies, chums. Sean thought the affair might make for good character observation, Jamie figured there'd be Ample & Easy Totty. For my part, I hadn't truly explored my motivations though probably Jamie and Sean were both right.

We arrived to a packed house, rammed stem to stern and floor to rafter. Bodies and beer, heaving, sod-all evidence of line-walking sobriety, and it was only 20 to 9. Arriving Fashionably Late was not a tactic that got you noticed, near on everyone seemed already too pissed to care.

Jamie suggested we U-turn and find something wholly more civilised on the Kings Road, but Sean was undeterred, had neatly inched himself on to an All Girl Table, figuring he could fight his way clear if things turned ugly, so Jamie relented and seated.

A waitress (dressed as Fraulein) took our order and within minutes our wallets were lighter and our arms much, much heavier. Clutching what need only be detailed as Fucking Massive Steins, we each paused at the sheer volume of liquid, and then like everyone else, began to swallow. *Though I may wobble through the valley…*

To get into the spirit, we drank, just drank.

Three Steins later: even Jamie was more in the mood, and "Tippage," conventionally a Cardinal Sin of Lager Culture had become a compulsory kind of initiation. Pouring a healthy pint of ale over yourself, a friend, or maybe someone you've never met was receiving not only social acceptance, but Buddy-Love Embrace. Vertical Beer Baths for everyone.

The rules of normal-place, normal-time human interaction were suspended. Circumstances were abnormal: it was OK to stand six to a table, unison jumping to a Euro-beat, with the collective purpose being to crack timber and give gravity its way. Never was Trestle Table Destruction so focused. Never was consequence so inevitable, so welcome, so comical, so pure, even fulfilling. Tables broke, drinkers did fall, cuts, bruises and dry-cleaning bills all a tomorrow realisation.

And everywhere you looked: similar antics by similar folk brandishing similar drunk-sloppy faces; but whether drunk or sober, the two events that followed I couldn't have predicted:

(1) Bucks Fizz took to the stage,

(2) Sarah crashed into my world.

"Come on then!," cried Sean, not caring to stifle a schoolboy enthusiasm woken from a ten year hibernation. Four characters in Bucks Fizz costumes emerged front and centre to a chorus of drunken approval.

Now I acknowledge that Revival bands have a purpose, make Easy Logic, fill an obvious gap left by some Grim Reaping Handiwork. Goodbye John, goodbye Jim, hello the Bootleg Beatles, welcome the Australian Doors; but where, I wondered, did the right-here-right-now emergence of a bootleg Bucks Fizz fit the equation? And what I really couldn't fathom was the reception they were getting.

"Come on then!," cried Sean again.

"I didn't realise you were such a fan?," I hollered.

"Bucks Fizz: Clean Bitch-Dirty Bitch. A fan? Oh yeah." Sean's gravity painted all manner of Pubescent Tissue-Moments.

"I'm guessing Roy Castles' able assistant was Clean Bitch?"

"You got it."

"In that case, I think I preferred Dirty Bitch".

Three numbers into the set, and I started wondering if there was perhaps a Bucks Fizz album waiting for call-up from the lower reaches of my tape collection.

Yards to our left, a black guy, with the face of a young Samuel L. Jackson and the rippling physique of an Early Years Apollo Creed jived and gyrated on plains that re-worked liquid bop. Neck tendons taught like suspension bridge cabling, sweat cart-wheeling off his noggin with the vigour of a garden sprinkler. Man, did this Top Cat ever feel the Euro-beat.

The Ladeez too, were more than getting in the groove. Chests lifting, bosoms heaving, hips working like pistons; Bucks Fizz had never been So Cool. Yes, I understood: this was The Outer Limits. Someone had screwed with the horizontal, fiddled with the vertical. We were skirting into the Realms of the Unreal, and then…

Then I saw her.

Her.

I'm not saying I heard trumpets, but all else was still (including the likes of Samuel) and all else was silent (including Bucks Fizz).

There. *She.* Was. This Absolute Honey, petit of frame though gloriously proportioned of chest, wearing tight – *Yeah Man, real tight* - but expensively tasteful togs that couldn't conceal long-standing gym homage.

I too was suddenly feeling rather up-standing.

She had a light tan, not dissimilar to that of a Milky Way chocolate bar (odd comparison, I know), with clean, smooth features that smacked of Cherubic Over-Bite but potential Sack Devilment. Pale blue eyes, and jet black hair that flashed obsidian-blue as it caught the light, *Oh, Meeeow.* (Footnote #1: Mercifully, I did *not* Meeeow aloud.) And she was even drinking Stein's, though only God knew where she was storing it?

Easy now, I told myself. Think: Cool. Think: Bond. Don't think: Austin Powers. You're not a Spy, and you're not a Playboy, either international or otherwise, but… she doesn't know that.

I was on my fourth flagon, and my forearm was starting to feel the efforts as much as my bloodstream. I was changing hands regularly, but wasn't going to resort to a double hand-hold, as favoured by many of the girls present. After all, I was not a girl, and it wasn't a mug of Bovril I was nursing.

What I was though, was Smitten.

She moved well, with confidence, dancing the way Properly Good Looking Girls dance. It fit; she was.

I had to speak to her. I stood marvelling, wondering, delaying. I could imagine her type – all pithy put downs and killer comebacks, churning a wake of bruised egos and broken hearts. My fantasy was seemingly fuelled by chronically hackneyed Country & Western ditties.

As nimble as 3-and-a-bit steins allowed, I pointed myself in her direction.

B-bum, b-bum…

I approach. She sees my approach, our eyes meet, I hold court, take a breath, assume Charm Mode, open with: "Hi" (short, concise, unambiguous), and flash what I hoped was my most winning smile. (Footnote #2: That smile of mine is always a risk. It morphs the drunker I get. It can look like a cheeky, dare I say Kinda Sexy grin. It can make me look a little like Tom Cruise, but depending on circumstance, it sometimes makes me look like a leering, lawn chewing Keith Chegwin.)

She says nothing, but neither does she just kick me in the nuts and turn away, so I figure I'm not giving it too much Chegwin.

My eyes feel greedy, want to slide down her half exposed cleavage, clock the Breast Potential, but I know that would send out The Wrong Message. Instead: I look her boldly in the eye, smile, and in the form of a question: "The Rotterdam Hilton, Spring, 1994, the Gunter-Ramsbottom Rooms?"

She says nothing, looks a touch quizzical.

I continue: "There was a slight mist in the air, and a definite chill… but no Moon."

Still silent, still quizzical, still Very Cute.

"What?," she asks quite rightly.

"You don't remember?," me hamming it up. "You were wearing a yellow dress with blue polka dots. I was wearing a purple jacket… in crushed velour. And a red carnation. The guy at the piano? You asked me to play *My Way* and, er, you sung it your way. You were unforgettable."

I pause. Tick, tock: she's either going to go with it, or she is not. She smiles, then broadly. Bingo.

"It's been a while," she says. "How are you?"

"A little drunk," I say, and now we're both smiling. "I'm Sam."

"Hi, I'm Sarah."

★

I don't remember how long we talked for, not particularly long in truth, but there was a very strong *something,* a strong enough something to distract me from the fact that we were not alone and that I was never going to get a chance to talk to her for long. When Samuel's young body-double (aka. Neck Tendons) came over, it was with the definite suggestion that I could keep all my body parts so long as I just fucked off. His head tilted towards Sarah's neck, whereupon he planted a light kiss that felt more for my benefit than hers and I understood easily, *this* was The Boyfriend.

He looked me over. More accurately, he squared his 6"5 frame of robo-muscle in my direction and narrowed his eyes. For a fleeting moment I did think he might just step on my head and have done with it, so it was with much relief that he extended an enormous dry palm.

"What's up?," he began. "I'm Eric."

I had to smile. Truthfully, I had to swallow very hard to prevent convulsion. Eric! Oh, dear, that's a bit of an equaliser. You're always going to be marching a bit of an up-hill struggle to Mt. Cool if you've been lumbered with a name like… Eric. Instead of sharing my thoughts, I opted for a neat: "Hey, pleased to meet you."

With Friend or Foe seemingly established as the former, Eric's face broke into a massive broad-backed smile, and I swear, somewhere in back a hunk of gold shone out at me. "So how's your evening going?," he inquired kindly enough.

"No permanent damage yet. I'm still upright and," I lie, "I've always had a bit of a thing for Bucks-Fizz."

"Oh yeah, which one did you prefer? Cheryl or Jay?"

"Jay," I reply, a little taken back by Eric's grasp of Song for Europe totty.

"Ah," he nods with what I detect is a hint of approval. "Dirty Bitch."

I laugh, he laughs, even Sarah finds cause to grin.

"In this place, I suspect we're not her only fans," I say, then: "It was fun meeting the two of you. I'll see you around."

I return to our table, thinking: that was not a winnable situation. In my absence, Jamie and Sean have each managed to drink another three Steins, and have been instrumental in the breaking of two trestle tables. Jamie has briefly snogged Some Random Bird with a Northern Accent; Sean (ordinarily quite placid) has taken issue with a member of the bar staff, nearly inciting Removal By Bouncer.

"Chaps," I suggest, "it's only wise to have so much fun in any one night. Shall we ditch?" I only hope I don't look as shit-faced as the two faces staring back at me.

As clocks all over London strike 1, and mini cab firms rub their palms with glee, we start walking, looking to put the booze-fuelled bonhomie behind us.

"That Northern Bird had a very tight looking arse," Sean remarks.

"She did," confirms Jamie, first-hand the wiser.

As we pass the coat queue, a hand suddenly takes me by the arm, turning me gently.

Sarah.

Blimey.

"The Rotterdam Hilton indeed," she says smirking, then: "We shouldn't leave it so long next time?"

I feel a square of paper being pressed into my hand, what feels like a business card, what I just *know* is a telephone number. I slide my hand and its new contents into my pocket, never once breaking eye contact.

"Hey, you're not *that* good looking," she points out in response to my goofy self-satisfied expression, then turns away, the moment over.

I race down the tunnel and catch up with the guys who'd walked on drunk and oblivious. The night air is actually refreshing because of its very clamminess and the prospect of an amble along the river feels good.

My hand still in my pocket, I finger the business card, the corner of the card crisp and pleasing to the touch. I smile and have no idea what I've let myself in for.

That was The Beginning.

That Was Then

It's morning. I'm awake. Like the Beer Festival, this, another memory.

I remember a morning, one of Our First, the early November light oozing through the open vein of retreating curtain, spilling onto the bed, falling over Sarah's shoulders and back. Nice shoulders, real tasty back. Yes indeed, I remember.

I remember Sarah, turning on her side, waking slowly, reluctantly, not yet willing to acknowledge the new day. The duvet moves with her, moves over her, her chest rising as she stretches, me sighing as the duvet falls away to reveal the immaculate form of Firm Ripe Breast.

Her eyes open, blink once, then twice, then open again. She looks at me, at my expression, and asks fairly enough: "What?"

I tell her: "I'm feeling very fondly towards you."

"That's better than badly I suppose. Why fondly?" At this point, I remember, she yawned, and I replied:

"For starts, you're looking very… nippular this morning. I'd planned to put some washing on later and was just thinking, I may chose to coat-hang a shirt or two from you."

"Nippular, eh?" She lifts the duvet, looks beneath, looking me down and up with mock theatre.

"Well Sam, you're looking very penile this morning."

"As in cocksure?," I suggest with a smile.

"No, as in you're such a dick!," she corrects, and laughs, pleased with herself.

I say, "Aren't we pleased with ourselves."

"Yes, very," she replies, still laughing, and still Very Nippular. We kiss, happy.

"Guys buy desert islands for girls like you," I tell her.

"In thanks for your breasts alone. You're breasts, they're like… The Best. If I was to spend a year in solitary confinement, but could take one thing from this room – in spite of all the accumulated possessions, luxury goods, techno-comforts – I would take your breasts. Assuming I couldn't take all of you that is."

"Sam, that's very sweet, I think?"

"And as for you lips…," I continue.

"Yes?," she encourages.

"Your lips are so very utterly and entirely kissable." I think for a moment. "Almost unimaginable, but I think they are even more kissable that your breasts are nippular?"

"Then kiss them," she instructs.

Good Cowboy, Bad Cowboy

Self-concept; it's a deceptive thing. You think you *know* yourself, have yourself down pat. Then things *happen*. Time goes by and as it does, you do *things*, things that surprise you, make you question who you are, that suggest you've *changed*.

I'd always seen myself as one of The Good Guys. Most people do I guess? How many perceive themselves as being bad, that their Core Self is, say, a little cheap, a little nasty? *Yep, I'm a bastard. That's me alrighty, hohum, there you go.* No, not many.

Most folk, probably all, reckon that deep down at the very least, they're Pretty Good Eggs. On the surface misunderstood possibly, perhaps with misguided intentions and bad influences, but at their very centre, actually quite nice, sweet, even innocent?

I always thought I was a Good Egg. When I was little, I like most other kids would strap on my hip holster when

Cowboys-n-Injuns playtime was called. (I never considered myself for the role involving tepees and Mohawk's. They were the Bad Guys, right?) If I was a trail-hitting Raw-hider, I figured I'd be riding with Rowdy or Woody, wearing my own white hat, waiting for the call-up to save a small Mexican village from Banditos, generally doing what a man's gotta do. And nothing much has changed in the years proceeding (until now).

Now I'm less sure, less sure of deserving a hip holster, like Rowdy, like Han Solo, the ultimate space cowboy. I have a concern, that maybe I've always belonged to the Dark Side, just had been kidding myself all these years, thinking that I was a force of good. Could it be that the ten-gallon hat I've been wearing (metaphorically you understand) has not been white, even beige, but instead a real light-sucking bad-ass black? And what I thought was me giving it my best Travolta nice-guy swagger was in fact no more than a cucumber-up-my-ass JR Ewing waddle? It could just be?

I'd like to think I at least fall into a middle ground, where I'm a not-that-bad-a-cowboy-really, like Butch or Sundance: fallible, but attractive and disarming for it, a likeable guy, packing charisma and charm as well as a quick draw. But I realise this could just be more of my bullshit, more self-deception.

So I've grown to know that maybe I don't know myself; that if judgement be by action, then I am The Asshole. And if not an asshole categorically destined for some serious subterranean roasting come the after-life, an asshole none the less, who may deserve a light flame-grilling?

Saturday, November 1ˢᵗ, 1997

Where I Met Holly

Location: Atlantic Bar; a party-hearty Saturday night crowd, very media, very wanabee, heavy on the lip gloss and swagger. The scene is typical: Guys *Giving It*, Girls *Working It*, wall-to-wall miniskirts, all slinky tops and slinkier smiles, many happy to give head to get ahead. Funny how it can work: some folk go down to go up in the world.

I'm drinking martini's and I'm probably only one more drink away from being the wrong side of sober, even though their pouring here is not particularly generous. I'm of the New York City School: if you don't spill the martini on that first lift to your mouth, it ain't full.

It's 10pm. Jamie is talking about some share deal he wants me to get involved in, do I have five grand? Jamie is convinced that he can make both of us some "really tidy" sideline cash.

"It's a small stake for high takes," he says.

Five grand is nothing to him, but a good deal more to me. I might give him the money, I might not.

Tam's on her way and she's bringing her New Boyf, some Nearly Forty (year old) called David who I'm disinclined to like, even pre-introduction. I'm feeling a tad territorial, even though I don't feel anything for Tam *that way*.

"So? You game?," asks Jamie, referring to the shares thing.

"I don't know. I'll sleep on it."

I look at my watch again. "Tam can get a bit carried away with her greatness for lateness."

"What do you know about the new bloke?," Jamie inquires.

"David," I answer and I think I sneer a little. "Apparently his family owns a good chunk of Leicestershire, something like a quarter, or slightly less depending on which edition of *Who's Who?* you read."

"I hate the Midlands."

"Midlander or not, his estimated net worth is £3.7 million."

The minute you start talking about someone, they show up. From nowhere, then right in front of us, like Scotty's just beamed them down, Tam, and next to her, the guy they must call David.

Tam looks Really Well (though she never looks unwell) and much as I'd like to think otherwise, David looks like the right kind of arm extension; tall, tanned, with squint lines at the eyes, a square jaw, and an expensive haircut. I'd like to say he looks old enough to be her father, but he looks nothing like. Firm hand-shakes for the boys, kisses for the girl and David offers himself up for bar duty.

Tam asks: "Sarah here?"

"No," I reply. "She's gone home this weekend to see her folks."

"So you're out on the tiles?"

"Just us boys," I confirm.

There must be something in my expression.

"Well Sam, be careful," Tam advises. "Those tiles can get hot and Bad Boys can get burned."

I've been seeing Sarah nearly a year. It's all going fine, though not the same fireworks as in The Beginning. She's been renting over in Richmond (aka. Nappy Valley), a fine domicile if you're a Thirty-Something Mother of Two, but an unreasonable schlep west if you're in any other life-stage. On my reluctance to trip beyond Zone 2, I have recently suggested that she moves into my flat. This Sarah is going to do and I choose not to feel anything about this other than acknowledge the Logical Convenience, like changing jobs and getting a shorter commute thrown in for free.

"It's been nearly a year hasn't it?," asks Jamie.

"A year, yes, pretty much." I do a poor job of feigning enthusiasm.

"Sure it's not getting past David's bed time?" I ask, changing the subject. "Guys pretty old, Tam. Looks old enough to be one of my Dad's friends."

Tam throws me a withering look.

"He's old enough to not be a kid," she retorts, "but he's not old."

"So you do feel the need to defend him?," I needle.

"I'm going to give David a hand at the bar," she announces, no time for me or my shit. "How many martinis is that, Sam? You sure you don't just want a glass of water?" She doesn't wait for my reply.

I turn to Jamie. "What the fuck does she see in him?"

"Good-looking, well-dressed, high-flying, beyond that, I can only think of another 3.7 million reasons."

I say nothing.

Jamie: "At Uni, did you ever nail her?"

"Delicately put, but no, Tam and I, we've only ever been mates."

Now it's Jamie's turn to say nothing.

"The share thing," I then tell him. "I'm in. Either way, it's only money."

★

With drinks refreshed, and having made brief talk with "Tam & David" (where I was polite, really I was, but distant), Jamie and I excuse ourselves and leave them to it. I figure I'm in such a charming mood I really should mingle a little, share my cheer.

Sophie Anderton saunters past, looking Just Amazing but exuding a glass tower ego and the kind of Higher Maintenance usually associated with crumbling stately manors. Jamie follows her bottom, but I inadvertently lasso him back.

"Who's *that*?" I simultaneously think and say, encouraging Jamie to follow my eye-line instead.

"That's Donna Air," he shares.

"No, who's that *next* to Donna Air?"

"That's Donna Air's mate."

"Thanks Jamie," I say dryly, but then add genuinely, "I just wanted to check she wasn't anyone famous."

Fast forward thirty seconds. My opening line is not: "You're not famous are you?," but it is: "Hi, I understand you're Donna Air's mate?"

If you're confronted by a celebrity and the Celebrity Buddy, I'd always say, assuming they're great looking, make a play for The Buddy, not The Celebrity. The buddy won't be expecting it, will always assume that you're just the latest in the Star-Fucking Line trying to angle an introduction with the more famous face. If you can convince otherwise, you could be on to a winner.

In this instance, the Celebrity Buddy may have been The Less Famous

Face, but it didn't take any smarts to appreciate that she'd had a life time of suitors and trouser snakes. Whoever this girl was, she was a cosmetics contract waiting to happen. Not meeting her was not an option.

Back to: "Hi, I understand you're Donna Air's mate?"

Response: "Fuck off." Facial expression: Contempt.

"Listen, I'm not trying to angle an introduction with your mate Donna, but I was hoping to chat to you. If we're to progress, it is important to stress that I am not a record producer or talent agent. Sleeping with me will probably not help your career in any way." I pause, then add: "However, if you think I'm cute, you should consider sleeping with me for this reason alone."

I know, the Cheeky-Chappy Routine can earn you a drink in the face, but it can also earn you a half smile, which is what I get.

"Hi, my name's Sam and I bet you one martini I'm worth chatting with for the time it takes you to drink it."

To whom it may concern: It's a Miracle. Half smile broadens. Ladies and Gentlemen, I can confirm, we have: Full smile.

"One drink?," I say again, smiling myself now.

"Okay, Sam, one drink. For what it's worth: I'm Holly."

And that's how I met Holly.

Holly

A little background on Holly:

Easy on the eye, easy on the mind, that's Holly in a harsh line – but a good many guys would consider the latter quality a great asset.

When we met at Atlantic, Holly's CV amounted to Sometime Model and Borderline TV Presenter, and I say *borderline* because she'd done some blink-and-you'd-miss-it presenting on MTV Europe (which means more pouting than actual presenting), and because MTV falls a country mile short of being a proper TV channel anyway.

To steal one of Holly's expressions: *For what it's worth*, Holly never once asked me if I had a girlfriend, and I never once thought to mention that I did.

A Kiss, Before Lying

The moment you kiss someone you cross a line - a line forever broken. You can never take the moment back (which can be a shame), but nor can you ever re-live it, not That *First* Kiss. That first kiss, that pause just *before*, that pause spilling with expectation and possibility? Eyes. Mouth. Parting lips. Anticipation. Closer. Yes. Complicity. A submission, a moment shared in time and trust, a kiss offered, a kiss taken; a first intimacy. You can never re-live it, and that is also a shame.

Kissing is The Business.

And *First-time* kissing is the business, And Then Some.

But of course, there is also a flip-side. Let me also say this: Kissing, I have found, is Trouble. Kissing leads to more, as if anyone needs proof.

Now I'm not about to kiss and tell – well maybe I am – but certainly I'm not about to tell "certain" people. I endeavour, most earnestly, for parties most interested to remain in the dark; the very darkest kind of dark.

I have this dilemma.

How can you spend time in the company of one woman,

one particular chick, one lovely, but all the time be thinking about another, completely and altogether different honey? For what it's worth: It is not a good Karma Hotel to go checking yourself into.

My situation: it isn't good for the conscience, downright terrible in fact. Matters are made the worse, when the thoughts one has are, let's say, kinda racy. Kinda racy, and kinda real. Flash-back thoughts, they're the problem. Snap-shots of what you *did*, most particularly what *I* did. Oh gee, oh baby. These mind-stills, they make me grin *and* grimace, make me feel ashamed - *almost* - for what I did, but oh-so-very-much hungry to do it again.

I tell ya: I'm in conflict.

I know this much: I'm heading for trouble.

How many times a day does the average human being think about sex? The number I read someplace glossy is 225, that's what *they* say. Who *they* are does not matter. It's the number that matters. Does 225 seem a lot, or not? D'you think it varies by gender? And how can you calculate something like *average* anyway? How big is the sample size; how robust are the figures? And does it really matter – I'd say probably not - because at the end of the day, when the night draws in, and you're thinking about that last or next great ride, you've thought a whole lot about plenty, and a heaving, pulsing, throbbing proportion of that plenty has been a touch spiced. That is life. Sex. Sex, is life. Thinking, talking, doing. Ssssssssex. Monogamy, polygamy, breasts, beaver, wick, wand, suck, fuck, bang, bang. Sex. Sex. Sex. Sex. Sex. Hmmmm. Oh sugar, oh sweetie, oh cutie. I'm over my 225 for the day, and the truth of it is, I'm doing a lot more than just thinking.

For what it's worth: I'm *fucking* someone else. Yep, Holly.

I'm fucking someone *other* that is, than who I'm supposed to be fucking (yep, Sarah), and this is bound to cause me hassles. I'm hatin' myself, riskin' a lot, livin' dangerously, knowin' it's unfair, and yet, I only want to keep on doin' it. Why? 'Cos I'm also lovin' it . My emotions are So Very Mixed, and I sense there's a comeuppance round the bend. I can just feel that there's a storm coming, and Man, I can fucking guarantee there'll be no storm rooms left for me when it does. Of this, I feel certain.

★

"I don't think my feet have ever been so clean," she comments.

"In that case, I'm glad to have shared this moment with you."

I continue massaging, lathering. The bath water is hot, the room steamy, the tub easily big enough for two.

"Ouch!," she says.

"What?," I ask. "Your foot, too much pressure?"

"No, the bath tap's just jabbed me in the back!" Holly scowls, but it's with good nature.

"Better than your ass," I offer helpfully with a smile.

"At least there's room up there". Mischief plays across her face.

"Darling, whatever are you trying to say?"

"Room up there... but not for long?," she suggests.

Saturday, November 7th, 1998

When I Lost Sarah

Saturday, 11:33pm. Storm Landing.

Location: The Golden Naan, New Kings Road. A good curry guaranteed, but…

Trouble. Big-Fuck-Off-Trouble: my own doing, my own creation, the blame neither adding nor detracting from matters dire. That storm is here, my rain dance to blame.

"What's wrong?" Directed at me, from across the table.

This is bad. *Die Hard* bad, *No Way Out* bad. I've crapped out, bottomed out, lost the lot. I'm rumbled, busted, badly. Right now, I'm the Cincinnati Kid, a handful of nothing.

From over the table again: "You've gone very pale. Sam, what is it?"

I laugh, more a giggle really, quietly, hysterically, the white noise in my ears thundering evenly. What rotten luck, but *so* inevitable. The Law of Sod, The Script of Circumstance: enter stage left, more precisely restaurant door right. Enter, Sarah.

Finally, opposite me and with impatience, "Sam, spill?"

I breathe deep, briefly option the filter tip rather than the papadum, then start: "The group who've just walked in…"

"Yes…?"

"The girl in the black jacket, I believe velvet, and the navy T-shirt…

"Yes…?"

"That's my T-shirt." Pause. Then: "That's my girlfriend."

Crunch.

"You're kidding?" Second pause, this time hers. Then: "You're not kidding." Then, in a near whisper, "Oh, Christ! Oh, shit, oh you fucking twat!"

"Holly, I can explain."

Up until then, I'd been on a roll.

★

Sunday, 12:43am. A cab ride later, me having tailed Sarah's cab all the way.

Location: In the flat; the face off.

Me: feeling drunk, but not so drunk that I don't feel a starburst of self-revulsion at the tired line, "Sarah, *I can explain*."

"Oh, really?," asks Sarah, dripping sarcasm and fresh, wet, unearthed contempt.

"Yes, I *can*," but then – fatally – I lose my train of thought. "Actually… I *can't* explain. Not. Right. Now. I'm not feeling very… loquacious. I know it doesn't look good, but… *Bugger*."

"You…*Fucking*…ARSEHOLE!", she says.

"Yes. I know. I am."

"I just can't *believe* you!" Sarah: now loud, hell having no fury, and all that.

"Can't? Believe me? No. Understandable really."

To me, screaming, "Stop talking like an imbecile! You can't "little-boy-lost" your way out of this one."

The depth of shit I've landed myself in is beyond my mortal understanding.

★

Holly, Midnight Hour.

Location: Outside the Sultan, on the pavement. Situation: Holly, building to a sonic-spin, still in the comprehending stage. Me, playing it stupid.

"We've known each other for… *how long*," she asks.

I know rhetoric when I hear it.

"TWELVE months!," she continues. "How many conversations, how many dates, how much time-invested emotion, how much *fucking*, and Me harping on to everyone about what a really good bloke you are?"

She's shaking her head, her lips thin (but still full, because she has very full sexy lips). She's doing the Math, calculating the magnitude, then, with the figures tallied, the summary. "Sam… YOU… CUNT!

"One big fuck-off lie, one well-played deception. Not once – ever - were you being yourself. Just a GAME to you – *was it?* - you cruel repugnant shit!"

I manage the cliché, "*I can explain*," feeling marbles in my mouth.

"Fuck YOU, can you."

★

Sarah, 12:45am. Cold Front.

"Sarah - *listen* - Holly and I - we're just friends. It's not like we've shagged; or kissed; or anything." Me: more lies. "For Godsake," I appeal, we were sitting down to a curry!"

"Do I look like an idiot? Has someone pinned me with your Moron badge? You were having a curry, with a girl! A girl I've never seen before, or ever before heard you mention, on a Saturday night, one-on-one over candlelight, when you'd arranged to be meeting me, and your friends, for drinks, on the other side of town, 5 hours earlier. It doesn't matter what I *didn't* see, or what you claim *hasn't yet* happened between you and…"

She pauses.

"Holly," I offer, trying to be helpful.

"…and *Holly*." The voice is killer; the inflection icier than a Siberian isobar. "Guilt isn't just a matter of deed, it's as much a matter of *intent*, and I'd have to be some kind of *fucking* retard if I were to believe that you haven't thought about fucking her. And seeing as I can't rely on you to make a drinks appointment, how the hell can I rely on you for the truth as to whether you have ever actually cashed it in with… *Holly*?"

And the Ice Storm slams me square in the face.

★

Holly. 12:01am. Sunday, But No Second Coming.

"It *wasn't* a game to me! Jesus, I'm not that much of a shit. I'm not the Antichrist!"

"Questionable," she spits.

"I wasn't trying to hurt anyone." Such a lazy line, jarring horribly in my ears.

"Then that's impressive, because it would seem you've managed to hurt everyone."

★

Sarah, 12:47am. He aims: High. He shoots: Wide.

"So this is about what I was *thinking?*" Me, knowing it's not what she means, but hoping to sidetrack.

"No, it's about trust, and complete betrayal," Sarah counters.

"But not through deed? *"Not a matter of deed,"* you said. Meaning the betrayal is one of *thought*? The impure kind, right? Making you, what? Captain of the Thought Police?"

Alcohol aside, the brain is starting to tick again. I'm thinking I might be in with a long-shot; might be able to pull this one round, go on the attack.

"You *are* guilty, Sam, and it doesn't matter how you try and spin it. It's not a question of what you were *thinking*, but it is very much a question of what your mind was *planning*. If you haven't shagged her, you were going to. If you already have, then I hate you with all my soul."

And my long shot goes high, yes, and very wide. No worming my way out of this one.

*

Holly, 12:03am. Just a Little White Lie.

"Now it's all thick red mist. You. Me. You, your feelings of super-grade hatred towards me, but if you… and I mean *We*, if *we* can just calm down a little, then I *really* can explain. Look, I really fucked up. I'm sorry – not that this is about me seeking forgiveness you understand? I just want you to *understand*. About this, about how it – *this* - happened."

"This should be good, because I *don't* understand, I *really* don't. *Why* have you done this?," Holly asks.

And all I can think, quite sincerely, is poor Holly, I'm sorry.

"I have a girlfriend – or at least had – but I then meet someone – you. I like them – *them* being *you*, that is - enjoy spending time with them, should have mentioned the girlfriend variable straight off, on Day 1, because that's The Done Thing, standard operating procedure, the only decent option.

"But I didn't option, didn't proceed decently. And then, as is the way, the longer things went on, the more we got to know and *trust* each other, the more impossible it became to say anything. So: a lie, spiralling out of control."

Whatever Holly is feeling, it's not empathy.

"What a White Knight you are! Such posturing! The defence of a white lie crusade! Wanker! You sound ridiculous: *"Hey Luv, it was best you didn't know. Best to protect you from the truth of what a grande shit I really am!"* Sure Sam. Like, thanks."

"Look, I wasn't thinking."

"Being thoughtless is no excuse."

"I wasn't using it as one."

"Yes. You were. *'I didn't think − I don't think − I have the emotional IQ of a Mosh Pit. What's happened is beyond my control.'* Fuck You, Sam. You've contrived this Dangerous Liaison, and it's backfired."

I want to suggest Valmont was a sympathetic character, but now is not the time.

★

Sarah, 12:50am. Group Hug.

"Let's not even get into the embarrassment of it all!," exclaims Sarah, before then focusing on the embarrassment of it all.

"Everyone pretty pissed," she details, "suddenly sobered, on tender hooks: bit delicate this, a rather tricky loyalty-to-betrayal ratio. The last thing anyone wants to do is *eat*! Everyone asking me if I'm *alright*, whether I just want to leave, Sean wanting to hold my hand, Jamie's new girlfriend Jane looking all sympathetic, Jamie fighting back a smirk but failing, and me trying to laugh it off, pretending like it doesn't matter or *mean* anything, an event of no significance; just a silly little in-joke even, and that I actually *do* know what's going on. Christ, I was only out with your friends because you were supposed to be meeting us!"

Sarah catches her breath. "You utter bastard."

I can't help but think: Of all the curry houses in all the world...

★

Holly, 12:07am. No Time for Humour.

"I'm totally stupid. I'm worthless. I'm..." Me, looking down, then inspired. "I'm melted pavement gum, that's been crapped on by a big dog." I pause, hoping for smiles, but getting silence, getting diddly.

"I can't believe you're trying to make a joke of this."

"I wasn't trying to be flippant. I was just trying to lighten the mood. Make you smile even." Me: now the Saint.

I didn't see it coming; didn't realise what *It* was until my head whipped right, the air flat clapped, and one half of my face – the left half – numbed, then exploded. I saw stars (not cosmic), realised Concorde hadn't just sonic-boomed above, and appreciated that I wasn't experiencing a stroke. Cheek/palm contact had been clean. It had just been a slap, but it felt like she'd doctored me with a blowtorch. I shouldn't have bothered with the humour, but it had kinda worked.

At last, now she was smiling.

★

Sarah, 12:52am. Last Minute Effort.

"You don't realise how utterly precious something is until you jeopardize it. I can't believe the sheer insanity of what I've done, of how I've jeopardized *us*." I think this should strike some sort of compassionate, even reconciliatory chord?

"Sam, you haven't jeopardized us. You've cancelled us. We're over."

"You can't be serious." Me, sincere, with no air of The McEnroe about me.

The reply, as if in Dolby, coming at me in stereo, very loud and clear: "Fuck You."

★

Holly, 12:10am. The Final Say.

She leaves me standing there, on the street, the red handprint aglow, looking like a Bambi-pal caught in a steel toothed snare. She's down the road. I put on my best speed walk and catch her up, taking her by the arm. She turns, all big eyed and tearful, her right arm lifting, considering a fresh swing. Looking into those eyes, I feel terrible. I can't hold the gaze, the situation sucks verily.

"Let me at least wait around with you till we find a couple of cabs. It's… *late*."

"Sam, it's a bit late for trying to do the right thing."

Good girl, I think, nice line. Holly turns away from me for the second time in less than a minute, and this time I let her walk, because I know she's right. Everything: far too late.

★

Sarah, 12:55pm. Status: Critical, Meltdown Imminent.

"I fucked-up – Royally, I know – but tonight was still *just* two people and a pile of popadums." Over indeed! I don't believe her, or believe she knows what she's saying. This is knee jerk stuff. Me, I accept, being the Jerk.

But Sarah is bristling, danger-zoning, right in front of me. "Denial," she spits. "Insulting. That's *all* I'm worth? Candle-light at midnight, quiet little table in the corner for two, one member of said party having blown out his girlfriend? Explanation?"

I figure it's another rhetorical.

"I know why," she continues. "He's blown out one commitment because basically wants, at the very least, to get blown by the girl he's with. No need to call out Columbo."

I'm in the rope-a-dope, then down, now being kicked by the referee too, in the head.

I try and launch some kind of comeback: "Look, this is all very, er… *charged* right now, very emotional, but it's of vital importance that you appreciate one very salient, very defining fact. *Nothing happened.* And of equal importance: *Nothing between Holly and I ever has happened!*" I wonder, can I go to Hell for this?

"Sam, you can't tell me you haven't entertained plans of getting in that girl's pants. If you hadn't got tangled in your own web, you'd have only come home drunk tonight and told a routinely worried but not surprised Me that you'd been out "larging it" with Sean, and sorrying every which ways about being thoughtless and such a shit. How many lies have there been? I don't want to know; but I know I can never trust what you say again."

This is Not Good. The look on Sarah's face is Not Good, and I realise I have No Comebacks.

She confirms, "You've blown it mate. It's *over*. We're *over*."

She's started crying now, but remaining strong, all resolve and defiance, iron still sounding in her words.

"You can't condemn me *before* the act?," I implore. I move closer, offering the possibility of a cuddle.

And then she hits me.

She's left handed, so it's a fresh cheek that gets it, a diagonal arc that starts low like an upper cut.

And then I understand: I'm history.

Where Sarah's words hadn't gotten through, her actions find their mark, and as I fall back over the *Konx* coffee table and skittle the *Arco* lamp so it lands on top of me (witness lamp and I hitting the floor in spectacular fashion), my understanding finds time to repeat, and repeat. I'm history, *I'm history*.

Fade to Black

I didn't black-out, not after Sarah thumped me and caused me to trip inelegantly over the coffee table, but I didn't immediately get up from the experience. In the horizontal, I made a conscious decision to embrace the darkness. I wanted to luxuriate in The Nothing. Me on the floor, *Arco* lamp next to me, the distant sound of the apartment door slamming, of footfalls on the stairs, then silence. Sarah had left the building.

Events had gotten out of hand, and for a while, I just wanted it all to stop. I hadn't found a way out, but I had managed to take pause, which I figured was something.

Monday, November 1st, 1999

Fast Forward and Fade In

Well, that was One-Helluva-Weekend.

Mentally, emotionally, physically, metaphysically, spiritually, psychically, on any fucking level, I cannot quite process the events that transpired. From my Saturday morning, I am left with questions.

1. Why did Sean kiss me?

2a. Did that Jenny girl come back to the flat?

2b. If the answer to 2a is Yes, did anything happen?

3. Why did Sarah happen?

The mental clip to Saturday morning, post Halloween party at the Bluebird, I keep playing over and over.

Scene: The doorstep.

Sarah: "Hi Sam".

Me: "Hi".

Sarah: "Sam, I wanted you to know…"

Me: "Yes?"

Sarah: "I'm getting married."

Me: "I see. Would you like to come in?"

★

It's Monday morning, I'm at work, the weekend has now passed, but I'm not sure how best to recap – for the benefit of the slower witted ones in the audience (such as myself).

Fact 1: Sarah is getting married. Arriving at Fact 1, the sequence of events goes something like this.

Sarah caught me over candle-light curry with a girl called Holly, whom I had been seeing behind her back for – wait for it – a year.

I know: I'm a shit.

At the time of the "outing," Sarah did not know the full circumstances pertaining to Holly, and I did my best to lie my way out of her knowing. Sarah then left me, moved into a friend's place for a week, Crisis Talks and Summit Meetings ensued, and we agreed to make a Fresh Go of It, Sarah returning once more to my flat. Things would be Different.

If I'd wanted Sarah out of my life, I shouldn't have let her move back in. At the time, I didn't know what I wanted, though on some level I suspect I wanted To Win, without knowing really what that meant.

The Fresh Go ultimately culminated in her… Ultimate Departure. *Things* were Different for about a month, and then I spent the subsequent 5 months pushing Sarah away, being nasty, trying to get rid of her. Holly was also over, and while I did miss her, I knew it would be kinder to pass, let her get on with her life and me not being part of it.

I know: I can be such a saint.

When Sarah moved out (for the second and conclusive time), she left me for Someone Else, which is the only way she was going to leave. The way she's made, her boyfriends are stepping stones. I had wrestled Sarah away from a guy who looked like he could have comfortably sparred with Mike Tyson, but who carried the life-misery of being called Eric (aka. Neck Tendons).

When Sarah started her new job in the New Year, she mentioned a guy she'd met (aka. The Third Party), who drove a sports car, who was some sort of ex-T-shirt model, and that little flash I'd seen pass over her eyes was enough to show me the way, to light it nice and bright. Eric, then Sam, then Hans, hop, skip, jump.

By June '99, Sarah was out the door for good, which is when I started feeling bad, as in: Guilty, Sorry For Myself, working up a frothy lather of self-loathing. If I could make myself Feel Bad, I reasoned, I'd be somehow down the road to atonement and full recovery?

I know: I can be such a loser.

Three months later, by the time Mein Gebürtstag swings around, I'm with Flu & A Groinal Boil, and a month after that, Sarah shows up on the doorstep announcing: "I'm marrying Third Party." Of course, she didn't call him Third Party. She called him Hans, which is his name. I know, *Hans*, like you couldn't write this stuff.

And the only point of cheer in all this? At least The Boil's history.

How You Should Play the Game

At work, I don't have a corner office, but I have wangled a half-decent window desk. Its appointment affords good distraction from all occupational matters. It's 11:05am and rain is lashing at the pane. The sky is dull, and the line: "I'm getting married" keeps slashing at my mind. In my diary, my

PA Charlotte has scribbled that I am expected in Meeting Room 5. The expectation is 5 minutes old. The phone rings.

"Sam?"

It's Charlotte.

"Sam's not here. Sam died."

"Sam, you were supposed to be down in Room 5 with Tracey at 11."

"Thanks Charley, I'm there. Where would I be without you?"

"Without a job probably," she suggests, then hangs up.

I smile, then sigh, then head to the lift.

★

In "Adland," it pays to be a good "Client Man". A lot of time is spent gaining the trust of The Client. The money and the glory are in the front office. There's no glory in being support staff. Be the guy who *gets* the support. Be Client-Facing, be good at inter-facing, strike the rapports, establish the comfort-zones, excel at Managing Expectations. Being a Client Man, a Good Account Man, is all about Giving Good Service & Saying The Right Thing.

Do what you say you'll do. Never say "A," and do "B"; never Under-Deliver. Even more importantly, never, if possible, Eat Shit. (Though some clients think shit eating's what they pay for.) If you like the people you work with, if you like your clients, tell them. If you think your clients suck, marginally prefer their company to a bathtub of monkey shit, and suspect them of (a) paedophilia, (b) necrophilia, or (c) a sick-fuck combination of both, then keep it to yourself. The rules here are quite clear.

Client-facing is about impressing, about (1) Straight Talk and (2) Sounding Smart.

(1) Straight Talk's good for conveying integrity: "I don't want to sound worthy about this, but if *we* don't do things *this* way," pause, "then *you're* just wasting *your* money".

As for (2) Sounding Smart, this is where the Poker Face comes in. Sounding Smart is not of course the same as *Being* Smart, but most marketing folk aren't All That, and the thinking prevails that most everyone feels better when things *Sound* Clever, feels more at ease after a luxuriating bathe in the BS. Consequently, in Adland everyone talks a Monumentally Large Amount of Bollocks. I'm talking Fantastical-Big-Kids-Havin'-Fun-Makin'-It-Up-As-They-Go-Along Bollocks, everything *meaning* very little, but occasionally sounding good and clever. In some cases, the concepts behind the words spoken are very simple, and where the concepts are simple, greater is the need to make them *sound* complicated.

If it is bollocks on which the world turns, I fear we may have reached a point where perhaps we are all just spinning in the void, riding this one big revolving testicle.

The irony amuses me for all of about 10 seconds, that "Advertising" is *supposedly* a Communications Business, yet all the time its practitioners use Non-Words, peddling the nonsensical, all in the name of self-justification, everyday producing more and more *Anti-meaning*.

Professional Self Concept is not without denial, but *admitting* that one's profession is sad, even tragic, clearly pathetic, and transparently meaningless-in-a-bigger-picture-sort-of-way, well, that's when my world turns and I start to feel queasy about what I do.

The simple fact of it is has become: I don't believe I can play this game much longer.

Mental Dissent in Meeting Room 5

"We're looking to dispose a high-tech culture in favour of a high-touch culture." To this, there are nodding-dog gestures of approval, especially from my colleague Tracey. I do not nod.

All I can think: This guy needs a very good slapping. He is called Marvin, a new client, this my first meeting with him.

Marvin's still at it: "We need to pilot some creatively strategic solutions: tailored events, ambient, contextual and field marketing. I'm using generic terms here of course, but I'm thinking of something *quite special*." Christ!, I wonder, can't somebody muzzle this guy?

Tracey is busy nodding again. It is arguably what she does best.

Tracey Boyle, colleague, , aka. The Royal Boil, aka. The Nodding Dog.

For reference: Tracey only ever flies Business, and always angles for an upgrade to First, decorated in Louis Vuitton at Check-In and flashing her BA card like it was 5 carats from Graff. She's 30, single, and I say Tragic. No one loves her. I fear no one will ever love her.

Tracey also has a permanent "cold," most probably one of the most expensive "colds" in London, if you know what I mean. Ultimately, it's not her pseudo Jet Set sophistication that annoys me, not her Cocaine Habit as Lifestyle Accessory, nor the fact that she's forsaken any soft-faced femininity in favour of becoming a hard-faced hard-assed aerobics addict.

What annoys me about Tracey is the way in every meeting she nods away in such earnest ass-kissing agreement. The only thing that puts me on the edge of my seat is the prospect that her head may one day fall off her over-flexed neck. Of her two nicknames, it is her second, the Nodding Dog, which is my preferred. It is the one I started.

Marvin's clearly swallowed the latest-print Marketing Manifesto and it's making my head feel numb, frozen with indifference to these lauded-round-the-room words of abstraction: *"Next Generation Business Models... Re-positioning Statements... Re-alignment Strategies... Differentiation Metrics."*

Marvin announces to all listening, he is a "Brand Purist". All I think: What a Cunt.

I'd like to fight Marvin. In fact, to everyone round the table, including the girls: *How about a fight?*

I say nothing, just conclude: I am a dissenting *mind*. I am no longer being a good Client Man.

I struggle.

I struggle to conceal my *thoughts*, my thoughts of objection, indeed borderline contempt for those sitting on all sides of the table to me. My poker face is shot. It can't be long before thoughts of dissent lead to deed.

"I'd like to talk strategy, not tactics," I hear someone say, not Marvin at least, but I wince, thinking: Stupid Fat Fuck.

My top lip Elvis', my right nostril flares. All involuntary, I fear it looks like I'm chewing on a turd.

Strategy, *not* tactics! *I'd* prefer not to talk semantics, but I know I don't have a choice. If I lived in the world of Orwell's *Big Brother*, I'd be toast, taken in the night, dead on arrival of the new dawn, but not at least attending the next day's meeting.

"Strategy-Only" Chap (dark hair, too-small features, looks like a worm in a wig) then says "vis-à-vis" for the third time in 30 minutes, before calling on the need for "more granularity" and finishing off with a "per se," utterly without any context or bearing on correct usage or meaning. Unlike: Idiocy per se. Once more, I wince, as if struck by heartburn or constipation.

"Strategy-Only" Chap has no idea what he's talking about and I'd like 5 minutes alone with him in a sound-proof room, just him, me and maybe my favourite crow bar.

Salvation briefly enters the room on trolleys, a short convoy of vacuum-packed sushi and stay-pressed sandwiches. The meeting's highlight, though a digestive low-light. Then it's back to more inanity and mixed metaphor, idiot remarks hitting me like a Mental Wasabi Slam: "We don't want to be blown out of the water like a dead duck," "Let's *press* the green-light," "In our waterfall of predicted effects, we don't want to end up too far down river," "Let's not try and boil the ocean with a Bunsen burner," "We don't want to cause a down-tools at the honey factory," "Do we need to plump the pillows?," "Should we keep our powder dry?". This last one, "Should we keep our powder dry," that was Marvin.

Marvin

"What do you think of Marvin?" The question, from Tracey. I think she may have asked me twice. "I think I can work with him," she then says.

We're out of the meeting, Marvin tucked safely in a cab destined to who cares where.

"I think he's about as impressive as a One Man Mexican Wave," I tell her.

"No, seriously," she insists, her face at least making the effort to smile at my half-joke.

My face turns serious. "Seriously, I think he's a lanky streak of piss in a poor fitting off-the peg suit. I think he wears a fucking Swatch and looks like he maybe ripped-off a strip of his bedroom carpet this morning and strapped it under his too-big collar… I mean, what was that fucking shag-pile tie all about?"

For a moment Tracey doesn't speak, but she, too, looks serious. "Thanks Sam, thanks for the professional point of view," she says flatly, then stomps off down the corridor

I shout after her: "My pleasure."

Why the Gym?

I need a drink. Marvin was Just Too Much. I was already on the edge and I feel Marvin tipped me over.

I call Jamie late afternoon to arrange a game of squash for later in the week and a stiff drink for as soon as possible.

"I can do now," he proposes.

"Now would be pretty perfect."

My gentle walk down Charlotte Street in the evening light is pleasant up until the point I pass a newsstand running with: *6 Year Old Boy Shoots School Girl Dead*. Perspective, I tell myself. It could be worse, I coach, but I can't encourage a cheerier disposition.

I meet Jamie at Bam-Bou on Percy Street. Setting is all dark woods, heavy silks and lacquered walls. I have this vision of Graham Greene, at night but lying on a day bed smoking an opium pipe amongst Quiet Americans. Bam-Bou's menu is French-Vietnamese, but I'm only interested in consuming alcohol so I head straight for the top floor bar.

"You look terrible," Jamie tells me on arrival.

""Do you enjoy your job?," I ask him as I take off my raincoat and throw it over the arm of a club chair.

"Of course not, no one does. What are you drinking?"

"Margarita," I tell him. "But what about self-fulfilment? Giving meaning to the gift of life, being a voice, leaving a mark, making a difference?"

"Listen, I just want to have lots of money and fuck about, and in this, I represent the majority." Jamie hands me my margarita, straight up, salt on the rim, the way it should be.

"Work aside," he asks, "what's been happening in your life?"

I'm far from sure I want to tell Jamie about my weekend, so I just deflect his question, suggest a topic truly dear to him, namely him.

"I'd like to say you look terrible too, but you don't look too bad."

"Sam, easy on the homo-eroticism, I don't want you going gay on me."

I don't want you going gay on me, a stock Jamie remark. I'm certainly not going to tell him about Sean just yet.

"But there's a noticeable difference," I comment, "Are you gyming more?"

"6 days a week. Today at lunch was Traps, Delts and Lats, with sadly no time left over for Rhombs."

"Jamie, you sound ridiculous. Explain exactly why you are embracing Gym Culture so passionately?"

"Pride," he tells me. "I don't want to be a bald pot-bellied forty year old burn out."

"How big are your arms?," I ask, baiting.

"15 inches".

"My God Jamie, you're actually measuring your arms! This is self love on an epic scale!"

"How big are your arms?," he asks.

"I've no fucking idea, I've never measured them," which is the truth, but I do add, provoking a little, "18 inches, you need 18 inches if you want to be a Super Hero. That's my target."

Getting to the nub of it, "You still seeing that dancer, Chloe?"

"Yes, I am," Jamie confirms. "I got an A minus for *Patriarchy & The Urban Form, The Need for Feminist Architectural Redress.*"

"Impressive, I think? And could Chloe have something to do with your new gym regime?"

Jamie just smirks, sips his drink.

"You've always had quite a hard-on for your reflection, but this I'm guessing is more than just the pursuit of lean 6-packery?"

"Maybe," confirms Jamie.

"And you're not gay, which would be a realisation which has struck late in the context of majority homosexual awakenings?" With much mockery: "Jamie, are you into guys, y'know, in a directional love wand kinda way?"

Jamie kids along: "Hey, the only way to get any bottom action is if you're in shape. Gay guys don't dig fat gays. I'm also about to start a bumper series of sun-lamp sessions and re-load my wardrobe with the latest in DKNY torso tops."

"Okay then, if I am to take your sarcasm as a form of denial, then it's The Chloe Effect, the root of which is insecurity."

"I'm not insecure!" guffaws Jamie, sounding just a smidgen insecure.

"Take your average, suburban, recently divorced male. He's 45, likely has 2 kids and maybe even a dog, but at considerable emotional and financial sacrifice, he's optioned pursuits less "Mid-life". He's moved back into town and - would you believe? – started dating a 25 year old. She may even be an aerobics instructor, or a dancer."

"Do you maybe work in Advertising, Sam? Is this one of those Adland archetypes?," Jamie interrupts.

"May I continue?"

"By all means"; Jamie sinks further back into his club chair, enjoying the open fire, enjoying his drink.

I continue: "Well, there's no way that this 45 year old can stomach a Sugar-Daddy self-concept. He wants another youthful blossom, and while Getting-It-On with a blossoming youth of 20 years his junior, he realises that he's a long way past his own first bloom. Still following me Jamie?"

"From a distance," he chuckles. "Please finish. Quickly."

"So, to rewind the years, 45 year old Love Rat starts clocking serious hours in the gym. That way he gets to nail a pneumatic babe while appeasing clawing insecurities and the sense that he could well be a perve."

"Just one thing. I'm not 45. I'm 27, I already drive a Porsche and I'm a bit young for a mid life crisis."

"Jamie, you're a younger variation on a theme. You've just taken up sack acquaintance with a professional hot body called Chloe. Without even meeting her, I know she's fit, she's sexy, and she's keeping you on your toes. It might not be a case of *'Be still my beating heart'* but it is a call to *'Pass me my pecs of steel!'* I figure, in 20 years we'll be having this conversation again - but hopefully it'll be *me* tucking into the 25 year old dancer."

"Well Sam, I was wondering if I'll have to wait 25 years before you get your arse to the bar. From here on, may I suggest: light on the psychobabble, heavy on the tequila. And when you get back, if you're lucky, I'll tell you how well your shares are doing."

Rage Against the Machine

Tuesday afternoon and my head hurts from too many Monday Night Margarita's. Added to which, my PC has just crashed…

again, for the third time today. I'm not in the minority. The network can't stay on its feet. Everyone on the floor is getting frantic and none-too friendly.

Someone in IT must have really Dropped a Bollock; they can't keep the network on its feet for more than 5 minutes. "Fucking IT!" has become Phrase of the Day. It can only be uttered with extreme venom. "Poor IT": today, their PR-rating has dropped off the scale.

...I jagged right while plunging the Tomcat's nose into a near vertical descent. A wingman would have thought the move crazy, but today I had No Wingman. This was a solo run and more importantly, I knew what I was doing. Negative G dives are always a rush, but at this altitude it was a good deal more. It was like mocking God. Training, talent, tenacity. The 3 T's. It's what lets guys like me do what needs to be done.

The Impossible, that's my line of work.

I do the impossible, like flying a $40million dollar fighter plane into the bulls-eye of a volcano and then blasting my way out. Yes my friend, that kind of "Takes balls the size of... impossible."

But Today, I was worried. This mission was beyond the remit of any mortal man, there was no way it could work; it was insane.

"So crazy, it might just work, eh Commander?" I said at the briefing, a half smile playing at my lips.

"Listen, I know it's halo flying at Mach 2, deep in enemy territory... but no one handles an F-15 like you," gruffs Commander Drexlar.

"That's true, but still..."

"Sam, you're the only one can do this. It's time for you

to play Hero again… and besides," added the Commander, "I know you like a challenge…"

An explosion of glass. Low level office noise, shattered, shaking me from Dreamlandia. A momentary hush.

Jonathan, a guy who performs much the same pointless role I do, has suffered a rush of blood; obviously feels his desk-top is victimising him, cannot take the prospect of having to re-boot 5 times in one afternoon, has found expression by putting his fist through the glass screen that filters monitor radiation. There is a brief silence, a degree of surprise, but people can appreciate where Jonathan's coming from. Aggravation is the order of the afternoon. Desk Rage is inevitable. Human nature, machine nature: seldom the best bedfellows. Just look at the Terminator movies.

Jonathan heads for some fresh air, and presumably needs time-out to remove the fragments of glass lodged in his right knuckle.

It's No Go on my screen either, and I suspect, No Hope. I phone IT. It just rings, then goes to Voice Mail. I knew when I dialled there'd be no one there, and even if there had been, I know what I'd have got. "Try turning it off… then on again." Yeah, thanks.

The IT Help Desk only ever does one thing: Points you in the direction of the power switch.

Fucking IT! And Fucking Bill Gates too!

A well-known moral dilemma: if you had the chance to kill Hitler before he became, like, famous, say when he was just a young boy playing out front of the house in Branau am Inn, Austria, would you take him out?

By extension, if you could get in your customised

DeLorean and past-blast to Seattle 1968 when a 13 year old William Henry Gates III was tucking into his first computer experience, would you run him down? I suspect there's a queue, and I know Jonathan would be in it.

E-Venting

My head's a muddle, thoughts gloopy, too sticky to pull apart. I need a girl's eye view. I decide to e-mail Tam, lay down the events, get a gauge with hope to getting a grip.

> To: tamsin.flint@londonlights.co.uk
>
> From: sam.grant@sdb.com
>
> Sent: 2 November, 1999 16:45
>
> Re: My Private Hell
>
> So, wanna know how my weekend started out?
>
> I wake up Saturday morning to a miserably pounding head and the realisation that Sean is kissing Me! For the record, I neither instigated nor reciprocated Said Kiss. Kiss is interrupted by doorbell, which I happily go and answer, until…
>
> I discover who's pressing Said Doorbell.
>
> SARAH!
>
> Yes, Sarah, like she's just come back from the dead. Knees knocking (mine, not hers), blood thumping at my temples, she follows me into the flat.
>
> I call out to Sean who's still in my bedroom but who

comes into the sitting room on my call. Sean clocks
Sarah, gives it: "Hi Sarah" followed by "I think I'll be off".
So then it's just Me and Sarah, standing there, like
The Old Days, but neither of us saying a godamn
thing, like we're both just too busy learning to breathe
for the first time.

Sarah looks around the room taking in the all-too-
familiar décor, then volunteers, "I hate this room". I
don't read this as much of a promising start.
I go into the kitchen, return with two tumblers of
Scotch. By now she's sitting in The Barcelona Chair
(which I am also conscious she has always hated).
I hand her one tumbler. "A bit early for this don't
you think?" she says, but she takes it from me
nonetheless. "Given the circumstances?" I reason.
Now, the bit I've been keeping back, for dramatic
effect, the REASON for Sarah's sudden visit.
SHE'S GETTING MARRIED.
Sipping her drink, she says, "I wanted you to know, to
hear it first from me, that I'm getting married…
to Hans."
"…I'M GETTING MARRIED!"
Yes Tam, that's what she said!
CAN YOU FUCKING BELIEVE HER!
While I could be a little hazy on this, I believe my reply
was: "I can't fucking believe this!"
And you know what she said to this?

"Maybe I shouldn't have come? Hans said it was a bad idea."

Hangover or no hangover, I believe a tirade of kinds then followed. Something like: Well fucking Hans, that big armed no brained Teutonic fuck can go fuck himself, and Sarah, what the fuck do you expect from me? Congratu-fucking-lations? Kooky and unpredictable is one fucking thing but rocking up on my doorstep after 4 months announcing engagement and wedding intent is fucking borderline nuts.

At this point I was so fired-up, the full verse of her response is something of a blur. There were a good few *How dare you!'s*, phrases to that effect, and there was a considerable quantity of venom to support the dictum, Hell hath no fury etc etc. I believe she called me a "cunt" on 1 or possibly 2 occasions, and a line from a Beatles song I recently heard kept occurring to me: "I'd rather see you dead little girl than to be with another man," but I didn't volunteer the thought, knowing I'd most probably just be called a cunt again.

Before Sarah left, on terms that were obviously not that amicable, she did share: "Sam, I trusted you with my heart, and you broke it. Not you or anyone else will ever do that again". I would have suggested the lather of pathos she was working up was excessive, but by then, Sarah had left and I was left standing in the flat, holding an empty whisky tumbler and still in my Calvins.

From then on, my weekend just deteriorated.

Yours, lost on the dark side of Adland,

Sam.

It's a Date

Five minutes later: "Christ, are you okay?"

It's Tam, only ever a phone call away.

"I dunno. Maybe?"

"Sounds like you're far from okay."

"It's hard to say how I feel." I look around the office, everyone rattling away at their keyboards or prattling away on the phone.

"Work isn't the place for an emotional outpouring," I say "and in truth, I'm not sure I want to talk about it just yet. Typing's easier, and it could be argued I've talked and thought about Sarah enough."

"There is some truth in that."

"But I would like to go out for supper," I suggest, "and it's my shout. Are you free this week?

"I can be free."

"How's this Thursday?"

"Thursday it is then."

"Where d'ya fancy?"

"The Ivy is nice," and Tam is being completely on the level. I have to smile.

"Yes Tam, the Ivy *is* nice, but *try* getting a table."

"Fair deal, I'll book, you pay;"Tam, still deadpan, and then the line goes dead.

I look out the window, my phone rings but the caller ID

that flashes up is not Tam so I let the caller go to voice mail. 5 minutes pass, Tam's back at my ear.

"Table's in your name, 8pm," she says. "And you're okay, right?"

"Yeah, I'm fine. But Tam, I don't know whether getting a table makes me love you or hate you more."

"Think on it till Thursday," she suggests, then hangs up.

The Kind of Place I Work

Somehow Tuesday afternoon became Wednesday morning and I'm back at my desk wondering, was there an in-between?

Of course, I don't have to sit at my desk, and I have all of twenty minutes before my next meeting.

At work there is a *Blue Room*, where people meditate, or cogitate, or just take time away from their desks and eat a yogurt or a banana or something, but the blue is *meant* to facilitate lateral thought, tickle the right brain, encourage *Blue Sky Thinking*.

You see, I work in an industry where "thinking" can come with a colour code. And people in Adland often discuss how *Blue Sky Thinking* can lead to the identification of *Green Field Opportunities*.

Currently in work, there is no Green Room. Should I suggest we paint one?

Blah blah blah

Opportunities-to-See. Opportunities-to-Hear. Coverage Bands. Frequency Rates. Penetration Levels. BOGOF's. Share-of-Voice. Tone-of-Voice. Advertorials. Infomercials. Blipverts.

Stand-Out. Cut-through. Front-of-Mind Awareness. Top-of-Mind Recall. Triggers of Action. Memory Decay Curves…

By all means, pause, take a breath, but then continue.

…Defoaming Studies. Tissue meetings. Beanbag rooms. Normalising Strategies. Discovery Strategies. Brand Footprints. Brand Architectures. Brand onions. Verbal Mnemonics. Sonic Logos. Mood boards. Early Adopters. Opinion Formers. Empty Nesters.

And there's more…

Volumetrics. Econometrics. Neural Networks. Alpha audiences. Broadcast Streams. Monocasting. Niche Targeting. Halo Effects. Generic Messages. Account Hygiene…

Words that sound *unpleasant*, that sound ridiculous, and most that don't mean *anything* at all: Welcome, to Adland, welcome to Anti-meaning.

Talk is getting cheaper.

It is now the afternoon, mid-way, and I feel a little desperate. I've just survived a 2-hour briefing where we proved the rule and devalued the currency. Talk has taken a major dive. At present, it's almost worthless. Ergo, the worth of my meeting? Actually, my meeting was less than worthless - a squanderous waste of time and words.

After giving Shop-Talk a serious airing, everyone, Me, Jonathan, Tracey, Barney, a host of nameless faceless others have taken away "Action Points," enabling much sharing-and-comparing for when we "re-visit" two weeks hence.

I can hardly wait.

My meeting was concluded with, "We've got some great *action points* here, but let's not start trying to *square any circles*."

Astounding, but no one laughed.

I just thought "Huh, what the…?," but the guy next to me, it was Barney, actually nodded, as if implying, Yes, that's a very good point, circle-squaring would be quite dangerous, quite wrong of us.

Barney is such a little prick.

Late Night Entrance

10:45pm and I'm in the flat, post gym visit. The gym closes weekdays at 10:30pm. I was the last one out the door.

The flat is the same as ever these days, hyper tidy, ultra quiet, eerily still. I switch on the TV, no kind of company, but an acceptable kind of noise. On MTV, *Duran Duran* with a comeback tune, a slightly melancholic ditty that's kinda catchy:

> *I turned on the lights, the TV and the radio*
>
> *Still I can't escape the ghost of you*
>
> *But I won't cry for yesterday*

Jesus! I decide, maybe the noise isn't quite so acceptable. I hit the shower (not literally).

While toweling off in the bedroom I can still hear the TV, now hear Ricky Martin telling anyone willing to listen how he's *Livin La Vida Loca*. Good for Ricky, who then gives way to the *Backstreet Boys* proclaiming, *"I Want It That Way,"* which I understand is also how Ricky likes it. The track finishes to a short talky bit, and this tune I recognise at once.

I run naked into the sitting room and there's Holly, saying how she thinks Ricky's Real Sexy and how the Backstreet Boy's do Such Great Ballads. Holly herself is making Real Sexy look Real Easy, and I conclude it's time to turn off the tube.

★

In bed I'm restless. Holly's late night entrance hasn't helped. I get out of bed and go to my briefcase, pulling out the latest copy of *London Lights*. Back under the covers, I leaf through to the latest edition to Tam's canon.

Problem Housing

A Girl's Eye View, by. Tamsin Baron-Flint

November, 1999

I'm trying to buy a home. In London, it's a Big Ask. And when I say "Home," I'm meaning 2-bedrooms, really rather modest, nothing sprawling, nothing Stately, though Ambassadorial would be nice, but I'm discovering that just about *anything* approaching *liveable* is beyond my budget.

I've been phoning Estate Agents, introducing myself as a Potential First Time Buyer, going through my wish list. Two bed, *not* lower ground floor, would like to actually live *in* London, ideally something with a bit of character. Say over 2 or 3 floors? A spiral staircase? A skylight? A Batcave?

The response: Politely spoken words that feel like abuse – like the voice of a tolerant, all knowing butler. *"I think Ms is possibly being a touch ambitious. Has Ms thought about moving out of town? I presume at your price band Ms is not entertaining outside space, car parking, "Period conversion," a property with windows, or four complete walls…? Perhaps Ms should instead consider a bivouac – very open plan you know?"*

I am told that the housing market is "Mad". It's true. House prices are crazy, Asylum-on-the-Hill crazy. Bargains are scarce. Unless you're willing to take on a place where there was a multiple-murder and the blood's still wet on the walls, then you have to accept it's a sellers market.

Properties are going on the market and being snapped up the same day! On first viewing, offers are being made for full asking prices. Prices are soaring. Percentage growth is double digit, and Big Digit. There's a mood of Panic Buying, and I'm thinking, *"people really are nuts; but how much can they be earning?"*

I'm trying to buy a place in London, and I realize, on my salary, I'm not a millionaire. I have clipped my champagne tastes, could even settle for non-vintage, but it's difficult to settle for a one bed basement box in Tooting. It's not a restful vision: pulling my bed out from the wall on an evening, falling asleep as the damp flavours my nostrils, ignoring the judder of the tube train as it passes over the ceiling but doesn't disturb the rat colony that lives beneath the broken sink. I might be able to stretch to a one-and-a-half bedroom pad, but to cover the repayments, I'd have to rent the half bedroom to a midget willing to pay full-grown rent.

It's always been "location, location, location," but it appears I can't even afford "location". My *realistic* options are potentially "life adverse". It depends where my level of compromise rests; it depends how much I'm willing to be abused by the Estate Agents and live cheek by jowl with The Hood. It depends what I'll settle for; exit the tube, kindly decline the offerings of the corner-dwelling friendly-neighbourhood crack dealer, do likewise when invited to turn tricks in the red-lit den of ill-repute that is my next door neighbour. Ideal if you need to pop next door for a bowl of sugar and practice your sack artistry, but not the urban life I have in mind. Surely writing this column doesn't pay *that* bad?

I covet the delusional urban ideal. A balcony flat with roof terrace on Pont Street – now we're talking - within minutes walk of Harvey Nicks, where I may gather design ideas for furnishing my split level open plan Gal-Pad that sprawls over 3,000 square foot. I'm thinking High Concept Living. I'm thinking the kind of place where James Bond would be a neighbour. I'm thinking I can whistle Dixie.

It also riles that while house prices soar, so estate agents can afford the most salubrious office footage space in London and indulge their most hungry and budding sales stars. Free ski trips await the high-flying chinless few who can pair hovels with hefty finance. I was driven to my last viewing by an agent who was so pure a version of his breed as to be undisputed Devil Spawn. Young, close shaven, ex-Public school, wearing a charcoal-grey chalk-stripe, he dressed like a merchant banker and spoke like he'd been too good for Eton. His name wasn't Giles but it could have been.

Giles shared with me that he'd just passed his 3 month period of probation. He was particularly chirpy because his employers had just announced that company Polo's (the entitlement of all employees) were being re-called and replaced with 3-series BMW's. There was a choice of green, dark blue or black, and Giles was in some agony. Yes, Poor Giles. When conversation finally moved to matters of the flat we were to see, "Tremendous potential" were his opening words. "South facing" he assured, and "very competitively priced" for such an "up-and-coming area".

Any warmth I may have had for Giles froze on arrival. "Total scary scum-hole" was my take. "Tremendous potential" for being turned in to a car park. "South facing" only if you happened to be lost, in dense woods, on a cloudy day.

The flat was above a Kebab Shop, and occupied by an old

man who wore trousers tied at the waist with clothesline. The old man kept birds, budgies specifically, that he encouraged to fly free and unhindered around the flat.

I wanted to kill Giles; for having hair that looked like Tarzan fresh out of the salon, and for giving me the material for a week of nightmares. However, a Big-Up-Thanks to Giles for inspiring my column.

Forever, 2 Fast 4 U,

Tam x

The Ivy

The table is a very fair one, affording a good sweep of the restaurant.

This evening, it's quite a Celebrity Chow Down and quite frankly Fucking Beyond Me how Tam managed such a good table at such a good time at such short notice?

Within my eye line, Danni Behr (C-list), and Kathleen Turner (Old School A-list, and apparently playing Mrs Robinson in *The Graduate* at the Gielgud Theatre next year). Kathleen is here with her teenage son, and Danni apparently with some footballer I don't recognise. Unless they've featured in a Nike ad, I don't generally recognise footballers. Some would suggest this is a failing, but I consider Not Recognising Footballers a Special Gift.

Although I can't confirm from our table, when I checked my coat, I overheard the check-in girl say to her check-in-girl mate that George Clooney and Lisa Snowden had just checked-in their coats. This impressed me greatly though I instantly hated myself for feeling impressed.

I'm trying to look seriously "nonch" about my surrounds,

and wearing a black cashmere polo neck. It is my opinion that I look Pretty Cool, even if the fact its cashmere makes me feel Actually Quite Hot. Tam looks Hot, but in the figurative rather than literal sense.

"What did you think of my article?," asks Tam enthusiastically.

"Haven't read it yet," I lie.

"Bastard," she says with a grin.

"Tam, you're a One Women Crusade, that's what I think."

"Someone's got to be."

The waiter drops off our menus.

"So where do we start?," she asks. "You had quite a weekend; how are you holding up?"

"Christ, I just don't know?," I admit. "Work is a joke, like the rest of my life, and Sarah's announcement makes me wonder, did I fuck up the only thing that actually mattered?"

Tam's shaking her head. "Sam, Sarah so wasn't The One, not for you."

"But the consequential logic isn't easy either."

"Meaning?"

"Well if Sarah wasn't The One, then I haven't yet met who I'm supposed to be spending the rest of my life with. So what's really putting me in a spin is this: Any wife of mine is going to be gorgeous, which means she'll be currently going out with someone. Which is to say: Somebody, perhaps this very moment, is nailing my gorgeous wife. My wife, whom I haven't even yet met!"

"Life can surely be unfair," sarcs Tam.

I continue, "So now I'm looking at girls on the tube, and if, like I say, they're gorgeous, and look the part, and aren't wearing a wedding band: I'M GAWPING AT THEM! I'm trying to force eye contact, and waiting to see if a thunderbolt strikes. Madness, I know."

"Sam, you need help. At this rate, you're going to become a fucking stalker." This time, I'm not sure whether Tam is being sarcastic or not.

The waiter arrives with our starters. Tam's taking the simple Caesar salad route; I'm going with Thai fishcakes. It is said that the fishcakes are Jack Nicholson's favourite starter at The Ivy, and if it works for Jack…

"How's the flat hunt going?," I ask mid-munch.

"You really want to know?"

"I know I want to change the subject, and I'm happy for you to cheer me up with your misery."

"My last viewing was yesterday evening, and it left me feeling… *unclean*."

"That bad?"

"Worse!"

"Go on," I urge.

"An estate agent calls; would I consider looking at "ex-local authority"? *Sure*, I say, not knowing quite what I'm saying sure to; not knowing that sure will amount to bed sweats, flash-backs and years in therapy; not appreciating that sure will afford a chance to sup of blood pumped from the dead heart of misery itself."

"I'm concerned you're straying into melodrama."

"Melodrama my brown eye!"

"That's not a nice turn of phrase, Tam; especially for a girl".

"The viewing was only 24 hours ago – I'm still not myself. This place, it… it… it was beyond Barton Fink," she shakes her head. "It was repulsive to an impossible excess!"

"Ex-local authority, once belonging to the Council, are you sure you're not just being a snob?," I suggest.

"If I was being a snob, I wouldn't have agreed to see it in the first place."

"So what happened?"

"The trauma's still too deep. I can't articulate."

"You've coped well so far."

Tam pushes her finished plate aside, lights a cigarette. "Okay, it went like this. I find the road – in fact it was just off the King's Road, which is why I thought the place was at least worth a look; the kind of address where you wouldn't mind getting junk mail."

"You're talking postcode pride, and you're telling me you're not a snob?"

"The address turns out to be one of those Mansion blocks, a touch austere and brooding, but it's getting dark and I tell myself, *Fuck it, how bad can this be?* It's a hop-skip-and-a-jump to the river, the King's Road is 200 yards the other way, and I'm thinking, *This could be a Winner.* The estate agent meets me out front, and he's all firm handshake, solid eye contact and a suspected Sandhurst drop-out background. I can't remember if he had a double-barrelled surname – or introduced himself *and his middle initial*, to make up for the absence of a double barrel. Anyway, he's a bit sheepish, and it soon becomes clear why.

"The area immediately around the building is, let's say, a little "ropey" – cracked cement, weeds, split dustbin bags - but I'm still coaxing myself: *Be open minded, you can handle this, you may even be pleasantly surprised?*

"Then I hear this wet, tar-heavy cough. The origin is overhead, and it's some guy smoking a fag out of a second floor window. A potential neighbour, no less! He's your regular fat old bloke with wet lips and a damp comb-over."

"I thought you said it was getting dark. Your eye sight is exceptional," I tell her.

"I assure you Sam, I am not exaggerating."

"The real icing on the scene is that Fat Damp Guy is wearing a string vest. He's the kind of character you never see for real, only in New York crime dramas, and typically as The Deceased, discovered by neighbours *once the smell's become too bad.*"

"Is Army-Boy-Estate Agent reacting to any of this?"

"Well he makes this small polite little cough of his own, then gestures me towards a small door in a wall. There's a small security key pad by the door, but before Army Boy has the chance to punch in a number, the door opens, and out shuffles a..."

Tam's sense of dramatic pause is really very good, as were my fishcakes. I join her in a smoke, cadge one of her smokes.

"...well, at first I wasn't sure," she resumes. "The light as I say was failing, but I believe the thing that came from within was human, of a sort at least: an old – gender uncertain – shrunken and shuffling *thing*, wrapped in torn oily rags. White strands of hair passed across what I still believe was the head, but very visibly, there were other, like, nodes and... *formations* protruding from the skull."

"Now you're making this shit up."

"If only."

Tam takes a long pull on her glass of chardonnay. (I've always thought chardonnay rather underrated in The World of White Wines.)

"This is the kind of story where nicotine's a comfort," I say.

"Wait till you get a load of Derek."

"Derek?"

"Derek was the vendor, the guy who owned the flat."

"But surely he can't have been as bad as the Thing with the Cranial Nodes?"

"In his own special way, I'd say worse."

"Shit."

I re-fill both our wine glasses, draining the bottle and nodding to the waiter that yes, another one will go very nicely next to the salt and pepper.

"So Army Boy waits for the "thing" with the "head things" to shuffle by, and then takes to the stairs. I at first wasn't sure my legs were going to move, but they did.

"The cement walls and floors echoed with every footfall. The doors to each flat were made of metal, but some had a single reinforced pain of smoky glass. We climb about three floors and reach a metal door that's ajar. This is apparently *It*. Army Boy again smiles at me politely, but to me it feels strangely vindictive, then knocks on the already ajar door and calls out, *'Derek, it's Rupert, I'm here with my 6:15.'*"

"A muffled *'Come in'* follows, and before I know it, I'm beyond the metal door, and all about me is Blood Red…"

"Red?"

"Sam, Derek's place was an apparition; possibly a Readying Room before madness itself. I can look beyond bad wallpaper… but this was an Essay in Evil. The front door opened on a straight corridor. The hall carpet was a thick, rich scarlet shag – which actually extended beyond the floor! – tapering at the half-wall point by a black painted dado rail. The top half of the walls was a woodchip in curdled custard affair."

"Fucksake."

"Yes, indeed. The corridor ended at a small kitchen, again of scarlet hue, but this time in *painted tile*. The tiles stopped at the ceiling. The kitchen appliances – ordinarily called "white goods" – were red. I didn't know you could get fridges in red!"

"I'm not sure you can. Maybe he'd painted his?"

"It's very possible."

"And what of Derek himself?"

"I'm surprised you dare ask. After the kitchen, Rupert - who by this point I'm wishing had met with a fatal firing range incident during basic training – shows me the living room. It's pure 1970's. The wallpaper is gold, alive with bold swirls of Paisley influence. There's a 3-piece suite, which also happens to be red velvet – *by this point there's no surprise left in me* – and sitting neatly in one of the armchairs is… Derek."

Tam pauses for the first time in what seems like a long time. The ash on her cigarette has burned almost to the filter.

"Derek is something out of a David Lynch nightmare. Derek, wearing white drain-pipe jeans, had albino skin, favoured a very bushy red moustache and the kind of haircut you have to put on each morning. Yes, what quite literally capped it was that Derek was wearing a red toupee, and it looked in need of a trim. The whole scene would have been hysterical if it hadn't been so… macabre."

Tam drains her glass, a good three fingers worth. I follow her lead.

"I think I might have smiled, greeted Derek with a very flat hello, then left. I hardly remember the staircase, or leaving the building, but back on the street - once more in *The Real World* - Rupert catches up with me. If he'd put a hand on my shoulder I think I'd have screamed. When he came out with, *Obviously it would need a bit of work*, I could have kneed him in the nuts. Instead, I just lifted a hand, and gave it, *Rupert, just… don't.*

"I'll give you a call when we take on some new instructions," he promised, and I told him it was a good job I don't know where he lives, but I hoped it was with Derek.

"So the search continues?," I suggest.

Tam sighs, pours more wine. "Actually no, the search is on hold."

"Instead?"

"So… I'm moving in with David," she announces squarely. My flinch is more than blatant.

"Personally, I'd prefer it if you moved in with Derek," I say.

★

Sensing the mains are on the way (Me: calf's liver & spinach, Tam: sausage & mash) I excuse myself and head to the Gents.

Standing against the urinal, I'm thinking: *David, he's such an Old Bastard!* My thought finds voice, "Old Bastard!" bouncing off the porcelain in front of me.

I become aware that someone has appeared at the urinal one across, so obviously I look across. George Clooney. Remaining nonch is harder than before but I'm mid-piss so at least saved the prospect of stage fright. I just nod, the way guys standing at urinals nod, hoping George doesn't think I've just made comment on his age or parental lineage; George just nods back.

George is David's age and is also wearing a black polo neck like mine. I zip, disquieted by the multiple coincidences, quickly wash my hands and take to the stairs.

Back at the table, Mick Hucknall (whose music I hate and whose talent is in my opinion highly overrated; quite unlike Chardonnay) has come over to say "Hi" to Tam. Fact: He so clearly wants to get into her Sloggy's. Further fact: I would so like to get into a rumble with Mick Hucknall. Instead I just smile. Tam introduces me, we shake hands, then Mick gives it "Nice to see you" and "Enjoy your meal," and leaves.

The mains arrive and I make no mention of George or David.

Fizzy Head

They say Madness can be defined as "Doing the same thing over and over again and each time getting a different outcome."

I do the same thing over and over again. I sit in meetings, forever talk round the same ideas, address the same themes, the same challenges, but the outcome is always the *same*: I remain indifferent. The *Same Outcome* can still lead to Madness.

This Friday morning I argued, or perhaps debated (more semantics that don't matter!) with 9 people for 60 minutes over a bullet point. Should we include it, should we exclude it, edit it, embellish it? The statement that accounted for the bullet point was in fact incidental. From the outset, it was acknowledged that the words were not the "right words". *That* we all agreed on. Then, we debated. 60 whole minutes.

You can do a lot in 60 minutes, change the nature of things, move Mankind along a little, make history in a very small or very big way. We didn't. We all sat around, taking turns to talk, no real linkage in commentary, just bubble comments, vaguely in reference to a theme. Everyone meant what he or she said, but no one was to sure as to the actual meaning. Everyone agreed that there needed to be a second bullet point, but no one knew what it should say.

My favourite quote of the morning: *"It's an issue, and I'm just challenging the issue, but of course, I don't know the answer."*

Just before lunchtime, we called it a day and I went back to my desk, logged out, told Charlotte I was feeling Unwell, which was a kind of truth.

"How unwell?," she asked suspiciously but in a hurry. Her boss, Duncan (who's the CEO so he's most people's boss) was taking her to lunch.

"Chronic melancholy, urban angst, jungle fever, that kind

of unwell, I'm going home to bed."

"Okay," she said, "I'll cover for you, but if anyone asks, I'll say your symptoms are hot nose, prickly eyes, and a fizzy head."

"Sounds good Charley, thanks."

I didn't make it home; I went to the gym instead. Right now, I'm on the treadmill, trying to run away from all the stuff that's chasing after me, seeing if I can make my heart explode, wondering if I can find the handle, seeing if I can clear my fizzy head.

My Weekend

My weekend is all about numbers, about units of time and items of consumption. I visit the gym twice, each session being just over 3 hours, which includes 20 minutes in the sauna. I sleep 10 hours on consecutive duvet sessions, and drink 2 bottles of red prior to each period of slumber. Saturday evening's 2x an okay Rioja, Sunday evening's 2x a pretty tidy Chianti. I figure two bottles a night is solid going, but they do say, "In wine is truth," and I figure I have every right to find out for myself. Prior to each stint of Vino Veritas, I take myself for a punishing 40 minute street run, returning to the flat and finishing my daily ration of Evian (3 litres). Lifestyle Brand Water is followed by a Lifestyle Brand Cigarette. The weekend's quota is one carton of 20.

The weekend is a self-imposed solitary, actual physical interaction being kept to an absolute minimum. At the gym, one of the Pilates instructors (female, French, early 30's) tries to flirt with me, and a small wiry Vietnamese guy checks me out when I exit the showers, but in each case I don't encourage. These episodes apart, my existence is within a vacuum.

Over Saturday and Sunday, my mobile phone rings a total of 6 times and I only pick up once. Tam calls once, and I ignore it. She's moving in with David, what more is there to say?

Sean calls twice, and I ignore it, not ready to face up to the previous homo-erotic episode or discuss all or any manner of sexual crisis he may or may not be going through.

Twice, my mobile rings and the number is one I don't recognise so I choose not to recognise the existence of an attempted call.

The sixth call is from my Mother, and possibly with the exception of Freud, God only knows why I decide to pick up. It's now 8pm Sunday and there are 5 cigarettes left in my original carton of 20. The way I can pace my cigarettes is exceptional. I've just started my first bottle of Chianti, MTV's providing backdrop and my mother's in my ear space.

"How's the boil?," asks Ma.

"Fine, gone in fact. How are you guys?"

"Very well, quite excited actually, what with the holiday being so soon."

"What holiday?"

"Haven't I told you?"

"No Mum, we spoke about a month ago, what holiday?"

"We're going on a cruise."

"Christ, aren't cruises for properly old people?"

"I'll tell you when we get back."

"Don't you have to sport a blue rinse, own a Zimmer frame, have confirmation of senility and be able to play shuffle board before they let you go on a cruise?"

"Maybe. Granny's coming with us, which should make our acceptance easier."

"Granny's cruising too? Well Dad must be just delighted! How long are you going for?"

"10 weeks."

"Excuse me. I thought you said 10 weeks?"

"I did," confirms Mum.

I must admit to being a little taken aback. I take a healthy slug of Chianti, light a less healthy cigarette.

"Isn't Granny too old to be let out the country? And more importantly, what am I meant to do for Christmas? Treat myself to a Bernard Manning Microwave Meal for One?" I am starting to feel very neglected here.

"Sam, you're a bit too old to start suffering from maternal deprivation," says Mum, and it's of my opinion that she's being particularly heartless. "You don't have to feel abandoned," she adds. "The cruise is around the Caribbean; the ship docks in Barbados for Christmas. We were thinking you could fly over for the holidays, should you want to?"

"When do you… set sail?"

"In a week's time."

"I'll think about it," I say, then after the usual sign-offs, I hang up and turn up the volume on MTV. There's very clearly a new sexpot in town and she does a good job of distracting me from irritating maternal phone calls. Moving like a well-oiled strumpet, but looking all of 14, she's called Britney Spears. A revamped Lolita for the MTV generation, her pigtails bounce as she twirls and gyrates, pouting at the camera, asking for It. The song's called *Baby One More Time*, and I figure this Britney chick could be Big. Just watching her, I feel I could do very dark deeds.

I retire to bed, but cannot sleep. Images dance and grind and morph, of Sarah, of Holly, of Britney, a hybrid taking shape: Sarah's head and breasts, Holly's legs and ass, Britney's tummy, pigtails and moves. I beat off like a fiend and sometime thereafter fall asleep.

Shop Talk

Man, I would so love to introduce the smell of napalm on a Monday. Such a shame I can't order in the jets, put All These Feckers out of their unrealised misery.

Brutal Truth: Mondays are one seventh of my life.

Venue: Meeting Room 9, and instead of Agent Orange, just a serious ordering of Blah going down.

Jargon used to amuse me. Now: I want to rid the world of Jargon Peddlers, scorch the sky above their heads, torch the earth beneath their feet.

I used to peddle the occasional slice of jargon, but I'd like to think I did it with irony. What frightens me are meetings where colleagues spiel so convincingly that one has to assume they're being *sans ironic.* Yes, utterly, *sincere!* They converse in tinny voices without even a smudge of "trace irony," astounding the hell out of me.

"Sam, thanks for joining us. To put you in the loop, I was just proposing a round-table brainstorm. Let's maybe do a quarter hour, and see just how many ideas we can download."

Tempting to say, *"What, you mean we'll all chat for a bit and you'll write down anything that sounds good on your flip-chart?"*

If you're going to use words like *download,* surely something should be plugged in?"

These days, I don't Deal Jargon; instead, I've started going for the Big Piss Take, wheeling out Jargon Double Headers.

My 2 efforts thus far this Black Monday:

1. *"We don't want to drop the ball anymore than we want to take our foot off the pedal."*

2. *"By ensuring we sing off the same song sheet, there's no
    chance of throwing the baby out with the bathwater."*

How silly did I sound? I would say: Very, but I kept a straight
face and (disappointingly) no one in the room Spontaneously
Combusted (which had been my hope).

Post Meeting Room 9, I return to my desk. Barney bounds
over, asks me quite sincerely what my "Key take out" from the
meeting has been? Barney's writing up some notes, going to
circulate them to The Team.

"That your head is invariably so far up your arse" I
speculate, "I imagine you can draw your lower intestine from
memory. Why not circulate that?"

Barney just stands there, thinking I've made a joke.

"Barney, seriously: Go away."

Barney fades out, as do I.

A Face Full of 44

Events sure suggest they're close to conclusion, and I must
admit… I'm far from fucking thrilled.

Looking down the evil end of a hand canon can be
surprisingly liberating; at least it can be if you're able to hold
down your lunch. The guy with the gun, Hector. He's an ego-
maniacal little prick whose company I've found loathsome
even in the short time we've been acquainted. Obviously,
this latest episode has not brought on any sudden warmth.
Normally I wouldn't invite a Hector into my social orbit, but
I'm undercover, or at least… I was.

"Cops," Hector shares, "you can't imagine how much I
fokin hate cops. Killing you, it's gonna be a thrill."

I just sit where I am, because right now, I have little choice.

Hector had one of his goons tie me to a chair — though wrists only, and not that well — and now he's waving a big ole gun in my face, acting Tony Montana tough, trying to scare me. Credit to the Little Guy, he's doing an okay job.

Big guns, tin-pot psychos and the threat of death will always be a scary combination for me, but giving Hector any sense of sado-satisfaction would hurt almost as much as the path of his bullet through my brain. Okay, maybe not quite, but I've gotta play tough too, stifle any urge to shit all things brick-shaped.

So I smile.

"Go easy with that shooter Hector," I say, "dinky wrists like yours, repetitive strain injury is a real worry."

Hector grins back, opens the chamber to his 44, and leering at me, pops out five hollow tipped bad boys. They tinkle as they hit the concrete floor.

"Grant, where you hiding the girl? She mine, I own her."

"You know me, Hector. It'll take a snow day in hell before I'll tell you a goddamn thing."

Hector rolls the gun chamber, snaps it shut, then squeezes off a round in my face.

Click.

Pre-click, all I could think was "Oh shit."

Hector's now enjoying himself.

"I'm gonna ask you maximum of another 4 times. You stay with your cocky answers, you get dead real quick."

"I appreciate the math, Hector."

Shit, this is all too real. If only someone would just shout "Cut," freeze time, tell me there's a chicken switch someplace or that SWAT's ready to bust down the door.

"Grant, where is she? I want her back… so then I can kill her!"

"Go ahead…" I say, "make mine a margarita."

Click.

Oh Boy!, I think. I can't keep playing Lady Luck this way.

Hector steps closer, sharing his bad Cuban breath, grinning from ear-to-ear.

"Maaan, only theeng I hate worse than cops," he shares, "it's fokin tough guys…"

Hectors only two feet away, and as I quietly wriggle my right hand free of the rope and memories of sacking quarter backs and killing Cubans flood back to me, all I think is, just a little closer little fella…

★

"Sam."

"W'W'What?"

"Away with the pixies, maybe?"

"Engrossed in some very high level strategic thinking. What do you want Richard."

I think I'd prefer dealing with Hector to dealing with Richard (aka. Dick). Dick has this ability to irritate me. He's my level, but sometimes tries to act that bit senior, and tries that bit too hard to always do the right thing, come over all Good Cowboy. He is also Very Good Looking, and Very Gay, though to his credit, he doesn't mince around in that OTT-Big-Limp-Wrist-Come-on-Girls! way

"Tracey tells me you're being a bit rough on Barny," says Dick.

In fact, although I say Dick is Very Gay, he hasn't come out. It's just his wardrobe, personal taste and grooming suggests to me he follows the Gay Way. He is too well groomed, his hair too perfect, his wardrobe too spot on. It's all Gucci, Gieves & Hawke, and Prada.

"Barney," I try and explain, "he's too gratingly keen. In all honesty, I find him a bit of an arsehole, and what we do, it's advertising, not proctology, right?"

Also, one occasion I was in a meeting with Dick, he openly admitted that he liked *The Pet Shop Boys*. Add all these things up, and in my opinion, the scales tip. Very Gay.

"Sam, stop chewing on the poor guy's ass, then I won't have to chew on yours."

I don't smirk.

"Richard, you don't manage me, you're certainly not my boss… but," I relent, "you do have a point."

I sigh, feeling like a heel, feeling like the Bad Cowboy I can be.

"Okay," I concede, "I'm sorry, you're right. I'll fix things."

"Barney's a good guy and very bright," he rubs in, before walking off.

In which case, I think, Advertising might not be Barney's smartest long-term plan.

Crazy Eyes

Current location: Momo on Heddon Street.

Momo's just opened and we had to blag our way into the subterranean Members Bar. I'm here with Jamie.

Jamie asked the guy on the door if Danni Minogue was here, told him he was her agent, that I was Danni's New Boyfriend (who he also represents). Door Guy looked like he snaps puppy dog spines for fun, had Death By Misadventure written all over him. To finish his performance, Jamie showed

Door Guy his new Black Amex and said, "This is not a mistake *you* can afford to make."

For a split second, I thought Door Guy was going to Truly Hurt Jamie, but then he just looked kind of tired or bored or both and waved us in. Now we're in the downstairs members bar and feeling quite A-list. All the girls in here are: Very Attractive.

"You ever bump into that Holly bird?," asks Jamie as we wait for our drinks and he takes in the room.

"Actually, I keep seeing her on MTV."

"Yeah, I thought that was her," he says.

"However, my last 3-dimensional encounter with her, she smashed me across the face."

Jamie chuckles. "Wish I'd been there."

"The scene just prior, in the curry house, you were."

"Yes, that was very funny."

"Back in the days of Jamie and Jane," I say.

"Inevitably doomed," he says. "Too alliterative," then adds, "like Sam and Sarah."

A girl who looks enough like Kate Moss to probably be Kate Moss sits carelessly wasted in a corner on some Moroccan version of a beanbag. Of course, her wasted demeanour could be for show?

"Oh, and guess what?," I say. "Sarah's getting married… and the guy's called Hans… and I think it's possible I might be having some kind of breakdown."

I choose not to time how long before Jamie stops laughing.

It's 9pm, and while the couscous craziness goes on above our heads, we opt for round-after-round of Mojito's. Tall glasses, splash of soda water, mint, fresh lime, liver-numbing slugs of Bacardi, and it's like a race. Jamie and I drink a new Mojito every 15 minutes and when 10:45pm hits, we're both frazzled.

"Ah… this could be awkward." Jamie looks suddenly uncomfortable. For the last hour, he's been telling me how work are cutting back and how he might just lose his job. Jamie looks more uncomfortable right now than he did talking redundancy.

"What?," I ask. "Where?"

"10 o'clock," he directs.

I look to my right.

"How many 10 o'clock's do you have?," Jamie asks. "To your *left*."

"Sorry, momentary hour-hand dyslexia. Is that…?"

"… Hannah," Jamie confirms.

Heading toward us like a Scud: Hannah.

"Fucking psycho," Jamie mutters under his breath. "I hear, even her therapist is pissed off with her."

"You hear from who?"

"From her, last time I spoke to her… just after I'd shagged her."

After Jane, Jamie was seeing Hannah for a while. Hannah is, I concede, certainly rather sexy, but I must also side with Jamie. Hannah is decidedly *wonky*. There is a scene in *The Outlaw Josey Wales* where Eastwood is facing off with three Union soldiers all itching to go for their guns. The awkward moment is witnessed by Eastwood's travelling companion, an Old Indian (real life name, Chief Dan George).

Squint, being Squint guns down the three soldiers. Afterwards, the Indian asks how he knew which one was going to draw first? Squint tells Chief Dan George that one of the soldiers, "he had crazy eyes," he was always gonna be the first to draw. I love that scene and it totally reminds me of Hannah. She's got crazy eyes too. She must terrify her therapist.

"Hi Jamie." Cordial. Cheek kisses follow.

Jamie tries hard to smile.

"When was the last time I saw you?," asks Hannah.

"Think: long… and hard," says Jamie, grinning, proud of his double entendre. "I've been meaning to call you."

"Don't beat yourself up about it."

"No, really, I've been overseas with work, but perhaps a drink next…"

"Sorry. Busy. Forever."

"Hannah, I'd really like to get together," he lies. "Get to know each other better."

"Jamie', says Hannah, moving closer, her eyes (in my mind) widening. "Have you ever thought about why we hardly know each other? It's because I don't want to know you. It's because I really don't like you. You're a fool… and a particularly uneventful lay."

Hannah smiles, a crazy grin to match the rest of her, then turns on her heel. Jamie and I slowly exhale.

"Could have gone worse," he says.

Not Myself

The radio triggers (though at what time I am not clear) and gradually I achieve numb awareness of a new day.

Holy Shit! What's all *this* about?

In short: *I'm not myself.* Doesn't feel much like my body (*goddamn snatchers*), and similarities with my day-to-day mind are slight (*bad-ass brain thieves*). Cognition's frazzled, needing urgent rewire.

Slowly, things start assuming focus. A misty, stodgy focus; not really much of a focus at all. Let's say instead, "An Understanding". Things are starting to be *understood*. Things like: *I'm still pissed*. As drunk as a skunk - a drunk skunk, that's had a Big Night. Even by skunk standards.

Next, I'm in the shower. How did I get here? As I suspected: mind and body working in complete *independence*. Working like when you're drunk, which I still am. The shower has little effect. It's wet, that I can appreciate, but little else. Besides, I'm distracted by the fact my genitals Feel Numb. I have Limited To No sensation in my scrotum, which *can't* be good. Not what you could confidently call a "good start". What was I drinking last night? I know the answer well enough: Mojitos.

I wonder if I can make it through a *whole* day, just the sheer number of hours, regardless of the location in which I have to bank them.

Could phone in sick? Tempting. Then again, it's not like I feel rough at this *precise* moment. Hell, I'll show my face. At present I feel fine... except for my nuts. God knows what's going to kick-in around Noon? Quite likely the Mother Of All Headquakes.

I'll just take things step-by-step. Next step. Clothes.

For the love of Christ, let me have an ironed shirt. If there's no ironed shirt, then I'm going back to bed. There is a shirt.

Cufflinks provide real adversity, but I overcome. To celebrate, I try and back flip onto the bed (it's not like there's anyone watching). I land on my head.

The tube ride is a joke. In the glass of the carriage my reflection spooks. In spite of the medium, my eyes look glassy, the lower lids an absolute spectacle; all folds of bruised skin like the belly of a rhino that's just come off a crash diet. I thumb the sockets, making it that bit worse, that bit more *remarkable*.

It's like everyone's occupying their usual temporal plain, and then there's Me, *Outer Limiting*, tingling away, a slight flush-on, occupying a dimension just out of synch with everyone else. I wonder, could I walk *through* people if I tried? I decide not to give it a go.

The train jolts unexpectedly and my legs nearly go. How the hell am I going to manage work if I can hardly stand? How will I manage *interaction*? I pep-talk: Sam, keep your eyes down.

Only option when AOA (Arseholed on Arrival): lots of coffee and a "Limbo Low" profile.

Out of the station, the wind is strong and bracing, the sky a heavy morning-black (much like my tongue). The *Evening Standard* vendor's at his usual spot. I skip by with my eyes down, smug that I've avoided the headline. I'm getting good at this.

With my desk finally in sight, I walk past Jeremy, who's busy barking down the phone.

"What is wrong with Capital-fucking-Radio? Those, those...*fuckers*! Why can't they play out the copy in even rotation. What's complicated about 1 to 1? I'm going to have a real sense of humour failure with those cunts when I see them." His knuckles are white on the hand-set. If ever a guy needed Anger Management.

I pick up my phone.

"Charley, when you have a moment, could I have a very very strong coffee please?"

Charley waltzes over.

"Out last night." Not a question, a statement.

"Why?," I ask, knowing I sound ginger as sin.

Charley leans across the desk at me, her eyes narrowing. She sniffs.

"Because you absolutely wreak of alcohol," she says matter-of-fact.

"Could be the new aftershave?," I suggest.

"Not unless you've taken to wearing Bacardi?"

"Please Charley, I implore you. One very strong coffee."

She smiles, disappears.

Two minutes later, Charley arrives with a brew thick enough to chew on.

"I think you're still hammered?"

"I'll have you know I'm on flying form," I tell her.

"I look forward to watching the crash land."

Charley leaves, and I feel it would be rude not to look at her bottom. It's exceedingly shapely. Before I can equally appreciate my first sip of coffee, the Nodding Dog appears at my desk.

"Hi Tracey." She looks in some distress.

"I've just had my ear chewed off by Duncan. I've got a whole heap of shit to brief you on."

"Tracey, I'm just not that inclined today."

"Save your sarcasm for someone else," she suggests, then plonks her Prada-clad ass down opposite me. Tracey's flat over-aerobicized bottom offers me nothing.

"We've got a stewing shit pot of a situation," Tracey begins. "Those see-through arse-wipes at McCanns are blaming *us* for the fact they're going to miss *their* copy deadline. No way the campaign will make launch date. Client's fucking apoplectic. They've already been over at McCanns – spot of breakfast and accusation - and should be spilling out of a cab and into Reception in about 5 minutes. Shoot-out's in Meeting Room 3."

"So much for "Limbo Low" profile," I mutter.

"Pardon," asks Tracey.

"This I could *really* do without," I say, but not caring a fuck about copy deadlines or apoplectic clients, only caring that I'm starting to feel sensation in my balls. My New Life Strategy: Not Caring.

"Yeah… well… unlucky," says Tracey.

I think, of all the Meeting Rooms, I hate Meeting Room 3 the most.

Damn it All to Hell
A new afternoon, an old format. Venue: Meeting room 9, Mojito Migraine still keeping company (unfortunate), but the morning's shit-storm and finger-pointing over. At no time were lives in jeopardy.

I want to define Marketing:

Marketing is…

Effort #1:
… a lot of confused people sitting around agonising over trivia.

Effort #2:
… a lot of clueless people sitting around brainstorming irrelevance.

I'm sitting in a meeting room 9, a 15x21cm white pad resting on my knee, wondering which definition I prefer. #1 or #2? Outside of my thought, in the room, other people, all talking (what seems) at once, filling the dead air with dead words and bad go-no-where ideas. It's a real Think Tank of Inanity we have going on. Tracey's adding to my pain, so is Richard, so is Barney. This time, Marvin's not part of the action.

With or without Marvin and his too-wide ties, I still feel like Sisyphus, condemned to forever push my boulder up the slope. The only difference: when my boulder rolls back down, I'm somehow already at the bottom, and I end up being crushed by the boulder. But then I start pushing again; Greek mythology meets Groundhog Day.

For some of the meeting, an hour or so, I sit there, just sit there, more time, passing in a way that I can truly *feel* my very mortality, can feel the dying going on inside me, a second at a time, and I just sit there, accepting the inevitable stroke of the death clock, as I use up my life in this limp, cruddy way.

Everyone starts speaking of "front-end bolt-ons," and of being mindful of how we "skin the cat," "bite the cherry," "raise our head above the parapet," "dip our toe in the water," while always ensuring "bums on seats". As we close, there is agreement that progress should be ASAP, even PDQ.

What I want to do is put everyone in a line and shoot them, one by one, gun 'em down without blind-fold or last request. *These people…*

The meeting ends. I smile at people, politely gesture with an arm for Tracey to leave the room first. All I can think is: *This is no way to live a life, this is no way to live a life.*

In the street this morning on my walk into work, I passed a great big billboard. Sharp white text on a bold red background, the poster advertised *The Economist* magazine, but this in itself is not important. What felt important was the copy line: *"Would the film of your life go straight to video?"*

Right now, I figure mine wouldn't get beyond pre-production.

Also in the street this morning, I passed an *Evening Standard* vendor where the morning headline read: *Flood Baby Born in Tree Later Drowns.* I'm convinced that "Flood Baby" would make a better movie than mine.

Law of the Meeting Room

Christ, where did yesterday go? I swear, I just blinked for a minute?

Current venue: Meeting room 9 (again). This morning, the *Evening Standard* ran with: *Cancer Boy's Dog Must Also Die.* Ever since hearing about Cancer Boy's chow, my day has just slumped.

I have come to a conclusion. The truth of it is this: It is not *what* is said, but simply *how much* is said.

Sensible Debate has given way to Volume-Driven argument. Say More and Win The Meeting, this is the Law of The Meeting Room.

Today's meeting is a kind of verbal *free-fall.* At one point, I actually experience a kind of vertigo.

My response: I drink lots of coffee.

Everyone talks endlessly and a couple of really clever-sounding words are given an airing. My favourites were: *panacea* and *patois*, the former from Richard, the latter from Barney. Obviously, nobody offered up any kind of panacea, but everyone did kind of speak in tongues. I'm quite in to my P-words at the moment.

The clever words stand out in a room of not very clever people, or people wishing they were doing something smarter than having really unnecessary debates about really unnecessary things, forcing themselves to use Smart Words in vain attempt to Feel Better.

I know: I am becoming bitter.

My favourite quote of the afternoon: *"It's not that I precisely disagree with you, it's just that I'm not actually agreeing with you yet."* This, from Tracey.

For me, runner up in the quotes stakes: *"You've got 750,000 customers standing at the foot of the totem pole all asking,* Which way do I wave?" This, from Duncan, our Idiot CEO who deigned to grace us with his genius (and heavy after shave) for the second half of the meeting.

If I have become bitter, I would argue it is with good reason.

★

When I get back to my desk, there's a voice mail waiting. From Sean.

"Sam. Sean. Stop avoiding my calls. Let's do beers, tonight, no excuses. Your Gay Mate."

I check my e-mails.

> From: sean@lbetheman.com
>
> To: sam.grant@sdb.com
>
> Sent: 11 November, 1999 17:08
>
> Re: Star Wars' Queen Amidala admits Twiglet addiction
>
> In extending the cyber arm of friendship, I propose we
>
> meet up – sic *Face time* – at your earliest convenience.
>
> Yours, unloved,
>
> The Coma Kid

I pick up the phone.

"I don't want to go drinking anywhere *nice, young,* or *trendy,*" I tell him. "I want *depressing* and *weird*, the perfect venue for you to share your strange new ways."

"Sam, I know the perfect place."

The Duchess of Percy

I meet Sean at The Earl Percy, a boozer just a little ways up from the tube station in Ladbroke Grove, W10.

Sean chose well. The venue is masochistic, an unquestionably crud pub; a nicotine crapped lung, a "Why aren't you dead yet?" dinosaur in an epoch of the All Bar One-style franchise.

We take a seat in "The Saloon Bar," no Young Guns in sight, but lots of Crazy Eyes. The décor's no more or less grotty than any other part of the Percy, just more frayed rotting velvet alcoves, peppered with cigarette burns, the stained windows turning the evening sky outside a malarial yellow.

"So, are you Gay or what?," I ask.

"Are you some kind of homophobe?"

"No Sean, I am not. Could just be that one of my best friends is Gay," I say pointedly, "which I would like to add, is okay with me, just so long as you realise I'm not much into snogging you... unless I get exceedingly pissed."

I slurp my pint, waiting for his reply, but instead, over my shoulder comes:

"Can I sit here? You don't mind do you?"

Sean looks up, I turn my head, and it's...

...OHMYGOOD!

Neither of us speak, but our faces must surely say it all.

Our screams are curdled, but silent. Whether the owner of the voice registers our discomfort, it is difficult to establish.

"Thank you," she says. "My name is Catherine."

We wouldn't have met her by choice, but Catherine hadn't given us any. I might have told Catherine to go back in her hole, if only I'd found my voice in time.

Both Sean and I sit there, and Catherine just starts talking.

"Had had him since he was a puppy," says Catherine. "He developed an unnaturally wide jaw."

Catherine isn't the kind of lass you tend to find in All Bar One. Developing that, she isn't the kind of lass you tend to find on Planet Earth; not at least outside the Hammer House café, where the blue plate special is always horror. I know I sound cruel, but it isn't my fault that Catherine looked how she does. A dog had done it.

Yes, that's what I said.

A dog.

"It was a very big dog," she says, "very large long teeth."

Catherine's face wasn't just uneven, but an event in two parts. Like two other faces had been merged. If symmetry makes the prettiest faces, go to the other place, go the opposite, go extreme, go a little further, and that's where Catherine's face lived.

"The owner knocked the dog unconscious, but his jaws had locked, you see? We were *attached* for two and half hours. I lost three pints of blood."

Catherine's right eye was pretty much where it should have been, at least in relation to her nose, but the left eye (goddamn that eye) had dropped a good inch and a half. This was more than the work of gravity, it was the work of…

"They called the dog Butcher," details Catherine.

I'm reminded of the Evening Standard headline: *Cancer Boy's Dog Must Also Die*. I shiver. Did Catherine meet Cancer Boy's dog?

We bolt down our pints, Sean runs to the bar and buys Catherine a very large glass of dry white wine.

"My, you're kind lads."

We say good night and hit the street at a run.

"You did say you wanted depressing and weird," says Sean.

"Yeah, well now I want nice, young, and trendy. I want to look at beautiful babes while you do the talking.

BBB

Outside on the street, it's freezing, like New York Cold.

By the time we've walked up to Beach Blanket Babylon (like after the San Francisco street, Beach Blanket Babylon

Boulevard), our faces are numb.

Oswald Botang's at the bar ordering some ridiculously named cocktails. Both the cloth and cut of his suit look good, but then again, it really should.

"What are you drinking? Another beer?," asks Sean.

"Martini Rosso," I tell him.

"How very retro of you."

Sean tells the bar man, "One Martini Rosso, one large glass of Rosé."

"Rosé?," I say, thinking, Christ, from that order, we really do sound like the biggest pair of flamers.

"Yeah Rosé," explains Sean. "It's a summer drink for fun people."

"But it's November?"

"Yeah, but I'm in denial. I'm championing the notion of the endless summer."

We get a table by the open fire.

"Right, second question, first. The other Friday, after the Halloween party, what happened to that girl, Jemima?

"Jenny."

"Right."

"You don't remember?"

"What's there to remember?," I ask.

"We all went back to yours, we all leaned heavily into Tequila and Jack Daniels, then we gave Jane…"

"Jenny," I correct.

"Right. Then we gave Jenny the kind of spit-roasting usually reserved for under-age models who fall into the cross-hairs of Premier league footballers staying at the Dorchester."

"Sean."

"Yes."

"You sound like Jamie. What really happened?"

Sean smiles like a goof-ball.

"Okay, the tequila and whisky part is true and I did raise the subject of a threesome, and in every truth, I think she might have gone for it… but you passed out and she called a cab."

Good enough for me.

"Okay," I say, "first question second. Rosé aside, are you gay?"

"No. Not as such."

"Not as such?"

Sean takes out a packet of cigarettes, lights one.

"Sean, are they menthols?"

"They are."

I must confess, I am truly puzzled.

"Sean, working to the thinking that what you smoke is a declaration of *who* you are; what sort of effete, big-girl, floral-dress wearing phase are you going through at this moment in your clearly confused life? You maybe want a nice long cigarette holder to go with that?"

"You've got it all wrong," says Sean. "In the nicotine/tar stakes, a menthol more than holds its own against a big mama Marlboro Red… but sucking on one of these feels like sucking back two dozen ice cubes through a polo mint."

"And that's a nice feeling?," I ask. "If I want a mint, I eat a mint. If I want to smoke…"

I shake my head.

"Sean, this is all very Twilight Zone. First the kiss, then meeting Catherine, then the Rosé, now the menthols…"

Sean grins, pats my shoulder. "Sam, I'm trying to broaden my horizons, trying to try out new things, like Tam with her Girl Kiss. It's an experimental phase."

"Like kissing me?"

"Like that. I was still a bit pissed in fairness. This scene I'm trying to write in my new script, it's where a guy kisses another guy. I wanted to inject some realism into my writing. It's a teen–monster movie, *The Breakfast Club* meets *The Thing*. Title: High School Blob Out"

"Sounds like injecting realism could be tricky?," I suggest. "Maybe you could get Catherine for the part of the monster?"

Un-momentous

I spend all morning "debating" with ten other people the difference between personal and *inter*personal. It proves a Linguistic Swamp, and we all drown, in an almost ceremonial kind of way.

My favourite quote of the morning is early on, only ten minutes in: *"These are the words we have. They're not the right words, but they are* The Words, *so I'll take you through them…"*

This afternoon, we – there are four of us - sit down to write a document.

"We need a document on this," someone, some fool had decided. "Okay, sure, why not," someone else, another fool, possibly me, then replied.

We trawled through twelve older documents: lots of charts, lots of Bullet Points, and Mission Statements. Stretch Targets all over the place. All twelve documents all said versions of The Same Thing.

Then: we wrote our document.

When we were done, we had thirteen documents… and everyone seemed happy, but this everyone did NOT include me.

I am now back at my desk. I consult my wrist. It's 6:25pm on a Friday. It is officially The Weekend.

I look around me. View: The Office-scape. Desks, swivel chairs, lap tops and desk tops, filing cabinets and large pot plants, all very generic and long leased. There are folk still busy beavering away. Jonathan is still hard at it (typing, not punching), and Charlotte is floating around, as are others.

I conclude: this is drudgery. Work is talked-up, fleshy, unnecessary, and *this* is What I Do. Hilarious, if it wasn't so terrifying. You get 3 score year and ten, ballpark, and this is how you mark it off: doing nothing worth a damn of anything; like, thanks for playing, buddy. I puff out my cheeks.

It is the weekend and I have no one to have sex with – except maybe Sean, which is not really an option. Sex is becoming a distant memory.

Friday November 14th, 1997

"Pretty Good"

It's Friday night, and it's Just The Two Of Us.

Occasionally, when it's just Me and The Doris (more commonly known as Sarah), I worry about what everyone else is doing. I fear that everyone else, that Tam, Sean, Jamie, and the Rest of London are all out having a Better Time, without me.

I suggest to Sarah that we go out; she asks we keep it local. The outcome is wine, pub wine. Hardly Jet Set, but actually fine. Sarah is hardly a connoisseur, and I'm plain thirsty. The first bottle – from New Zealand, a quite buttery chardonnay – is sliding down at a steady rate, and by the time it's up-ended, Sarah wants to talk Sex.

"Earlier today," says Sarah, "I was thinking about when we had sex last night."

"Last night? Did we?" I jest.

"Mmm," Sarah purrs, pauses, then: "Didn't it feel different?"

Question or rhetoric? With Sarah, sometimes it's difficult to establish.

I assume it's a question, but request elaboration. "Different, as in *literally*?," I ask, hoping she means literally, and not say, *spiritually*?

"Yeah, literally."

Phew.

She adds: "By you being there, and me being... like that..." The words are accompanied with sign, Sarah making a kind of double-scissor shadow puppet. "...you're going in at... *that* angle." Her hand movements continue to elaborate. She is very dexterous.

"And that's good, right?," I ask, hoping it's good (it felt pretty damn good last night).

"Very good," she confirms, then continues her trigonometry based discourse on the angle of hypotenuse necessary to calculate and – eureka! – stimulate her G-spot. It's all rather encouraging stuff, sounding like last night's performance received good, perhaps even rave reviews.

Aussie Bar Bloke comes over, and I wonder how much he's overheard? Then I think, who cares? If my appraisal had been bad, it would be a different matter.

"Do you guys want another bottle?"

I turn to Sarah, and it's all "Sure's," "Why not's," and "Cheers, that would be great".

Bar Bloke departs with empty ice bucket, Sarah proceeds: "So, it felt very different for you too?"

"More pressure at the sides." I answer, the half bottle of Kiwi grape assisting my candour.

"Better, worse, different?"

"More, er, different," I say.

Her eye-brows lift. Why they lift, I'm not sure, but I'm fast getting the feeling that our Shared Intimacy did not afford Shared Perspective. Clearly we are once again coming from different angles.

"Don't get me wrong," I say, not quite stuttering. "It was very enjoyable. It wouldn't have been the same without you."

There is no good time for cracking a bad joke.

Sarah is silent, holding the almost empty wine glass close to her mouth, but showing no sign that she's ready to see it off.

I chose to talk on. "It's just that there have been two *other* occasions – recently – which *really* stand out."

Sarah smiles – albeit only a little – so I continue: "There was…"

As I lean perceptively forward, my eyes widening, she corroborates with a "Uh-huh, *that* time was great!"

Alrighty now, we're back on the same page; very much in agreement over "that time".

"…and then there was last Friday when…"

"Yeah, that was pretty good too."

Hold everything. *Pretty good*? So, not *as good* then?

"Pretty good?," I ask with heavy inflexion, the call for explanation quite obvious.

Bar Bloke returns with the second bottle, new bucket, heavy on the ice. "Yeah, it's a pretty good drop," he contributes. "Enjoy." He smiles at Sarah. She half smiles back, then drops her lids. He walks away and I let it go. However, this "Pretty Good" business is much unfinished.

Now I am silent, forcing her not to be. "Yes," she says, holding my gaze, "Last Friday. Pretty good." Her upward inflection attempts for up-beat.

Spiralling through the windmills of my mind: So, not life-defining then?

"Pretty good," I utter back, like the words aren't fitting right in my mouth. "As in ,'How was your starter?' 'Oh, it was *pretty good* - considering it had broccoli in it...'"

Sarah smiles: "If you want to go with a food analogy then yes, pretty good sex, in spite of the broccoli."

"So, what was the broccoli?"

"Sam, I have no fucking idea what the broccoli was. It's

your analogy!"

The humour is there, but it's thin.

"Bullshit. I suggest you have every idea about the broccoli. So talk. Give up the broccoli."

She pauses, composes, then: "Last Friday you had drinks after work with Sean – many drinks – caught the last tube home – shit-faced – fell into bed – suit on the floor – and announced – fortunately absent of drunken slur – that you had to Have Me right there and then. This, I didn't particularly mind, although I had been fast asleep and dreaming pleasantly."

"What about?," I ask absently.

"What, the dream?"

"Yes."

"Flying kites and an old man with a kind face. I didn't know the man. The kite was yellow."

Once again amongst the windmills: Why the hell did I ask?

"Oh," I say.

"So, you wake me from my kite flying, and we have sex. Friday Night Sex: drunken, wanting, passing directly to 'Go'. It lasted a *pretty good* while; we built up a *pretty good* sweat. As for the seven or so stage checks prior to 'Go', there weren't any. Just a lot of "Go". Hence, *pretty good*. Would you prefer if I rank it as *pretty OK?*"

I consider this, then decide, Sarah's assessment is close enough. I had been out last Friday, and I did get back shit-faced, but I *hadn't* been out with Sean. Two weeks ago, I met this Absolute Honey called Holly, and last Friday night, I was on a date. I had a great time, but I *didn't* get to "have" Holly, and when I got home, I was damned well in the mood to have somebody.

I lean across the table to our untouched, uncorked second bottle.

"More wine?," I ask.

Saturday November 14th, 1999

No Fun Zone

I spend the best part of the day at the gym, trying to find outlet to my sexual frustration. The bench press is hardly a Fun Zone, but lifting helps. The treadmill is not my preferred way of working up a weekend sweat, but again, I have little choice. I return to the flat via the off-license (bottle shop if you're Australian, Liquor Store if you're a Yank).

Once back in the flat, a broody looking Cab Sauvignon uncorked, I consider a night of MTV and mind rot. My phone rings.

"Hi Jamie," I answer.

Jamie has called to tell me how truly "bendable" Chloe is, how his new found upper-body strength is being really put to the test, and how his essay writing skills have never been better.

I hang up on him.

Twenty minutes later, my phone again rings.

"Jamie…," I start, but Jamie hasn't phoned back to chat.

On the line, I can just hear grunts and moans and "Oh baby's!" and "Yeah baby's!" and what might be a squeal (which

I presume is Jamie, not Chloe). I decide that Jamie's humor is unusual at best.

When my phone rings a third time I am ready to throw it out the window, but it's Tam so I pick up.

Tam's Friend

I sigh, possibly with my entire body. It's 12:30am. The evening: a disaster. All the Great Girls spoken for, all that was left unspeakable. Except for one girl, and it's a miracle I didn't murder her.

"Come on Sam, come out, have some fun," says Tam, three hours earlier. "There's an old friend of mine I really want you to meet…"

I leave the flat, leave a half bottle of red just sitting there and flag a cab so easily I think, maybe I'm in for an okay night? Me, such a fool.

Indeed, my evening did feature this girl, Tam's friend, Tam's "mate," long-standing. Tam had known this girl since the school playground, which is where I wish Tam had abandoned her (possibly throttled). Alas.

Tam & Co (which included her 40 year old boyfriend David) were down at a pub round the back of High Street Ken. I didn't know the crowd. The gathering had something to do with one of David's good friends, who was celebrating a birthday. I think maybe a 90th or something?

I arrived. David's at the bar slamming tequila's, Tam's talking to a group of gal pals.

I recognise two of the three girls. Helen, tall, half-cast, a model; the second girl, dark brown hair, Sloaney, very healthy looking and called Sophie. Helen is always sadly going out with a Society Someone (make that, No One), but her choice in Men aside, I find her Very Sexy (she has great pins). Sophie, I once sadly snogged (pre-Sarah) on a skiing trip following a Very Enthusiastic bout of vodka shots. Sadder still, Sophie is a Bad Kisser (I'm not being nasty, she just is) and when we returned from the slopes, she called me a few times with what I can only imagine was a view to a date. I never returned her calls and she is only ever borderline civil when our paths now cross.

The third girl in Tam's gal-pal clan, I don't recognise and have never met… but sadly it doesn't stay that way.

"Sam, this is Miriam…"

Tam's friend was single, so she was a logical girl for introduction, what with my status being the same.

Only… logic sometimes shouldn't come into it.

Problem was, Tam's friend (and I think it was her Very Being, rather than any One Individual Thing) pissed me off royally.

To define Miriam's being, and pinpoint what I found so Fundamentally Irksome was simple. It was her "Singleness". Her singleness, which absolutely, unequivocally played like a blunt cheese-grater making repeat passes over my tits. I nailed four vodka and tonics in forty minutes.

"You have quite a thirst on you," commented Miriam.

"I was at the gym earlier, and I'm still a bit low on fluids," I jested.

Forty minutes was long enough to get the Life Story.

Miriam had been single exactly 9 months. Previously, she had moved to Tokyo with her Banker Boyfriend, Roger. In Tokyo, they had been engaged, they had talked of children, and they had never once talked about the many other women in Roger's life. The Other Women was something Roger had kept to himself… until one afternoon, when Miriam returned home from the International School (where she was an English teacher) and caught her fiancée in bed (such a cliché) with his boss. His boss was a chick. Suddenly, all Roger's late nights in the office and weekend business trips threw up rather cruel images.

Trapped at the bar, Miriam competed with the aggressive decibels of the sound system, less shouting, more throwing words towards my left ear on waves of hot breath, while (whether aware of it or not) pressing her right breast into a point just above my left elbow.

Oh. Dear. God. It was all so depressing. Lenny Kravitz just jibed me, singing his new tune, *Fly Away*. Occasionally, I looked up, wishing for a skylight, praying for wings.

"But now… I'm so happy," Miriam chimed. "Really… I am; at last so happy - so much happier than before. I can't believe what I went through… but now I'm *really* happy."

Good for you Miriam, I thought, and also, you are such a lying cow! Miriam went to painstaking lengths, saying the same sentence using a selection of the same words, only in different orders, assuring me that she was Absolutely & Truly Happy.

Looking along the bar, I see David's still slamming back the shots. A shot. I so needed a shot.

"Miriam, do you want a shot?, I asked. "I could really do with one."

"Great!', she said with a grating put-on perkiness.

Having clearly been briefed by Tam about my Relationship Breakdown, the way Miriam was trying to assure me that everything would be okay, would turn out for The Best, that there could be a Happy After was, to no small degree, Very Annoying. Especially Annoying was that I didn't give Two Shits for her assurances, hadn't welcomed them, sure as hell hadn't invited them.

Truly Vexing was Miriam's paper-thin efforts to appear happy. The self-deception was pathetic. *I'm so happy-happy-happy!* No you're fucking not!, I wanted to scream. You're alone and shitting yourself Miriam; shitting it that you're going to die alone, where maybe no one discovers the body for weeks. Epitaph: She always said how happy she was.

"Your boy… I mean, ex-boyfriend?," I asked, very aware of what I was doing. "Is he still seeing his boss?"

I didn't know whether Miriam had been mid sentence, or come to a pause. Either way, my question was enough.

"Hmmm, I believe he still is; someone who's willing to at least for now be treated like a doormat."

Then I asked: "Do you think he treats her how he treated you?"

"Why wouldn't he be just the same with her?"

I couldn't help myself.

"But *she* is *his* boss. Maybe," I hypothesized, "it was just the rapport the two of you had? The way you connected, or didn't connect? Maybe your boyfriend…

– note the deliberate omission of "ex" –

"…and his new girlfriend are a perfect match, wonderfully happy, neither wiping their feet on the other, but both willing to lay down their coats so the other may be saved stepping in a puddle?"

At this, Miriam frowned.

Yes, the sound system was loud but I, like Miriam, could make myself heard when I wanted to. At her crumpling brow, I offered a sympathetic, slightly knowing half-smile. "When people aren't meant to be together," I added, "when they don't love each other, that's maybe when they treat each other poorly, like doormats."

I patted her kindly on the shoulder and I could see the

welling of tear along the bottom lid of each eye.

I finish on: "Miriam, he couldn't have loved you."

That did it.

"Excuse me," she said, "the ladies are over there aren't they?"

"I think so," I said, having not the faintest, and watched her hurry, excusing herself between clusters of drinkers, no longer looking quite the same Happy Miriam she'd announced earlier.

I couldn't help myself.

Miriam was thirty, just turned, and had probably in her mind wasted the last 6 years of her life with some tosser called Roger. From Word 1, Miriam hadn't fooled me, and I'd hated her for her false attempt at Being Happy. I didn't want her thinking she could get away with it, at least not while in my company, not on my watch.

A pretty-looking girl, a little over-weight, staring dumbly into a fresh and scary new decade of life but deluding rather than dealing with it all: that was Miriam, and that's why I'd wanted to make her cry. Besides, she'd trapped me at the bar.

I didn't feel I could spend a life-minute more with Miriam and I wasn't going to wait for her to come back from the toilets.

I finished my drink (knocking back half of my comically priced Vodka & Tonic) and turned to leave. Turned out, by then Miriam had already surfaced (a little red eyed) and was talking with Tam and David.

I go over to them, kiss Tam gently on the cheek. I can feel the voodoo vibe David's trying to give out.

"Tam, sorry, I have to go. I've got a big day at work tomorrow."

"Tomorrow's Sunday, Sam?"

"I know, just imagine how busy that must make me? Seriously, I'm working on a pitch. The whole team's involved in a run-through tomorrow. The pitch is Monday.

"David," turning to David, "good seeing you… as always." I shake his hand.

The guy has a firm grip, too firm, like he's trying to prove something, say something.

"I didn't even know you were here," he tells me, grinning.

I smile back knowing I can handle his handshake any day of the week. "I'm not surprised. Guy your age, failing eyesight must be a real worry."

I turn to Miriam. "Bye Miriam," I say gently, then lie: "It was nice meeting you."

I leave, not waiting to see if she bothers to lie right back, keen to find a cab before the pubs close. Of course, all the cabs I see are taken and I spend forty minutes walking home, which I figure is absolutely what I deserve. I know the score. Make a girl cry, don't get a cab, I'm such a long-time resident of the Karma Hotel, it's not like much surprises me these days.

Ariel

Ironically, my Working Monday proves a Significant Improvement on my weekend.

This afternoon, I was in a 2 hour meeting with what started as 15 people. For the first hour, Chronically Disconnected and struggling to care, there was no real level, other than the physical, in which I was actually present. It was like killing time in a waiting cell before being allowed into Hell proper. Sartre portrayed Hell as three people in a drawing room. I'd say, the more people you get in a meeting room, the More Hellish life gets.

Mercy came in the second hour, when salvation entered the room. 15 people grew to 17 and I spent the time staring at this Properly Fit Brunette who took a seat across from me. She was from some or other PR-agency.

She had straight jet-black hair to her shoulders, almond-shaped blue eyes and there was a suspicion of a nose job about her. Her colouring and dimensions: much like Sarah's.

I put her at 24, a North London Jewish Princess indulging the working drama for a couple of years, either because Daddy thought it would be good for her, or because she wanted to prove to Daddy that she was an Independent London Girl; all before she married a Good Jewish Boy, moved to Hampstead and dropped a litter of sproglets who themselves would likely require nose jobs 17 years down the line.

Looking at her, instinctively, I wanted to Do Things to her (my hormones are thermo-nuclear right now), and while she knew I was staring, she smiled back. Whether she guessed that I was mulling the minute details and possibilities of her nakedness, I could not say.

As a consequence of the Properly Fit Brunette, with 10 minutes of the 2 hours remaining, I said something Deliberately Intelligent.

I might have spoken for 5 minutes, holding court, telling everybody how I believed it should be. There were lots of nods around the room (go Tracey, go!), and afterwards, it was decided that things should be "Actioned," that we had some excellent "Next Steps," and the brunette gave me her business card (name: Ariel Cohen), insisting that we should "liaise".

Will I try and make "liaise" vernacular for something else? I put Ariel's business card in my wallet and return to my desk full of questions. Am I taking control of my feelings, am I on the up, having crossed paths with a fellow traveller I'd love to screw, or am I just kidding myself, like the Miriam's of this world?

Everything is Confusing

Ariel or No Ariel, I remain baffled and confused, life continuing in a tail-spin.

Riding home on the tube, another day done, I wonder?

Can I blame The Post Modern Condition? I can try. I say: it says a great deal for where we are right now. It says that collectively, that mentally, we are All Unstable.

Definitions are broken down, swapped around, fragmentation all embraced, borders becoming hazy edges when what is needed is clear mandate. Sing it; *Deeeee-Con-Struc-Tionnnn*.

The New Reality is that everything's open to interpretation, everything negotiable, nothing assured, granted as fact or truth eternal – like having, then not having a girlfriend,

Nothing is any longer certain.

Cast-iron truths have grown rust. Black and white has merged, receiving each other like the union of two fast-spreading ink blotches across a tissue paper terrain. There is a bastard big grey area that didn't used to be there.

I say: The World is more in need of a rhyme and reason than it has ever been. Ideas abound, scenarios are stock-piled, theorists reveal a car boot full of possibilities. Everyone seems to have an opinion, but no one knows for sure, and everyone knows that too.

Collective forces have given way to eclectic suggestions.

All we do know… is that we don't know.

Is it just me or does Social Evolution seem to be loitering, waiting for a jump-start, waiting for something Quite Epic to happen despite the lack of immediate prompts or pointers?

Boundary shrinking and interactive technologies lay the world open to Global Scrutiny. Meaning: Everyone is an

Informed Observer and Opinionated Critic. How many of us still participate or have we all become spectators?

Fibre optics and satellite link-ups make everyone a potential witness. The world is a more naked place; we watch the cultures it supports being disrobed and dissected. International events start to feel like Special Features, their protagonists like daytime soap opera stars. The *real world* feels increasingly *less real*. We view newsreels, war, famine, and disease, all the Malthusian Nasties, with an almost painless detachment.

We see so much, supposedly know so much and we just grow ever more numb to what we see and do.

Everything is Pulp Fiction, everyone seems to covet Supermodel Stardom, everyone accepts Media Manipulation and Tabloid Truth. Techno-Dudes are In and Internet Millionaires rule. Everyone plays the main lead in their Own Life Movie, walking through a world where there is death, destruction, misery, but a groovy soundtrack and sponsored messages at every turn.

Finally, as the train lumbers into my station, I ask myself: How will any of this help me get a date with that Ariel bird?

Man on Fire

On the street this morning, I passed a police van. Written on the side: *Underwater & Confined Space Unit*. Now, in meeting Room 3, as the walls draw in and we Play Semantics I wonder, *Do they know I'm here?*

Today, the *Evening Standard* read: *Suicide Dad Gases Family*. I have decided, I am going to make a very active effort to avoid reading future headlines.

My favourite quote already, despite this meeting being

only 15 minutes old: *"We have a theme, but the question is…*
What theme do we have?"

A tremendous contribution from The Nodding Dog.

Inside: I also think my head might explode.

Marvin is here, torturing me with his very existence and
his ridiculous tie. Ariel feels like a memory that may not have
ever been real.

I am on fire, *and* in a confined space, *and* underwater.
Yes, it takes some doing. The utter and immense triviality
of this working day is almost beyond words. Meetings, then
more meetings, with so many words being used and no
one, absolutely no one (especially Tracey) moving anything
forward. I want to scream. My head is a Munch painting,
totally freakin' out.

On the outside: My God, even more terrifying: I'm smiling
at Marvin. It's almost sickly it's so serene, this sublime smile of
mine, so composed, like a Monet, this myopic view of sunlight
playing over near-still water.

And still: no one knows what theme we have.

Walter Mitty

You know Walter Mitty, ever heard of him? Danny Kaye
played him in the 1947 movie; James Thurber conceived the
original short story. Walter Mitty, a fearless naval commander,
a fearless WWII bomber captain, a world revered surgeon,
the world's finest pistolier, a legend, but only sadly in his own
mind. In reality, Walter was a hen-pecked husband escaping
his reality, spinning story strands amidst the turning windmills
of his mind. When I first read the short story I knew exactly
how Walter felt. He was trapped too.

*

Marvin has suggested "taking the conversation off-line," to be continued when he gets "back to the ranch". I have no objection. I rarely answer my phone these days (unless it's personal), and maybe The Theme is hiding out at The Ranch?

Marvin leaves, but the funs not over. The meeting continues.

I sit back and try very hard to fade out.

FADE IN:

INT. BRIDGE - NIGHT

Light drizzle hangs in the air. Evenly spaced street lamps produce small orange balls, but cast little shadow.

A solitary figure stands, then leans at the railing of a wide bare-backed bridge, then looks down.

Beneath the bridge, a brown murky sludge passes with unbroken flow. Somewhere beyond the curtain of mist and drizzle, the horn of a tug boat breaks the silence, but the intrusion is flat and brief.

Tight on: cupped hands light the end of a cigarette.

Tight on: lips pull on the cigarette; smoke jets out through the nostrils.

Pull back: disarmingly handsome, SAM GRANT
stares out into the night. His raincoat and trilby keep
the damp and drizzle at bay.

SAM (V.O.)

Circumstances: you do what you can to prevent them
turning into one unholy head-on super-charged shit
storm... but sometimes that's just how things turn out.

Usually: it starts with a girl, always a
good-looking one.

Next: you're slip-sliding down a whole new destinial
chute – one most likely sprinkled with razor blades.

And what then?

The inevitable: you're left staring at the darkness,
seeing what shape your demons take. If all this was
written in the stars, I should have chosen a clearer
night to look up.

"And... CUT!"

"Sam, you were great! Just GREAT!"

Immediately, a cast of thousands flurry into life, so many
lights, cameras and clip-boards.

"Ridley," I say. "We happy?"

I flick the end of my cigarette over the side. The ember tip
spirals into the dark.

"Happy?" he exclaims, like I even had to ask? "Sam, we happy. You. Nailed. It.

I smile, he continues.

"It was everything: enigmatic, charismatic, poignant. The way you smoked that smoke, it had stillness... it had a sublime grace."

"Ridley," I say. "You're too kind, even if you are full of shit."

"I wouldn't say great if I didn't mean GREAT."

"Hey, I know, I know. It's just... all I had to do was stand on a bridge smoking a cigarette."

"Wait till it's overlaid with your voice-over." Ridley shakes his head, marvels. "Sam, you're a rare breed. I've never worked with a two-time Oscar winner who's so humble."

I smile, humbly.

"Just wait till you see the dailies," Ridley adds excitedly, "just see what you give off, in the face, in the eyes, a vulnerability somehow blended with this brutal masculinity..."

I really don't know how I do it.

From somewhere: "Mr. Scott, we're setting up the next shot."

"Sam, I won't need you for two hours. I understand Cameron Diaz is swinging by your trailer to maybe – if you're not too busy – say Hi and get an autograph. I'm sure you can entertain her for a couple of hours."

I smile. I've admired Cameron's form for some time.

"Just let me know when you need me Ridley."

"Sure thing Sam. Y'know, I'm so glad you left the advertising racket."

"Ridley, I'm glad you did too."

No Meetings?

This is truly a miracle.

I walk over to Charlotte's desk.

"Charley, I've just checked my diary."

"Yes?"

"I've got no meetings in for today?"

She clicks away at her screen, then looks up with a smile. "That's right. You've got a clear day."

I am almost overwhelmed, as well as being delighted by Charley's choice of wardrobe.

"Nice top by the way," I tell her.

Today, Charley has selected to wear a fabulous and fantastically little top/vest/thing. Lycra-stretched and brandishing a desert island "rack shot," complete with arching palm trees and white sands. She is totally distracting. Despite the sun-drenched scene, Charley looks a little cold, her nipples poking out like bullets. I marvel at the power women can have over men. I marvel at how older guys get to employ young girls as their PA's, and how PA's know they should and don't seem to mind dressing just That Bit Dirty.

Duncan appears from his office, stares unblinking at Charley's palm trees (read: tits). Would she mind fetching him some lunch in an hour or so?

"Of course," she smiles, all innocent, like she has no idea what her nipples are up to.

Duncan so wants to go beach-combing, and a thought comes to me. Has he already?

★

Hilarious. Allegedly, which is to say I heard it on the grapevine moments ago, I'm possibly in line for a promotion. It's a three-way race between Dick, the Nodding Dog, and Yours Truly. I'd say Dick's got the racing line.

Personally, I wouldn't promote Me. Hell, I'd fire me. All I can say, if I get promoted, it shows what dickheads I work with.

I spend the afternoon flicking through 3000 photos on greataupair.com. (Way I see it: I get paid to sit at a desk, irrespective of what pointlessness I pursue from behind it.) Au pair 20948 is seriously hot, and I may send off for more details. If I get promoted, who knows? Au pair 20948 would be money well spent.

Booze & Talk of Blood Cops

I arrive late. The restaurant: Osteria Basilico for a "tastes authentic" slice of Real Italy in W11.

Everyone's already nibbling on garlic breads and bruschetta.

"You live the closest," comments Tam, "and you arrive the latest?"

"It's a skill," I confirm.

The table: Tam and Sean, Tam's friends Sophie and Helen, Tam's senior citizen boyfriend and now housemate, David.

Under the table I imagine Helen's long brown legs stretching on forever. I smile warmly at her, nod (in an indifferent guy way) at David, and manage "Hey" to Sophie through what feels like a plastic mouth. Helen smiles back, David replicates my nod, Sophie wears the kind of scowl that it probably took most of the day to apply. Mercifully, my seat is in between Tam and Sean. Tonight, I suspect it will be a table of two halves. I'm guessing David is here under some duress and will spend the evening flirting with Helen and/or Sophie. He will drink heavily, and I may just try and better him.

Two tables away in another group of six, Stamp Heir and Over-Tanned Smug Mug Tim Jeffries. His group does not include his Alleged Intended, Claudia Schiffer. Personally, I don't see 'em tying the knot, but I also don't really care.

I take my seat, and pour a very large glass of white wine, slowly easing myself into Sean's mid-rant. I may be later than I thought. Sean already sounds drunk.

"Quite simply, I don't wish to be an A-list underachiever in a world littered with all these catwalk harlots and Brit pack starlets!," announces Sean.

Tam nods sympathetically. She can be good like that.

"Honestly," he continues, "reality bites when you realise you are notable only for your lack of notability. Mary Shelley penned Dracula when still only a teenager. Orson Welles gave the world Citizen Kane before reaching his 26th birthday."

"But Sean," I say, "you've got notoriety. You're The Coma Kid."

Sean doesn't acknowledge. "The fact that I have not yet *Arrived*, it gnaws with acidic, cramping frustration in my gut."

"It could be the wine?," I suggest. "How much have you had?"

"Sean," says Tam in a way that doesn't sound patronising, "isn't this something you should have got out of your system in your teens, early twenty's latest?"

"Yeah," says Sean, "I thought I had. It's just… I've had a lousy few days."

"Sean," I say, "you can want it all, the Girl, the Goldwatch, *and* the Diamonds – and that's fine – but I struggle to see how you're going to achieve heights of Art House excellence with the likes of *High School Blob Out?*"

"High School Blob Out?" asks Tam, eyebrow lifting.

"And," I continue, "if you want fame, your name in lights, to be the young blood with the column inches written about him, then *finish* one fucking script."

"I have."

"High School Blob Out?" asks Tam again.

"No," says Sean, "Blood Cops."

"Remind me, which one is that?"

"It's a vampire movie, but where being bitten by a vampire is reversible. There's a clandestine cell, the Blood Cops, who carry vials of Pure Blood, and if they can reach the victims in time, they can save them. Think: *Lethal Weapon* meets *The Lost Boys.*"

"Could work," encourages Tam.

"Sadly," counters Sean, "*Working Title* doesn't seem to think so. They've had the script for the last month. Yesterday, they called, told me to piss off."

★

Our food arrives; all very Italian and authentic looking. I'm not the slightest bit hungry, but I order more wine for everyone.

"Maybe you'd be better off telling My Story?," I suggest to Sean.

"Your story Sam," he says, "it's not a compelling one, and nor is it sympathetic."

"Oh," I manage.

"He's right," backs Tam. "Boy meets girl, boy loses girl, boy feels bad for treating girl like shit. This Sam, happens all the time."

"Yeah?"

"Yeah," says Tam firmly.

"Well, unlike Sean here," I say, "it's how I tell it that sets me apart."

Tam continues. "Please Sam, tell me that you've faced facts and moved on. You cheated on Sarah, she left - which is what you wanted - and now she's getting married."

"She's getting *married?*," asks Sean.

"Yes," says Tam.

"Buddy," says Sean. "You didn't mention it?"

"What's there to mention?"

Tam again: "That your past with Sarah is just that - The Past. Her getting married has a nice finality to Your Story."

"He's called Hans, for chrissake," I say.

"Well if you do still feel any animosity towards her," Tam adds, "the fact that she's going to have a husband called Hans should delight you."

"Hmmm," I say. We all drink our drinks in brief silence.

"Sam, maybe you need some help? Professional help."

"Help, professional, Tam, what are you talking about? I'm fine, or at least, fine about not quite being fine."

Tam presses: "I'm talking about therapy, about maybe you talking to someone who has a business card with *cognitive* in the title. A couch, a soothe calm 'I'm listening' voice. Maybe someone who has studied psychothopy?"

"Yes. Very amusing, but I'm not that fashionable." I refill my glass, top up Sean, top up Tam.

"Is psychothopy even a word?," I add. "Seriously, therapy! Do I look like Ally McBeal?"

"Well mate," says Sean, "you are starting to act a bit like her."

★

The plates cleared and the wine still flowing, everyone is starting to look a touch round bellied and glassy eyed. Sean goes to the gents.

"So, how's living with David?," I ask. "Is all his messiness getting to you?"

"He's a very tidy person," defends Tam.

"Give it time. All that anal overly-attentive tidiness will start to annoy."

"Hmm."

I know that Hmm.

"Hmm… *what?*," I ask. "What's up?"

She looks (pains me to say, it could be *lovingly*) over at David. He looks content and animated, drinking away and no doubt talking no end of Big-I-Am Bullshit.

"I've found bottles of booze," she says.

"Found?"

Tam sighs. "I think he's an alcoholic."

"You… think?"

"I've stumbled upon bottles of liquor all over the apartment. Stoli in the top of the wardrobe, Jim Beam behind the hi-fi, tequila…"

"Tequila?"

"Jose Cuervo," Tam details, "behind a book case. Some people stack a heavy drinks cabinet, but people rarely secrete hard liquor in bathroom cabinets and behind boxes of Kelloggs."

"There too?"

"There too," she confirms.

"Was this some sort of major dusting session?," I ask.

"You find two bottle's of gin hiding out behind the Frosties, you start to wonder what's lurking elsewhere."

"Once you start living under the same roof," I say, "that's when you really get to know a person, all their dark little secrets.

What are you going to do?"

Tam takes out two cigarettes, hands me one.

"Thanks," I say.

She lights, inhales deeply, then: "I'm going to talk to him about it."

"I see."

"What else can I do?"

I take a heavy slug of wine. "I guess, if you love the Old Bastard, you're gonna have to confront him."

Sean bounces down in his seat, back from the gents. "What did I miss?"

Monday, November 22nd, 1999

Picture Imperfect

This is too much…

Thirty minutes ago I was snuggled beneath a thick, fluffy (very fluffy) 20-tog duvet. I was at rest.

Then: the radio came on. LOUDLY. Then I became aware of the heavy-weight rain pellets rapping at the window. Then I remembered who I am and what I do.

Now: I'm here, on the station platform, living my life, doing what I do 5 days out of 7, doing what countless others do.

Standing with others, I await the train. We all stand together, and we all wait alone, trying hard to ignore Another Less Than Perfect Day. It's as if the world spent last night pure-lining on an excess of uncut grey. The texture is grainy, like maybe Day 2 of the Apocalypse.

Someone has been busy with a spray can. Peeling ad sheets promoting the latest play/movie/mag/retrospective are covered in the laziest graffiti I've ever seen.

Everything: the buildings, the people, look tired and wasted, too low on life. Faces are numb, expressions resigned or indifferent. This is the drill. This is the deal. This is: How It Is.

People hide, lost between the pages of their latest paperback (Barnes, Banks, King , some Cussler) or engross within the daily column inches, drifting from outrageous photo stills to salacious celebrity gossip.

Those with nothing to read zone out, maybe Walter Mitty-ing, perhaps rustling up a little Lottery Fantasy?

A tube train clunks and grinds its way into view. Alert to the familiar rhapsody, small, stunted rats scuttle between the tracks.

The carriage windows are a caked veil of condensation and grime. Heavy droplets (the product of someone's bronchial sneeze?) race each other in spastic parallels.

Commuters surge forward, claiming turf adjacent to where they predict closest access. The carriage doors open, unleashing a damp, body odour belch. *What joy.*

The doors open and NO ONE gets out!

The commuter scrum-down begins, middle-aged bankers forming a tight ruck with middle rung managers. *I WILL get on this bastard train! I MUST get to work! I CAN'T be late!*

Passengers who already felt sardined suddenly realise their former "luxury".

There are protracted groans and moans. *Oh, how rude, how selfish! How impossible people are! Can't you see there's no room?* My expression is equally candid: *Fuck off - breathe in.*

Total strangers stand with less than an inch of unfamiliarity between them − as if they are but a heartbeat away from sealing that first kiss − and share the pretence is that it's not happening, that it's Not So Bad. Face-offs are so close, people can examine each other's nose hair, test the success of their deodorant, observe their choice of perfume.

I look at the ads. Panels peddle a carpetbag of pharmaceutical relief. Alka Seltzer, Lemsip, super-strength vitamin pellets − Christmas is a'coming. Up-market holidays and ski-insurance, date-lines and phone tariff deals also have heavy profile. The ad boys know their audience.

A gaggle of Foreign Students get on at Victoria, and during the next three stops incant *"Mind The Gap. Mind The Gap,"* like it's the only English they know. An Early Bird American tourist remarks to her Blue Rinse Buddy how she'd imagined Big Ben to be, *"Like, bigger"*.

We pull into the next station and suddenly a seat becomes free. The seat is close, but to secure it, I'll have to knock over someone's Granny, and by the time I've decided it's an acceptable casualty, a Pregnant Women has eased into it instead. I smile kindly at Pregnant Women, thinking: *FAT BITCH!*

Instead of a seat, I get some suited punk (with a bad case of bed-head) share the events of his previous night. Bead Head tells his buddy that last night was so "LARGE," his first act of this new day was some "serious churning" in the bathroom. Allegedly, the bounced Madras still contained "fully-formed mutton chunks".

What sort of start to the day is this? How long can I do this for? How long have people done this for? THIS is why people grow old, their faces becoming craggy and scored. THIS is why people die early. The endless, pounding routine makes ghosts of us, these one-way zombie shuttles turn us to worm chow. London kills me.

Nearly there.

I alight at my allotted station, re-button the overcoat, straighten the tie. Me: ready to get back on the ladder and back in the race. I take the station steps two at a time and come to A Decision.

This Stops. Getting on and getting by, working hard, playing tough and fighting through, all That Shit.

I've decided. It all stops, I need out.

The Dead Granny Excuse

First thing I do when I get to the agency: "Charley, what time's Duncan in?"

"Sam, are you okay? You don't look too good?"

I'm hardly going to say: I'm sick of the commute. Instead, I lie.

"My granny's died."

"Oh… Sam." Charley's face crumples, looks genuinely sad, like dead grannies and dead bunny rabbits are the very worst things in the world.

"It's okay Charley, she was old," I say, thinking, I wonder how Granny's enjoying her Caribbean cruise?

I add: "But I need to take some time off work, some of this week, maybe some of next, and I just wanted to clear it with Duncan."

"He'll be in at 11," says Charley.

"Right, can you put me in his diary for then?"

"Of course. And if there's anything I can do to help?," she offers.

I just smile, while thinking, showing me your puppies would cheer me up.

Jamie at Jamie's

I meet Jamie at Jamie's, an okay-but-no better bar on Charlotte Street.

"I get to hear you fucking her," I say. "When do I actually get to meet her?" I refer of course to his weekend phone call.

"Chloe?," he asks.

"It was Chloe you were having sex with?"

"Hannah."

"The psycho?," I say, taken back.

"And she really is," says Jamie, shaking his head.

"I don't understand."

Jamie helps me out: "Turns out Hannah's just joined my gym in South Ken; her flat's a two-minute walk away. After seeing her in Momo, then seeing her working out in this very tight and tidy cat suit number, I thought I'd ride the coincidences and chance my arm."

I frown. "That time in Momo, she didn't look like she wanted to have sex with you?"

"Maybe the endorphins helped me out?," suggests Jamie. "All I know is: one minute I'm saying Hi and buying her a mango smoothie, 10 minutes later, we're back in her flat and she's licking my arsehole." Jamie shakes his head in wonder. "Some girls, they just don't mind doing stuff, y'know?"

"Not really, no," I say. "And what about Chloe?"

"As bendable as ever," Jamie leers.

"Everybody on the planet is having sex but me," I say, resigned.

"Probably," considers Jamie. "The fact that you're an annoyingly good looking bastard just makes matters more amusing."

We both drink, then Jamie asks, "Other than not having any sex of any kind, do you have any news?"

News? I ponder a moment.

"Well...," I say. "I keep fantasising about my secretary's breasts. She's not even officially my secretary, she's the CEO's; though I suspect her breasts are remarkable... Tam thinks David's an alcoholic and that I need counselling for past, present and possibly even future breakdown, and I think she could be right... about booze-hound David, not about me needing counselling... Sean assures me he's not gay, though he did try and snog me the morning Sarah rocked up to tell me she's marrying Hans... I'm about to blag a few days off work because – with increasing dread - I realise work has no meaning, and the general desperation of living an unremarkable life I don't understand is starting to *upset* me."

"Good outpouring," Jamie compliments.

"Cheers," I say, before adding, "I feel like some sort of amnesiac, no longer sure of who I am or what I should do." I swig my beer, grin. "Maybe I've got Millennial Angst?"

"Sam," says Jamie, "very simply, what you need is to get laid."

I have to laugh.

Jamie asks, "You gonna have a punt at your secretary?"

"I don't think so, no."

"Do you want Hannah's number?"

"I need catharsis; I don't need Hannah."

"Okay, then you should start," suggests Jamie, "by going and getting seriously shit-faced. And you can explain, if possible, why Sean tried to snog you?"

When we leave Jamie's, I decide Jamie is right. I'm feeling pretty drunk, drunk enough to think getting shit-faced is an okay plan. Jamie jumps in a cab and I wander out of Noho, down into Soho, deciding to drink on while thinking, I'm no further on than I was 4 months ago. It's like I'm trapped in a One Act Play that refuses to end.

So Not In The Mood

Morning talk agonizes over targeting Urban Youth, then Middle Youth, later Middle England. Everyone pigeon-holes like crazy, speaking of "The Consumer" as an Alien Form, but one that we *must* get Raving About The Brand!

With a headache the size of Africa, I am seriously under-whelmed with it all, so not in the mood. It is a good job that I am not coming in tomorrow, that I spoke to Duncan and he bought The Dead Granny Excuse.

I make a note of the morning's Meeting Room Phrases, my contempt rising like a tsunami of boiling blood.

(1) "I don't want to cover the waterfront."
To which I thought: *Good, but I wish you'd drown in it.*

(2) "This is where the rubber meets the road."
To which I thought: *Can't you just say "crux"?*

(3) "Now folks, this isn't Rocket Science."
To which I thought: *You idiot.*

(4) "I don't want to teach anyone to suck eggs?"
To which I thought: *I'd pay good money to watch you suck an egg, right here, right now, you Mother Fucker.*

The Name Giver

Last night, I left Jamie, and it was as if I became an Urban Commander, no longer an Ad Man but a Super Hero maybe, like a Lone Star passing through the Shadows of Night?

If Other People Are Hell, then I am in luck, I thought. I am alone, have no one to drink with, except the strangers I encounter. Bring on the adventure, I asked.

I wandered from bar to bar, place names that never registered, locations that will always be lost to me. I introduced myself to everyone, gave people names that looked right and I found funny.

I met two Norwegian girls who I tagged Honey Lips and Sweet Pants.

"What's your name?," they asked.

"Me?," I said mysteriously, "I'm The Name Giver."

They thought I was Hilarious. Of course, they were right, and while their English was poor, they were expert at drinking shots. I paid for all the shots.

I moved on, standing or sitting at other bars, calling fellas things like The Gator Man, Mr Machismo, and Dr Fear.

No one seemed to mind being given a name for the night. I got chatting with a Blaxploitation Heroine Type who I insisted on addressing as Candy Girl. Her boyfriend had The Biggest Fro Outside of 1974 and while he didn't warm to me, she kept stroking his shoulder and assuring him I was Harmless, and of course, she was right.

Admin

Two hours and you're out the door, I coach myself.

Planning my return (I'm such a Seasoned Exec), I make a series of Important Looking phone calls. In reality, I am setting up a week of lunch dates starting Monday December 6th. I've decided to *brand* the five days therein, "Eating Week". After all, "Branding" is what I do.

Tracey comes over to my desk, trying to convey Some Kind of Emotion? Unsure, I think it might be *kindness* she's shooting for?

"Busy, hey?"

"Yeah, I've got to take a few days off," I say, and I don't say, l still haven't fixed a lunch date for Friday 10th and I was thinking maybe I-Thai?

"I heard," says Tracey. "I'm sorry to hear about your Granny. How old was she?"

"97," I lie. "It was a climbing accident."

Tracey doesn't know how to take it, doesn't know what emotion to fake.

"I warned her," I continue, "the north face of the Eager is a hard climb for anyone her age."

Tracey: silence. It's like teasing a small awkward animal. I sigh. "She was 86," I then say. "Natural causes. The funeral's this Sunday in Durham."

A good lie is in the unremarkable details.

"Well, I just wanted to offer my condolences," says Tracey. "See you when you get back."

I return to my phone calls. I'm tempted to call Jenny from Vogue (at last I remember her name!) but flicking through my Voluminous Address Book, I find alternatives. One conversation later and I-Thai is fixed for the Friday, then (with Jamie's comments of the previous evening still stalking me) I finish with a call to Ariel, the Very Fanciable girl from the meeting whose business card I'd stuffed in my desk drawer.

I get Voice Mail, so just leave my name and number and ask her to call me when she can, all in a tone that I hope sounds like I'm the Greatest Guy Since Jesus. Phone duties over, I swing on my jacket and taking Elvis' lead, leave the building.

Not Angelic

I wake to a New Day and a small smile forms but then departs my face.

Under the pretence of a Dead Granny, I am Saved From Meetings and Meeting With Idiots (cue: trumpets, hallelujahs et al). Conversely, it dawns that I have Nothing To Do, No Place To Go, no one to be with.

★

I tube to Angel, via a branch of the Northern line that was carefully designed to confuse. Minutes spent on the Northern line pass slower than those on the rest of the planet; I'm sure I've read of Time-Space Tests that prove it. And if you happen to be taking the branch to Angel, then I'd advise taking a snack pack (and maybe a torch) because you could be hanging out beneath the streets for longer than you'd planned.

I'd phoned Tam earlier, told her I was bored, that I had taken time off work and that I am… adrift. She suggested that I should go visit the Business Centre in Islington, check out their Design Fair.

"Go and buy yourself an expensive lamp or something, that might help? Retail is always a good way to fill the void."

"I believe Karl Marx called it The Fetishism of Commodities," I'd mumbled.

"Well I bet his pad looked the pits. Alternatively," she'd suggested, "you could just stay home and ease yourself into a marathon tantric wank? See how long you can go before it falls off?"

"The calluses haven't healed from last time," I'd joked, thinking, I shouldn't have phoned her.

I hadn't spoken to Tam since Osteria Basilico and didn't want to ask about David on the phone. Instead, I'd asked whether she was free for lunch.

"I can't, Sam, I've got this bloody deadline baring down on me. Tomorrow's better, but you'll have to schlep over Wapping way."

I'd said that was fine.

It's now Noon, and when I emerge topside, Angel Islington all around me, I wish I *had* taken the wrong branch of the Northern; the line that maybe ends in downtown Beirut?

There's nothing cherubic/angelic/divine about Angel Islington. Its Monopoly Board value is clearly over-priced, its buildings crumble and keel with intent and the people look "wrong". Every other pedestrian has a Flawed Walk - either cheap fitting shoes that drag, or a faulty ball-and-socket joint which forces them to lilt much like the buildings they shuffle between.

Are these people trying to freak me out? I wonder. I do feel a little freaked. North *North* London, I decide: too many zombies, too many people with Odd Shaped Heads. "Odd" as in funny-looking, not humorous. I'm not joking. Either a forceps-delivering sadist had been working the local hospitals for the last forty years, or there's something wicked in the water supply. Maybe I 'm on edge, maybe I exaggerate, but you ask Fox Mulder. I bet there's an X-File tagged "Angel".

I realise, my need to buy a New Lamp is Not That Great. I'm sure there are easier ways to Fill The Void. Instinct takes hold. I turn and face, needing to get back underground, closer to the Earth's core.

Back in the station, the tannoy greets me with: "Be alert. Professional beggars are operating in this area. We would ask that you do not give them money."

Professional Beggars? Are there any other kind? I reason, Amateur Beggars, who don't make or beg for money would surely be Dead Beggars, and therefore not much of a nuisance? Either way, I don't enjoy visiting postcodes where I have to be warned about the beggars.

I vow never to return to Angel Islington, it just so isn't my cup of Darjeeling.

I should not have left the flat. Unless everyone else in the city coincides a holiday or sick-day with yours, I say, stay off the streets, especially in Angel. There are too many freaks out there, too many people with scary shaped heads walking in ways that are funny but won't make you laugh. It's too unsettling.

A train pulls in, a set of doors pull back, and Unsettled, I step over The Gap, a memory taking me back.

Monday, November 24th, 1997

The Gap

I'd had this meeting, OK? Not particularly important; insignificant in the context of Land Mines, Ethnic Cleansing, and all such Global Atrocities – but still a meeting where I was Taking The Spot Light and Holding The Mike, and no one likes being late for those kind of meetings. This was back in those Working Days when I gave a damn (or at least half a damn).

I was running late, so I was running. Down the road, into the station, at pace, travel card inserted and collected with Flamenco-Style Fluidity, shoulder – *"So sorry!"* – against a sea of people who had just stepped off an arriving tube train. Jump the final few steps, land: with panther-like balance, pivot, and prepare to dart through the doors of the nearest carriage. Time saved, meeting made, all going so well.

On the platform, I recall, propelling with the left foot, landing on my right. It is of vital significance that I tell you I had just had my shoes re-soled.

My foot (the right one) hits the carriage floor, Forward Momentum over-rides Traction Control (re-soled leather not being Dunlop-assured), left foot is ready to counter the slide, but left foot finds nowhere to land.

Wait for it…

My left foot goes… *down* the Gap.

As in The Gap we are so often told to "mind," the one between Train Carriage and Platform Edge. And it does not stop with my foot.

Shin follows foot – as is convention – connecting lustily with train metal as it Begins The Descent. The blow is more than slight. The pain is slightly awesome. I begin to keel backwards, right leg crumbling like a seafront hotel in a long forgotten resort. Left knee gets in on the act and strikes the same point as my shin, thigh going vertical, left thigh finally interfacing with the Platform Edge. Me: a cautionary urban tale. Arse finally halts proceedings, right buttock splayed along with right leg *inside* the carriage, left arm outside the carriage, left leg (up to the hip) down The Gap.

It was one of those moments when time stopped - which is fortunate, because if the carriage doors had closed there and then, Scrotal Bisection would have become a Serious Reality. It dawned on me – like straight away – that I'd fallen *down* the Gap. Not all of me, granted, but enough.

A woman screamed. Another wailed. Somewhere, a young child began crying, possibly? In truth, there was silence, but all eyes were most definitely on me. Wide eyes, Double Door Wide, all distracted from their typographic routines, all looking down at the young guy in the suit who'd just gone most of the Way Down the Gap.

I was shocked, down, but not out. Like a cat (perhaps an old slothful over-fed cat that feels a delayed scalding), I lifted myself up and out of danger. My arms, you see, felt fine. The nearest person to The Incident, to Me that is, broke the

Astonished Silence.

"My God, are you OK?"

Well, she wasn't likely to say, "Gee, *neato*, can you do it again?," and at least she hadn't said "Christ, that had to hurt!"

I assured everyone far too quickly. "Yes, absolutely fine." Then: a forced laugh. Then: "Never done that before," suggesting I'm bionic, didn't feel a thing, took it all in my stride, something so trivial as a Gap-trip.

No one looked convinced. All eyes remained firmly fixed. The train hadn't even threatened to move, the carriage wasn't commuter-full, the driver waiting to fill up a little, in no hurry. Bastard. All that haste, for what?

Gazes began returning to newsprint, assumed I wasn't offering an encore, but I didn't feel so good. The Adrenaline Dump was massive. I could feel Rubies Of Sweat break on my forehead. A quite stirring Chord Of Pain played down the length of my left leg. The nerve endings then went symphonic, my head swimming in time to the tides that rolled through my stomach.

I realised that if the doors shut, and the train pulled away, I was odds-on liable to faint – but only after bringing up whatever was left of last night's meal. Which had been Chow Mien. Possible I would even Crash Land in my Vomit Patch, which would really bring the gazes back.

I stepped out of the carriage, felt curious eyes scrutinize each step, felt too much pain to suffer any Real-Time Embarrassment. I climbed the station steps – the one's I had minutes ago taken in a near-single bound. I climbed the steps slowly, one at a time, the way you're meant to climb mountains, my breathing coming in big, unsteady gulps.

"Sam?"

I looked up. It was Sarah. Why aren't you on the tube?"

"I…"

"Christ, what's wrong?" She appreciated that my green pallor was not the norm.

"You're shaky and sweating."

"I'm fine," I'd said, for the second time that morning.

"Fine, but green?"

"Well, I , er, just fell down the Gap."

"Christ!" She took my arm, her forehead folding with concern.

"Yeah. I guess I should have been more mindful."

Thursday, November 25th, 1999

The One

I meet Tam for lunch at a small deli/bistro type place in Wapping (of all places), just round the corner from her offices. She looks a little wired, her head obviously whirring a little with whatever she's working on.

"The quiche here is excellent," she says.

"Real men don't eat quiche," I explain.

"So two quiche then?," she suggests.

Now that we're face-to-face, I ask after David.

"How's David? Are you going to chuck him for being an old hopeless soak?"

Tam sips her low cal latte, then tongues a touch of froth off her top lip.

"We've talked; he's going to AA," she says.

"Just like that?"

"Just like that."

"What about indignation, denial, all the standard responses?"

"I told him I loved him and I wanted to marry him but I couldn't be with him if he was an alcoholic. You've never seen anyone turn paler or look more sober. He said, 'I think maybe I do have a problem with drink. I think maybe I've been waiting for you to come and rescue me? I'll do whatever you want. I love you and just want to be with you.'"

"You're serious?"

"Yes, he went very pale."

"No, that you want to marry him?"

"Yes," she says, "that too."

"Christ! So David's The One?," I say, not knowing what else to say.

"Yes," she confirms.

"You're certain?"

Tam smiles. "Utterly," she offers, all dogmatic. "You know when it's The One. You get this moment, and just everything about them is perfect, even when they're imperfect, and they're all that you want, and more besides. They are The One. And you just *know*."

Tam's words are dreamy, but her face is almost grave. I find myself frowning, not wanting to be sold.

"Let me guess…," I sarc, "You feel complete and as if life is suddenly given purpose and direction? You feel as if everything before was directionless or at best, just a rehearsal?"

"I see you continue to be bitter, Mr Grant."

"Just realistic, Ms Flint." I shake my head. "Hopeless romanticism," I say. "*Hopeless* is about right. True Love sells movie tickets and poolside paperbacks. One in three weddings end in divorce Tam, and absolutely nothing lasts forever. *Super Toys Last All Summer Long*, and at best, so does love. If you can sustain delusion and raging hormones for 3 months, you should consider yourself lucky."

"I say there's such a thing as an Endless Summer, Sam."

"You should drink Rosé," I say, shaking my head. "Tam, you're very sweet."

"And you don't believe a word you're saying."

Our food arrives. Being the Tough Guy, I've ordered salad.

I Have a Dream

4:03am. I wake up sweating. Profusely. That was one hairy-ass REM episode.

I'm in a tube station, specific station unknown. There is no one else, just me and I'm running, like a madman down a sterile white-tiled tunnel. I can hear only my panting.

All else is like a vacuum. No sound of my footfalls, just panting. Then I realise, this panting isn't my own. It's the *thing* chasing me that's panting. You see, being chased is what accounts for my running.

The tunnel snakes on. I race past signs directing to Meeting Room 3, Meeting Room 7. My lungs are burning, my hands tingling now, and I can feel my back being scraped and clawed, but I tell myself, it's scarier not knowing what the monster is, so turn round and take a look.

It takes some balls but I steal a look over my shoulder.

The Monster is… Very Much a Monster; a kind of Cerberus, and though it has the body of a dog and the tail of a dragon, the three heads are human. One head is Holly, the other Sarah, the third head Ariel, and they are all barking and grinning these crazy salivating grins at me.

Then I had the good sense to open my eyes.

Make Someone Happy With a Phone Call

"Hello Sam? Hello!"

So Loud it's like some sadist's shoved a bongo stick rather than a cotton bud into my left ear. The line is crystal clear, no time delay.

"Granny, we might be three thousand miles away," I explain, "but there's really no need to shout."

"I can't hear a thing," I hear Granny say. Then Mother comes on the line.

"How are you, darling?," she asks.

"Just fine," I say. "How's the cruise?"

"It's wonderful!" Whatever, I think.

Mum continues: "First St. Barthelemy – great shopping – on to St Lucia, where there's currently a Jazz Festival taking place, and then we go on to Barbados for Christmas - and Granny's having a wonderful time. She's really enjoying the Jazz festival and is rather partial to Bajan rum."

Contrary to certain rumours, it sounds like Granny is very much alive and well.

"And how's Dad?"

"He and Granny are getting on famously," assures Mum, not that I was needing any assurance. "Partly because he's either on a golf course, walking up a volcano or getting lost in a rain forest," she adds.

"That's all just… splendid," I say, feeling very neglected. "Right, I'm off to the gym… I'll speak to you in the New Year."

"Darling, there's no need to be like that. Listen, like I mentioned last time, we think you should fly out to Barbados for Christmas. I'm sure you'll enjoy it. Your father's reserved you a seat on the mid-afternoon flight leaving Heathrow Christmas Eve."

A sudden wave of unselfish emotion swells over me. I love my Dad.

★

I wasn't lying to my Mother. After her call, I do option a workout.

I go heavy in the gym, focusing on the bench press, incline, decline, on the flat, every imaginable angle of misery.

Middle of the day, a weekday, and the place is heaving with young girls trying to outrun the treadmills and young bucks flexing and flouncing in the weights room. Don't any of these people have jobs?, I wonder. Employed or otherwise, no one looks destitute, just buff.

Leaving the gym, I check my phone. Two missed calls, two Voice Mails. The first from Sean, suggesting drinks tonight in town.

The second message is from Ariel. Walking along the street I nearly slip off the curb, almost drop my phone down a grate.

I call Sean to confirm, then punch in the number Ariel left.

"Hi, it's Sam Grant," I say, voice strong and even.

"Hey Sam, you well?"

"Yeah not bad. Listen, I'm out of the office for the next few days," I explain, "but wondered whether you'd be free to meet up next week? Either your offices or mine is fine."

I decide not to also mention that she has just featured in a dream where she played one head of a three-headed Guardian of Hades.

Apart

I tube to Piccadilly Circus and spend the afternoon acting like a tourist, going to galleries, walking slowly and trying hard not to get creamed by any buses or cabs. Hey, it happened to Sean.

I drift from location to location, an urban willow the wisp, a spectral force without purpose or destination. I revel in my Contrived Disconnection, my sense of being *apart* from things, turning my collar high to a damp wind, dropping my shoulders and smoking my smokes the way James Dean once did in Time Square. I go to the movies, catch *Fight Club* on re-run at the Prince Charles Theatre. I loved the way Ed Norton took care of his boss.

I sit drinking strong coffee and watch the pavements, everyone else getting on with their lives, moving through time and space with apparent meaning.

What is my purpose? I have no immediate answers; instead spend long stretches of time floating among the music aisles of large stores that employ too many stoned teenagers.

In Leicester Square I sit on a bench and watch the dusk settle and the street acts entertain. I wonder, *Am I even here?*

A little Chinese boy holds hands with his father, while his other hand holds a violent pink candy-floss even tighter. I smile at the kid and he just deadpans me back, that genius way little kids find so easy. I wish I could get that look for meetings.

Night Time

Darkness falls and I leave my bench, wander up into Soho, wanting to bare witness to the seamier and more uninviting side of life, to watch it seep up through the gapes and tears of this badly frayed world, to observe Jekyll give way to Hyde.

I walk the Wrong Streets, the neon-lit, cheap thrill sleaze strips with their peep-shows, junk food eateries, and arcade gallerias, the unadulterated concentrations of vice, corners of prostitution and circles of porn.

Odd how daylight can temper everything, The Streets seeming Relatively Safe and Reasonably Clear-Cut. Odd how Night time can morph the world into this Dinge-Enthroned Tomb, resplendent with dark alleys, jagged edges, sinister corners, and social undesirables.

Odd, too, how the darker it gets, the more you can see the grain and grime, the more likely the disaffected and the depraved come out to play. Am I one of these? I mull. Am I called by the night to bark at the moon and drown my sorrows? Do I by day sleep between the cracks only ready at night to join the Crazies on Parade? I pass shop windows touting terrifying-looking items that guarantee terrifying pleasures. I think of the Little Chinese Boy, and I too stare deadpan at the world.

Wanting to spook myself, I keep walking the walk, amongst the Key Hole Loiterers and Dirty Raincoat Wearers, the Pimps, Psychos, Sickos, Wierdos, Wackos, and Waistoids, the flotsam and jetsam who sunk or started at the bottom of the barrel, but either way found they quite liked it down here, and I realise, this may be where downward spirals come to rest, but this is no resting place for me.

Out in the Cold

A light rain starts up. I turn up my collar and light a cigarette in response. I smile, suddenly feeling Noir-ish, and I imagine myself, the gritty Anti-Hero, enduring the November Cold and fighting a Cold War all on my own. I think about Burton's portrayal of John Le Carré's spy who didn't quite make it in from the cold, of Deighton's Harry Palmer and his penchant for Gauloise and cooking.

People shuffle by and I wonder, does anyone suspect that I might be a spy?

I used to love reading all those Cold War yarns, where Governments played their ill-gotten games behind closed, leather bound doors and concocted their Machiavellian plots from the security of soundproof, oak panelled studies. Fleming, Follett, Forsyth, Higgins, the Dudes who could draft a Double Cross of Byzantine complexity, where people were pawns and life was chess and espionage was all bold gambits and intuitive counter-moves. Yeah, I was a sucker for all that jazz.

What a world, where the enemy was always evil personified, where life forever 'rested in the balance' and 'teetered on the brink', and the women were always beautiful and dangerous and often carried with them deadly secrets.

I lean against some brickwork, looking over and down an alley, and my Spy Mind wonders, what intrigue and deception toys in the dim light? What secret schemes will be executed in those shadows?

I flick my cigarette at a puddle, the tip hissing brief protest.

"Can you spare a smoke?"

A bum, short and dressed in bum regalia, aged anywhere from 30 to 90, with lank dark hair so greasy the light rain hasn't managed to take hold. His shoes don't match, but somehow, one brogue and one high-top pump look kinda funky.

Is this my contact?, I consider. Is this The Cougar, International Assassin & Master of Disguise, here to pass on the Soviet microfiche designs for the Next Gen nuclear sub?

"Here," I say, giving the bum the packet of cigarettes,

concluding it's not The Cougar. He is notorious for having much larger feet.

Mac Attack

Along with needing to buy cigarettes, I realise I'm hungry.

Minutes later: "...would you like fries with that?"

I haven't been here for years. I can't remember the last time.

I take a window seat, trying to ignore the fact that every imaginable surface appears caked in burger-grime and contentedly dig in, enjoying the taste while suspecting there's more nutrition in a cup of river water. Still, I marvel, Mass-Consumerism is kinda fabulous.

I recall, back when taking a blow-torch to the 'Cold War' had fuck-all effect and dear old Ron Reagan was calling Russia the 'Evil Empire', the Other Ronald (who also happened to be a clown) had found no problem pitching camp next door to the Kremlin.

The Storm Troopers of Consumerism landed the day Macky D's first opened in Moscow, and I reckon it was the beginning of the end for the Old Order. Socialism was sentenced to drown in a sea of ketchup, mayo, and discarded gherkins. All those burger-hungry Ruskies formed a nice orderly 'McQueue', and a few years later, The Wall came tumbling down. Turned out "Big Mac" kicked the ass out of "Big Mo".

I eat my fries and form a tentative socio-political theory: Maybe Ronald McDonald was a Double 0?

My phone rings. It's Sean, already bar-side and waiting for me.

"Get me a Vodka Tonic," I tell him, then: "You feel in the mood for some big drinking? I feel like leaning into a few."

Legendary

Last night, from what I can remember, I was Drinking.

I drank with style, flair, finesse, élan, even perhaps a little Je ne sais quoi, that if you were really pushed, you'd probably label 'panache', maybe sell in a bottle? Yeah, *that* was Me, last night, the way I drank.

I was The Guy To Be With and The Guy To Know. I was The Man on Campus, Man-With-A-Plan, yes wearing a tan, giving it the BIG "I AM". It was like I was on a mission, raising the stakes and mocking the odds, seeing the angles and doing it *because* it was hard, taking no easy way out, while facing the music, staying on my feet and standing tall, never once going to the corner or leaning back on the ropes, playing the long game, drinking through, all the time ploughing towards a bold new dawn. Oh yeah. You betcha. That was Me.

Last night, I had a *taste* for it, a heavy thirst for it, feeling a lot gung-ho, climbing into every pint then tumbler, eating it down, going the distance, upping the ante, lifting the tally, suggesting those whole nine yards were maybe somehow short? Even after the band had packed away (despite assuring they'd play on), the pianist declared too tired to tinkle on, there was still Me, propping up the bar, with my stories to tell and my audience eager to listen.

Are you getting a sense of how it was, the scale of it, the epic qualities of it, of Me, this drinker, this tour de force, a legend in the flesh, giving it as large as can be, drinking like I was wearing 3 Lions on my shirt?

Last night I was breaking all the rules, making up new ones. I was Jimmy Belushi; I was the prototypical hard nut, hellraisin' king of comedy and swing. I was a Richard Harris, Olly Reed, Dennis Hopper Triple Decker, a deluxe at that, and say my good man, go heavy with that extra fire sauce. Me, a Wild Bunch of One, trailing a blaze of glory, saying, Yes, tonight Matthew, I'm living on a prayer. I was winging it and it felt like it was working out, Me, squaring off with fate, dialling my date with destiny, letting my ego write the cheques, going eye to eye, punch for punch, drink for drink with the ruffian on the stairs.

And when I was done, there was no need to look back in anger, because when I was done I couldn't look back at all.

And then everything faded to black, which always serves as a kind of plan.

Not an Epiphany

I wake up with The Worst Hangover of My Life, but curiously, somewhere else deep deep down in a far off recess of the soul, I feel… better.

Time away from the Chalk Face has actually helped. At least, I'm telling myself it was productive. I think maybe I've reached the Tipping Point, born of too much time on my hands, too much melancholy, and too many nights on the liquor.

I wouldn't call it anything so grand as an epiphany, but I do decide to make some decisions. Then I go ahead and make 'em.

First off, I ask myself, why should Life Without Sarah be Such a Trauma? What is So Suddenly Terrible with Being Single?

Most of my life, I've been single. Even when I've been in relationships, I felt Independent, liked *asserting* my independence, enjoyed flirting like hell and doing my own thing, like a Jungle Cat, sure as hell no Domestic Pussy.

I went out with Sarah for shy of 3 years and I Felt Independent, but the circs blind-sided me. You see, in 3 years changes happen, little ones, day by day, the smallest increments that you don't notice as they dig in with their very many sharply filed teeth. So nasty and sharp, the kind Stephen King likes writing about. Then, if after 3 years you part company, all those little changes that took place in you present themselves. They reveal their very large bite marks and you're left feeling bruised as fuck with chunks removed. This is how I figure it, but surely it gets to the point where enough is enough is enough?

I say, it has. Hence, my Tipping Point.

So, my decisions are these:

1. Sarah is Not The One and it's time for the bruises and bite marks to fade – because Feeling Miserable and Lost and with No Sense of Future is… Very Dull.

2. My Shit has been Hemispheres Apart – it is time to Gather My Shit Together, to move forward with Steam & Gusto, to come in from the cold.

3. Work Sucks and I find the people who orbit it Contemptible – measures must be taken.

4. Now, Dear Friends, it is time to bury Walter Mitty – because in reality he was a hen-pecked Miserable Nobody, and I've come to conclude, Doing it will always be better than Just Dreamin' it. See points (2) and (3).

I realise, it's time to Break the Downward Spiral and get Way Out Ahead of the Curve. I'm re-starting my life by opening my eyes. Maybe a little like Keanu Reeves, I've decided on the red pill.

A Farewell to Walter

My name is not Walter Mitty. My name is Sam Grant, I'm 27 years old, and I'm not a Top Gun. I'm no Undercover Tough Guy, no Soldier of Fortune nor Super Spy or Movie Star, but I am this much: I'm ready to make things right, to show some flair and finish where necessary with a bang.

★

DECEMBER

Wednesday, December 1st, 1999

A Jedi Lesson

Guess what?

During my absence from work, Nothing Changed. There were many meetings of Mind & Ego, lots of hot air spoken, words/theories/models and paradigms expounded, but no one figured a cure for cancer.

I am serene to my reality, quietly going cuckoo in the cuckoo nest.

The other cuckoo's are also as I left them:

1. Charley: tits still look amazing in her funky-thread tank tops.

2. Tracey: still nodding.

3. Dick: still… in Prada.

4. Jonathan: still angry.

5. Duncan: sadly, still the CEO, still the Smuggest Man on the Planet, still dressed in Aquascutum suits that don't quite hide his pot-belly.

On a white pad in front of me, I've just being Doing Some Math. Get this.

I work an average of 8 hours a day. Here I use the word "work" in the broadest possible terms. Regardless, that's 8 hours times 5 days a week, making a 40-hour Weekly Total.

Times 40 by 52 weeks a year, subtracting 6 weeks for Annual Holiday leave and National Holidays. That's 1,840 hours a year, in work, of Forced Attendance. Not a gun to my head, nor a ball and chain round my ankle, but it's compulsory attendance none the less.

Say a typical person, degree level, starts work as late as 25 years old, works till he's 65. That's a flat 40-year straight, making a total of 73,600 hours of Forced Attendance. Each lived as a tick and a tock.

I may even have rounded the numbers up in places, but my point remains this: 73,600 hours is a Shit-Load of Hours, especially given that (in my case) it's spent in the pursuit of doing Seriously Very Little.

★

The first job I ever did, my Dad got me. I was 16. It was a Summer job working in a factory that handled and "processed" poultry. I think Dad's plan was that it teach me The Value of Money and Hard Labour, and that maybe if I wanted to earn lots of money, I should work hard and avoid hard labour. My old man also hadn't been quite up-front with me. He didn't mention what I was going to be doing.

I turned up in a linen suit, very Our Man in Havana. I was issued a rubber boiler suit and boots. My job was shovelling chicken carcases into a vat, some kind of extreme temperature acid vat. I believe the vat stripped the last remnants of meat from the bone and melted any remaining bits of chicken that refused to melt at temperatures shy of molten. The melted contents became a gloop that was then coloured and scented and fortified and I'm afraid to say most likely ended up as somebody's ultra-low cost chicken burger.

I put on my boiler suit and boots, grabbed my spade, started shovelling away, and didn't utter One Goddamn Word. At any moment I figured my old man was going to come round the corner, smiling like hell, having enjoyed his little gag. I thought he was going to take the spade from me, pat me on the back, and we'd walk out of there laughing and wincing then laughing some more.

Minutes became hours. At no moment did my Dad spring from behind a piece of machinery chuckling like crazy. It dawned: this is fucking It! There is no joke being played and no one is coming to rescue me. I think that was the lesson Yoda had in mind.

Fast forward just over a decade, and I'm sitting in Meeting Room 3 with Marvin and my Jedi Dad's lesson returns to me. This is It. You have to rescue yourself because no one else is going to suddenly appear, tell you you've been Candid Camera's Longest Running Chump and that actually you never had to work because you're from Impossible Independent Wealth, only your Dad wanted you to first learn to value money and appreciate the curse of the working man.

Here in Meeting Room 3, Tracey nodding as Marvin speaks, I realise Marvin is also a kind of curse, along with being a moron. While perhaps cruel, I would testify that I've eaten tired-looking side salads that concealed a higher IQ than Marvin's.

The only thing I do enjoy about Marvin is his Remarkable Wardrobe and never ending selection of ties. Along with

Talking Tripe, he is a shambolic, almost breathtaking apparition of anti-style, an unashamed outburst of anti-fashion many steps beyond clueless. Today's Tie is of such enormous proportions as could be mistaken for a bib or even a windbreaker.

Marvin asks me what I think. Sadly, he is not looking for advice on his wardrobe.

I pause, adopt an expression of someone who has many Long & Intelligent Thoughts, then put my back into it, pacing out few Brand Footprints, sketching a rather impressive (yes, I do say so myself) piece of Brand Architecture, evoking a workable Brand Archetype. In short, I enthusiastically push The Frontiers of *Anti-Meaning*, airing words like "Holistic," "Visceral," and "Bespoke," and Marvin loves it. I then tell the Wide-Tied Loon I think we should be "very *up-stream* in the way we tackle this project," and there's unanimous agreement, Marvin grinning with real lame-brain delight.

★

"Sam."

"Yes Charley?"

"Ariel Cohen in reception for you."

"Very good," I say, while thinking, Oh Shit!, but feeling at once predatory.

Expectations run high but as I cross reception, Ariel delivers. Taller than I remembered, as cute as I remembered, fuller lips than I'd dare recall. I thought it was my imagination playing pesky tricks, but here they are, lips as full as can be.

"Hi!," I say, shaking hands. "Listen, all our meeting rooms are full. Do you fancy popping round the corner and grabbing coffee?"

Her smile is Truly Disarming, wide and sincere, reaching

the eyes and saying, My favourite animal's the unicorn. An image comes to me of Ariel in pigtails, dressed like a schoolgirl cutie, following Britney's moves while purring *Oh baby, baby.*

As we step onto the street, a thunderclap signals on call and rain starts falling. I turn up my jacket lapel, hoping this looks A Little Rakish while Ariel fishes a compact umbrella from her bag and triggers it skywards. She turns to me, her brolly arm out.

"It's okay," she offers, "you can come under me."

I offer a small grateful little smile back, my erection instant.

Isola

Venue: Isola Bar, 145 Knightsbridge, lots of chrome, plenty of red leather, looks like the fella that set-designed *Space 1999* now does bar make-overs.

Scoping the room, in search of Tam, I'd say there's something of a Famous Dads to Daughters theme going on tonight. Emilia Fox is in a small circle over by the window. She's just done a Dickens-TV-effort, *David Copperfield* I think, and looks cute, but not cute enough to be My Type. Stella McCartney, who looks too much like her old man to be anyone's type is also here, no doubt air kissing the ass off everyone. There's talk (according to Tam) of Stella moving to *Gucci*, but *Chloe* (it is said) are "very keen" to renew her contract. I couldn't care whether Stella McCartney stays with *Chloe* or moves to *Top Shop*… or *Burger King.*

Working through the crowd, I reach Tam.

"What are you drinking?," she asks.

"Was planning making December a Martini Month."

"Absinthe Martini?," she suggests.

"Sounds suitably destructive, but I'll get 'em in. What you drinking?"

"I'll join you in the same."

Bar Dude is trying hard to look Seriously Dolce & Gabana. Tall, high cheek-bones, slick-back hair, all-black outfit. I could forgive The Attitude if only he could serve a drink in less time than the half-life of a plutonium rod. If Bar Dude could unleash the short pour contents of his speed tray with the laser-accuracy of a Cyborg Shootist, then I could tolerate his whole puckered lip hollow cheeked demeanour. As it is: there'll be no tip for this wanabee.

Announcing himself, Jamie gropes my arse. I turn round; he is not alone. For the first time he has wheeled out Chloe. He introduces and it's difficult maintaining eye contact. I try my best, returning her sweet smile and asking what they want to drink. Orders relayed to Bar Dude, she slinks off to the Ladies.

"My word, Chloe's certainly got *something* about her," I remark. "She's had quite a boob job?"

"A small... actually very sizeable detail that I'd held back until you met her."

"I'm astounded you could keep it to yourself."

"You should see her lying on her back."

I swear, the smile of a small and very naughty boy passes over Jamie's face. "They don't move," he adds, "they just *sit there*, armed and if need be ready to prop up the ceiling. You'd be astounded."

"They are quite remarkable," I agree. "She's like, what, as size 10 with a D-cup?"

"Size 8. I don't mind saying it, I'm really smitten."

Love comes to us all, I decide, in many shapes and augmented sizes.

"Are you now?," I say.

"Really Sam, she's the most pneumatic, sack-skilled girl I think it's possible to meet. Can you imagine the kind of tit wank she gives? I think I'm in love…"

"What you are Jamie… is seriously beading."

Across the entire of Jamie's high forehead: multiple and truly huge beads of sweat.

Jamie takes a paper napkin from the bar, mops his brow. "You try wearing cowhide action pants in this fucking sauna."

"Jamie, why the fuck do you even own a pair of leather slacks?"

"Chloe bought them for me, says I look sexy in them."

I just look dumbfounded. Confirmed: love is blind as well as big-titted.

"Hey," he underlines, "if they work for her…"

"Maybe for *Ah-ha*, more than a decade ago, maybe they worked then," I say. "All they're doing now is helping you work up a Monster Bead."

The barman finally does his thing and I pass out drinks.

'Thanks," says Jamie.

Chloe well out of earshot, I ask: "And what about Hannah?"

"What about her?"

"No more Brideshead's? Not going to be *revisiting* that particularly psychotic terrain?"

"No, it was a one-last-time sport fuck. I just wanted her to check out my improved bod."

"You're beautiful, Jamie."

Jamie smirks, tastes his Stoli and Slim line.

"You'll think I'm beautiful when I tell you how our shares are doing," he teases.

Me, gullibly, "They've rallied?" This would astound me more than Chloe's chest works.

"No," he grins, "I'm just joshing with you. They've gone through the floor."

I sigh. "I guess I won't be buying that summer home in the Caymans just yet. I hope you're better with other people's money than with ours."

"Actually, I'm usually worse. The way it's looking, I don't see me still employed come the new millennium."

Chloe returns and I pass her flute of champagne. It cost about the same as buying a whole bottle at Dubai Duty Free. Although impractical, flying from Isola to Dubai may only have taken slightly longer than it took for Bar Dude to get his arse in gear.

Chloe says Thank-you and I'm about to make small talk on the merits of leather fashion apparel when someone catches at the corner of my eye.

"I'll be back in a minute," I excuse. "I've just seen someone I should say Hi to."

★

"I haven't seen you in…?"

"A while," she says, trying hard to sound cold and bored. She looks Very Catwalk, all long limbs and angular poses, hips thrown forward, shoulders slung back.

"Though actually, I am seeing you on MTV quite a bit. It's obviously going well?," I say.

"Yes, it is." Holly semi-smiles, now looking less bored, more uncomfortable, like she's suddenly grown extra limbs and is unclear where to hide them or how to fold them.

"I'm in the new FCUK campaign too," she adds.

As if seeing her mug on MTV isn't enough?

I'm about to tell her, That's really great!, when a tall blonde

Scando-lad appears beside her, a territorial arm slipping round her waist.

"Hi, I'm Jorgen."

For what it's worth?, I think.

6' 2, worked out, I'd say about 190 pounds. Yeah, I can see how Jorgen could be Holly's Type. He's probably in the new FCUK campaign too.

Being a sophisticated, complex, evolved human being, I consider: Yeah, at a push, I could maybe take Jorgen down. It wouldn't be an easy scrap, but I reckon I could drop him. We're broadly the same frame, though my colouring's at the other end of the scale. Dark hair, a more olive skin, green eyes. Often, people would mistake Sarah and I for being brother and sister. Then we'd start getting touchy-feely and they'd conclude we must be from one screwed up family.

Jorgen's introduction isn't the kind where he's looking to get to know me better, but I don't knuckle him. I do the Gracious Thing. I say "Good to meet you Jorgen," "Holly, lovely seeing you after so long," then I excuse myself and turn away, mulling, perhaps I'm even more evolved than I thought?

I make it safely back to the bar, put Jamie beside me, notice he's still sweating, see Chloe chatting with Tam, wonder what Tam makes of her?

"Was that who I think it was?," he asks.

"Depends on who you think it was?

"First I thought it might be Ivana Trump, then Imelda Marcos, but my final guess is… Holly."

"In which case, yes, it was who you thought it was."

"How'd it go?"

"As a social interaction, I'd have to say it felt like Gallipoli for one."

"Shame, incredible looking calves."

"You were checking out her calves? Of all her things to ogle?"

"Sam, *always* check out the calves. Working bottom up has never let me down. The calves are a giveaway. If the calves are suitably and seductively shapely, you know you're in for the goodies upstairs."

"Well, it's now Jorgen who's tucking into her goodies."

Work Gum

Monday morning. I pick up the phone and dial Ariel's number. She's off site all day. Frustrated, I leave a message on voice mail, but try hard to sound up-beat, easy-going and a Real Nice Guy. I return the phone to its cradle with more force than is absolutely necessary.

"How was the drive back from Durham last week?" asks Richard (aka. Dick).

"It was as it was," I say.

Dick perches himself on the corner of my desk, looking in no hurry to go anywhere. He spies a pack of chewing gum by my phone and helps himself. He doesn't say, May I? or Thank-you, just takes a stick like we're good friends and I won't mind in the slightest. I don't say anything; just wonder what he's up to. Taking a piece of work gum with Such Presumption, trying to infer he considers us buddies without the formality that constrains others, it screams to me that there's something on his mind. Stealing work gum attempts a weird intimacy.

"You'll have heard," says Dick, "Duncan's announcing a series of promotions just before we break for Christmas."

"I heard and I heard who's in the running," I admit, "but I won't congratulate you until it's formal."

Dick smiles, playing it cagey, not wanting to hex his chances by saying, Yeah, I'm rather looking forward to being your boss, Sam.

I get up from my desk. "I've got to run," I tell Dick, hoping to sound a little mysterious, "I have a lunch appointment."

This week (as you may recall) I've arranged to be taken out for lunch *every day*, a full sweep, all five in a row.

Hey, I figure, it's nearly Christmas! Also, I like the idea of utterly abusing The Corporate Lunch, really milking it dry.

Perhaps I am subtly making a comment on Capitalist Excess and how there are starving Ethiopian children in the world (most of them in Ethiopia)? How eating in a litter of Posh Nosh Palaces is going to bring down The System, I am uncertain. Realistically, I doubt whether making my stomach very full will bankrupt the Capitalist Machine.

It may just be that I wish to indulge in some Gourmet Gluttony, see if I can provoke anyone to comment, encourage someone to take me to one side, take me to task, say "Steady there Sammy-boy, you don't want to go taking the piss *that* much."

Eating Week

It's Friday afternoon and Ariel has not returned my call (the slut!). No one beyond Charley has said a thing about me being so often out of the office. I'm not even sure if anyone has noticed? Maybe everyone else has been on lunches all week, or in meetings, or in lunch meetings? I'm back sitting at my desk, 4 in the afternoon, surely half a stone heavier than I was on Monday morning? My 5 in a row, with plate highlights reads:

1.   Monday: Criterion, in Piccadilly.

I went for their signature starter, a seriously yolky
eggs Benedict served with enough hollandaise
to drown a Large Cat. The place is Full-On
Byzantine, a golden mosaic ceiling, pillars,
paintings & drapes. It's how I would decorate my
bedroom if I were a Sultan.

2. Tuesday: Asia de Cuba, Ian Schrager's "Flash… if
    you like flash?" effort on St. Martin's Lane.

    The scallops with Tokyo Caviar & Chilli lime
    stood out; the company did not.

3. Wednesday: Mezzo, on Wardour Street.

    For a while the biggest restaurant in Europe,
    Mezzo is now Not The Biggest and is no longer
    particularly trendy, but they still serve up a pretty
    tidy Bloody Mary, along with over-priced after-
    hours Vodka & Tonic's, should you find yourself
    thirsty in Soho after-hours. On the lunch with
    a guy called John who worked for the cinema
    distributor Pearl & Dean, I remember eating
    an enjoyable pan-fried lemon sole with parsley
    mash. I remember nothing about John, beyond
    his name, but that for me is progress.

4. Thursday: Langan's on Stratton Street.

    I ate a skyscraper of a burger, smothered in
    melted dolcelata, then smoked a Monetcristo
    number 2. Instead of making it back into work,

I drank lots of port and made empty promises
to my lunch company, a really rather pretty
girl called Cheryl, me saying that I'd absolutely
recommend Her Client (this bright young thing
film director) to My Client (an old fat thing
who's marketing director of an arms-around-
the-world-large Japanese car manufacturer). Fat
Old Thing doesn't know one film director from
another, and insists only that the shoot is in
South Africa. This I did not share with the girl
called Cheryl.

For interested radio fans out there, the DJ known as
the Ginger Whinger, but more likely known to his
mother as Chris Evans was on the next table, and
when I left Langan's at 5, I could see three of him.

5.   Friday: I-Thai in the basement of The Hempel
     hotel on Craven Hill Gardens.

     I-Thai is so called because the menu is Italian-Thai
     fusion. Yeah, I know, what next? Today, I drank my
     body weight in Sake, and all I can now recall, only
     hours later, is scoffing course after course of really
     expensive sushi, which I'm not that partial to, but
     told everyone that I love because it amused me
     despite irritating my taste buds.

*

Meal Mussing over, I see Jamie has e-mailed.

From: jamie.sykes@gs.com

To: sam.grant@sdb.com

Sent: 10 December, 1999 17:52

Re: Man Squash – Be Afraid

Have survived 8 days straight at the gym. Currently
have pectorals of galvanised steel; am walking around
the office like Robocop. I am ready. Tomorrow evening:
Man Squash?

The Cross-Court King

I reply:

From: sam.grant@sdb.com

To: jamie.sykes@gs.com

Sent: 10 December, 1999 17:55

Re: Man Squash – Match Stats

Sykes vs. Grant

Played: 95

Grant: 92

Sykes: 1

Drawn: 2

Am good for tomorrow evening; and afterwards?

I have a hankering for something dry and distilled.

Proposed: Rivoli Bar, at The Ritz, for a pleasingly dry
and awfully self-assured Gin & Tonic.

Sambo

PS: Just remember, only a loon brings a tub of
marmite to a jam fight.

Jamie calls.

"The Rivoli?"

"Yeah," I say.

"It's possible to be too Old School."

"Alternatively," I suggest, "All Bar One do a very pleasant gammon platter… and you get a choice of relishes."

"Hardly something to relish. You, my friend, are the saddest kind of loser freak."

"Okay Jamie, I don't mind where we go… so long as it involves high-class hookers and high-grade nose candy at over 30,000 feet."

"Like your style – but it could be a bit tricky to arrange at such short notice. I was thinking, how 'bout Zander, near St. James?"

"I've never been."

"Zander it is then," declares Jamie, "and by the way, your match stats…"

"What about them?," I ask smirking.

"They're such crap."

"Oh?"

"Yeah, I've drawn at least 3, and we've played a shitload more than 95 times."

I log out, mulling, what shall I do now? Another weekend is upon me. I consider phoning Sean but before I'm able to dial, The Nodding Dog appears and asks whether I'm coming for drinks at the Sanderson. I tell Tracey No. I get my coat and passing Charlotte's desk wish her a good weekend.

"A bunch of us are going to the Sanderson for drinks. You fancy it?"

I consider for a moment, trying not to look at her breasts.

"Just one, maybe?," she persists with a smile. "Duncan's buying."

"I dunno…"

"C'mon Sam. As Duncan might say, Let's make Friday count."

"Okay," I relent. "But if you see me talking with the Nodding Dog, you have to rescue me."

My Feelings on Duncan

The Sanderson on Berners Street is currently a fully accredited pit-stop on the see-and-be-seen circuit. It has Serious Pretension on the inside despite the outside being a Miserably Crumby 70's prefab.

No sooner are we through the door than Charlotte is bouncing to the long bar, joining a number of Office Faces I recognise but couldn't put names to.

Duncan is indeed buying drinks and Acting Important. Next to him, Über-Cad James Hewitt is chatting up some Ra-looking 30-something. I also recognise two pint-sized TV presenters who are rumoured to be gay, and not far from them another daytime TV celebrity and housewives favourite who (depending on one's circles) is more renowned for groping just about every pretty girl in London. Tonight, I imagine his hands will be most often full.

Many of the girls here are over-dressed, making it difficult to distinguish whether they're Friday Night Bridge & Tunnel or Hi-Class professionals. It could of course be that some are both.

Sipping my Sake martini (thanks, Duncan) I speculate whether the slice of star fruit floating on the surface makes any difference to the flavour. Behind me, two toss-pots discuss the merits of the Shrager hotels they've visited; London's St Martin's lane versus the Sanderson, the Delano in Miami versus the Mondrian in LA. If I was a few more Sake Martini's down the line, I think I may turn round and slap either or both toss-pots hard in the face.

I talk enthusiastically with people who offer me nothing. Time passes, though not quickly enough to suggest I'm having any real fun, but Duncan's card is still behind the bar and I'm raking up the Sake Martini's so successfully they may have to order out for more star fruit.

"You don't like Duncan do you?"

It's Charlotte, her girl-purr in my right ear.

I beam. "I certainly don't like the *name*, 'Duncan'. It's a terrible name. It suggests deep-seated parental spite. It's like the female equivalent of calling one's daughter Ruth."

I quickly consider: Sake Martini's are surprisingly punchy.

"Who's Ruth?," she asks.

"I don't know any Ruth. In fact, I've always done my best to avoid meeting anyone called Ruth."

"Stop trying to change the subject," she says, herself showing the hint of a pink-drink slur. "We were talking about Duncan. Actual *name* aside, I get the distinct impression you don't warm to Duncan the *person* either?"

"No more than his parents, I suspect. But *warm* to suggests emotion, Charley. I don't *feel* emotional towards Duncan full stop. Very simply, I just think he's a first class wanker."

I drain my Martini, immediately catch the Bar Girl's eye and gesture for a new one. I lift Charley's drink by lifting her wrist, requesting that the round be two more very expensive drinks on Mr Duncan Boyd's plastic.

"Why do you care what I think?," I ask.

Charley doesn't answer me straight away, just looks over at our Esteemed Leader, then back at me.

"Are you just resorting to name calling because you can't be arsed to explain yourself, or do you mean 'wanker' in a first person have-lent-a-hand kind of way?," she teases.

"Listen," I say. "In my opinion the guy strokes Big Time – but No, I've never offered my services. Have you?," I challenge.

Her look borders on the cold.

"Personally," I continue, "I'm not Duncan's number one fan. I think he's…" the aggressive edge of drink coming through, "… fucking redundant."

"Redundant? He runs the company."

"Still makes him redundant; as in, *surplus to planetary requirements*. As in, 'Duncan, you have no role, get off my world, go walk in space.'"

"I see," she says.

I elaborate on my feelings, although there is absolutely no need: "Everything that's wrong with the agency, everything that's bad, that's evil, that's poisonous: that is Duncan. Duncan is the embodiment, the very archetype of All That Bad Stuff. In fact, he's not just the very worst of this company; he's the very worst of being human. Like Hitler was."

"So, you don't like him?," Charley giggles.

"Who? Duncan?"

"Yes, Duncan."

"No, I fucking hate him," I say. "Liking him doesn't come into it."

More time drains away, like strong martini's slipping down the throat, and I reach two decisions. One, it's time to leave. Two, Charlotte is very sweet and very impressionable. At 22, I suspect she is too young and too attractive to not become a victim, but what do I necessarily know? Maybe she knows what she's doing?

For SDB, Charlotte's a very obvious recruitment choice, a fine example of the agency's very Active Recruitment Policy. "Who wants to look at dogs all day?," that's what Duncan once told me at closer quarters.

There are a whole host of reasons why Duncan employed Charley, all of them anatomical. Looks Highly Fuckable in fuck-me-boots, preferences great wet-look lip-gloss, wears short skirts and only occasionally demure blouses while still managing to look very un-demure. Although in a Slightly Obvious way, I will give Duncan this much, he has Solid Taste.

Nocturnal Cliché

Back on Berners Street there is a customary dearth of cabs, and to neatly cap it off the heavens open all at once, from nothing to a deluge, strong diagonals of rain falling like pool cues. I feel for my phone, feeling impatient but resigned to calling for a minicab. It's then that I notice my pen isn't in its customary inside pocket. I reason sensibly, despite a Martini fug, that I must have left my pen on my desk. My Mont Blanc was a gift from my Staying Alive Granny and the thought of a light-fingered weekend office cleaner treating himself to My Meisterstück compels me to take a late night walk back into work.

The office is a strange place to be in the dead of night, a dead place, hollow and still where time seems to hang. If I wanted to, I could really spook myself. I shiver, but partly because of the current downpour, and run a hand back through my wet hair. I need a cut.

Shafts of street-light cut through the half-open blinds, showing my pen to be on my desk just where I'd forgotten it; a Happy Result. Rain continues to shock-test the windows but otherwise there is silence. Pocketing my pen, I turn to leave, but above the noise of the rain, a Small Groan crosses the office floor, reaching me before I make it to the lifts. I am compelled to investigate.

Stepping through the shadows, following the trail of repeated groans and now moans, I pass desks and pillars, curiosity high. I turn the corner and then quickly drop to a knee behind the nearest available desk.

"Ohhhh… ahhhhh… urghhhh…"

Peering above the desk and in the direction of Duncan's office, Duncan is clearly in residence. He is not alone. In it: Duncan and Charley. In Charley: Duncan. The sounds and silhouetted form show them to be enthusiastically engrossed in the Oldest Act. Duncan stands with his broad back to the window, little Charley pushed forward over his desk. If I were Charley, I wouldn't want to look at him either. They seem to compete to see who can make the most remarkable farmyard noise. This is a Bleak Result. The Boss & His Secretary, what a disappointing cliché.

Quietly, I retrace my steps, keen not to interrupt their late night consult, feeling saddened but not surprised. I try to block out the groans and moans and the aural indication that he's started slapping her arse. As the lift doors close with me safely inside I tell myself, there's still cause for faith, at least I have my pen.

Kevin & Gideon

"I can't believe you beat me again?"

"Believe it Jamie," I tell him. "I always beat you."

"Once; I've beaten you once."

"It's good to have something to hold on to, isn't it?"

"Once can become twice."

Jamie's so dogged. Perhaps it's to compensate for all those failing follicles?

"Not in this lifetime," I tell him. "I don't care whether you can bench-press a small planet. You just don't have the speed, and might never have the touch."

We take a perch at the bar, which is long, very long, a real Manhattan-stretch affair. The bar stools are clad in soft brown leather, making the perch bearable. After the on-court clash, we despair for some serious stomach lining assistance. Sustenance takes the form of ham (Iberian), cheese (manchego) and enough honeyed quince cubes to keep our glycemic index through the roof. To compliment, we hit the wine list hard, thus ending my martini-themed month.

"You seem of better cheer," says Jamie. "Any interest on the totty front?"

"I've just come to the conclusion that life is too short to spend it sulking and skulking."

"A kind of epiphany?," he suggests.

"Jamie, your right shoelace," I point out, "it's come undone."

"Hmm," he replies, then forks a chunk a manchego towards his chops.

"Jamie, you should do it up right now."

"Okay, in a moment."

"No right now, at this precise moment."

"Can't I finish chewing my cheese?"

"You can do both," I tell him.

Still chewing, Jamie bends down and rectifies the errant laces.

"Happier now, Rain Man? You fashioning some sort of obsessive compulsive disorder?"

"Just a weird memory," I explain.

"A weird memory?," says Jamie.

"Untied laces, it reminds me of a of a kid in Primary school."

"In Primary school?"

"Yes, Primary school. Well in-between, actually. Kevin Partridge. On the first Sunday of the Summer holidays, secondary school in the September a distant concern, a group of us went fishing down by the Old Mill."

"Sam, tell me you didn't drown this kid?"

"No," I say, "but I'd never really been fishing before, and it was the first time I'd really spoken to Kevin Partridge. He turned out to be an okay lad, shared his crisps with me and a tin of multi-coloured maggots that he was very skilled at piercing with a fishing hook."

"Buddy, talk of multi-coloured maggots does not endear me to my quince cubes."

"Do you want to hear about Kevin Partridge or not?," I ask.

"Is Kevin relevant to your Spac-Attack over my shoelace?"

"He is."

"Then progress."

I continue, "The relevance is that what I really remember about Kevin Partridge was his trainers. The basketball kind: high tops, lots of eyelets, really long laces. All that afternoon we were fishing, his shoe laces were undone, dragging in the mud, dangling beneath his feet, sometimes catching the surface of the water while his legs swung over the river bank.

"When we walked home I remember those long laces, with his every step scraping over the pavement in great sweeping arcs. I never asked why he hadn't tied them, and I never suggested that maybe he should. But I remember the noise they made skating over the concrete in the fading July light."

Jamie looks at me, oddly. "This is all very evocative."

"We planned to go fishing the next day, everyone to meet at my house as I lived closest to the Mill. I decided that I liked Kevin Partridge, and that in the morning I'd ask him about his laces, but I didn't get the chance.

"That next day, Kevin was cycling through the village, from his house to mine and was knocked down by a car.

The driver wasn't local. Some Sales Rep late for a Monday morning appointment who thought the village would provide a nifty short cut. It didn't of course."

"I lose at squash, and now I get to hear 'bout Kevin-bloody-Partridge!," Jamie appeals.

"The Rep wasn't even going that fast, but Kevin as I understand went airborne and landed on his head. He didn't die instantly but if he had woken during his last 3 days on life support, he'd have been cabbage, unable to tie his laces even if he'd wanted."

Jamie drains his wine, his eyes slightly bunching. "And the purpose to your story Sam would be? To depress the shit out of me?"

"If there is a moral," I tell him, "it's that bad things can sometimes happen to people who don't tie their shoelaces. But it's okay, I made you tie yours."

"Thanks for that."

"Hey, you asked why I was of good cheer."

"Because of a Dead Kid memory?"

"Because life's too short to angst over an ex-girlfriend and not take control of a life you don't like."

"So you have had an epiphany," confirms Jamie. "I guess Kevin would be proud of you."

★

"Jamie, have you ever read the Bible?"

10:45pm: unless I am mistaken, this Senoma County chardonnay is Bottle Number 4.

"Actually, I did pick it up once," he says. "but couldn't get past the first line. I was on a training course in Stalingrad. Staying at a pre-Perestroika hotel where my room was gulag-inspired. Broken TV, I wasn't in the mood for a five-knuckle shuffle – because I'd just had one – and I'd already drained every thimble-sized vodka bottle in the mini bar. It was enough to get Tom Thumb or a fetus pissed, but no one that clocked in a body weight that exceeded a small bag of sugar.

"I read *"In the beginning…"* and in my head, I sounded like Richard Burton, gravel voiced and backed by the opening bars to *War of the Worlds*."

"I don't think that's usual," I say.

"I figured, even the most devout atheists would have cringed at the piss take."

I suggest, "Maybe coming across an English Bible in a Russian hotel room was a sign?"

"Maybe a sign that I should have left well alone. I put Gideon back in the drawer, reasoning that if there is a God, I didn't fancy explaining myself or spending eternity masticated in one of the three jaws of Satan."

"Understandable."

"So, No," says Jamie, "I've never read the Bible and if St. Peter asks, it's all Richard Burton and H.G. Wells' fault."

Walking The Bridge

It was the kind of day you really wanted to ignore, only there was no chance of it letting you.

Glancing to the heavens, the monochrome sky is bruised, not quite to a pulp. The air is clingy, keen to offer a cold clammy embrace. My tube carriage houses the usual: a breakfast order of sandwiched secretaries and florid-jowl pinstripes.

Topside, I pass an *Evening Standard* vendor, but avoid

yesterday's headline: a Genuine Victory. Rain falls carelessly and sadly I have no umbrella.

Walking the bridge at Blackfriars is like trying to make headway through liquid cling-film. The going isn't impossible, just dismal. Louis Armstrong was full of it; the world can fall a long way short of wonderful. Through it all, I smile, because that's what the New Me does. He smiles.

The Thames ebbs and flows underfoot, showing a turgid persistence. The water, a silty-putrid brown, looks on the verge of boiling. I wonder: what would happen if I just jump in?

To my left: the faintest outline of Tower Bridge, and beyond that the citadel of Canary Wharf, though Today's Grey is too thick to afford an outline. Ahead and just to my left the *Express Newspapers* building wears a temporary crown: a countdown clock stands proud and prophetic, the number 16 glowing in the morning dim. 16 days until the Zero Hour, 16 days till the end of the world.

To my 1 o'clock, the Oxo Tower, where their brasserie is okay but their restaurant over-priced, unless someone else is picking up the bill – and there should always be someone else to pick up the bill.

Feral-eyed couriers on their flimsy cycles zag and jag between cabs and trucks. Legs pumping, their mouths are hidden behind pollutant-filtering masks, but underneath, they sport grimaces, hard and drawn. Even though it's the New Me, I feel I can relate just a little.

I rally myself. Though the prospect of the day ahead is hardly mouth-watering, I endeavour to find sport in it.

Training Guy

9am. *Mood Boards*

We've just been told to "give good meeting". There's this Training Guy, trendy looking, you can tell he reckons he knows lots of stuff, really has that INSEAD MBA Attitude about him. He's standing in front of the 12 of us. There's me and the usual crew, Tracey, Dick, Jeremy, Barney, and 7 others who work on different accounts on different floor who's names I find it impossible to remember, and there's Training Guy, who's just said one should always look to "give good meeting".

There's been this date in my diary for the last 4 weeks, and I'd been doing a very good job of ignoring it, but then the day came - being right bastard now. My prospect: 8 hours of Latest Thinking management psycho-babble with Training Guy at an off-site address in Waterloo.

I couldn't feel less touchy-feely. I'm into my third minute of "listening actively" and in things warm-n-fuzzy, it turns out I'm already running on empty. I just know, this bloke's going to really get on my tits.

"We're going to do a little warm-up exercise?," says Training Guy.

I'd been ignoring the pieces of paper and the chunky marker pens on the desk in front of us. Sadly they are not just decorative.

We have to do what?

"Using your markers, I'd like you all to draw... how you *feel*?"

Certainly, my feelings for Training Guy are developing quite rapidly. Turns out the pieces of paper aren't just pieces of paper, they're Mood Boards.

Fuckin' Mood Boards and fuckin' Training Guy, with his Soho shaved head, his thick-framed Gucci specs and his trendy Big Collared & Shimmering shirt.

I ask Training Guy, "So this is like, Sketchy-Feely then?," and while one or two in the room smile, Training Guy does not.

I'm tempted to draw a big thundercloud with cartoon lightning bolts, or perhaps Mother Earth retching magmatic fury, but the lightening cloud feels hackneyed and wouldn't go down well with Training Guy, and I haven't the colour range for the volcanic scene I had in mind.

I settle on a simple black-markered Question Mark, and when it comes time to present My Mood Board, Training Guy's eyebrows are already racing north.

"I'm feeling… enigmatic," I tell everyone. I think I'm being pretty clever actually, but it's clear Training Guy prefers my colleague's efforts: lots of thick tipped beach scenes, sunshine dispositions, drawings of sporting apparel, etc. More "Hobbies & Interests" boards, I would say.

"Of course we could address the much wider existential issues," I then suggest in regard to my "?". "It just depends on what level you want to discuss my mood… board."

"No, enigmatic is fine," says Training Guy, mentally noting me a Potential Problem Case.

10:30am. *Crap*

"I'm sorry. I appreciate it's always easier to criticise… but that's just crap!"

Training Guy's made a suggestion, and I've decided to disagree. (It's not so much that I disagree with his suggestion, more I just disagree with him.) I think he's starting to get a little rattled.

We've just had our first coffee break, returning supposedly

"re-charged" to the challenges in hand, and straight-off, Training Guy's first "downloaded thought" is Borderline Nonsense.

"Sam, can you build on crap?" There's no hiding his tone of condescension.

I consider for a moment. "Well you can, but I wouldn't recommend it. Crap's not the best foundation."

"You understand me perfectly," counters Training Guy. "Crap is just a little bit lazy and dismissive and insensitive. Can you elaborate on your remark, but instead of criticising, I was hoping you could build? Be encouraging. Compliment with a spade, criticise with a teaspoon."

"I should encourage, even if an idea's truly terrible, like this one is? I'm not sure encouraging bad ideas is a particularly good idea." I think my words are almost reasonable, though of course, I may be acting rather immature. I know I'm being immature.

I am told: "It's about Friendly Evaluation."

I answer, "What you're saying then, is it's in the *phrasing*?"

Training Guy gives a hint of a nod.

"In that case: It's not that your idea is bad. It's that it's *not good*. I would *encourage* that next time you think a little longer and try a little harder."

Okay, not so much Friendly Evaluation, more Friendly Fire.

There is a pause. Quite a long one. Some of the group are looking uncomfortable. Dick is smirking, Tracey's head is uniquely still. Barney isn't sure where to put his eyes.

The potentially difficult character, namely Me, has gone from "difficult" to "rude," and Training Guy's thinking: what to do?

10:38am. *Personally*

"Everyone has a role, right?" I'm making speeches now. "Individuals within any group situation assume clearly defined roles. Leader, facilitator, jester, etc etc. Right? Well, in this situation, as I'm sure you're aware, I'm your proto-typical "Difficult bastard". Now, it's your job, as "Trainer," to handle me, to manage this "Group Moment". The question is, how are you going to diffuse this moment?"

I smile. "Relax, this is a non-threatening environment… but I am challenging your credibility."

Training Guy's shaved noggin is really starting to shine. Through clenched teeth, "It isn't your place to question my credibility."

"It is if I have a lack of confidence in what you have to say. It is if you're wasting my day. It's fine for you to be here, you're charging a hefty hourly rate."

I'm starting to enjoy myself. This is turning into quite a fun little bun fight, but…

Training Guy isn't happy. It's obvious. He's scowling at me, his eyes wide behind his glasses. I'm reminded of those times in school when we'd try and get a rise out of the teacher. It was always, how far do you go, before going too far?

I continue, "Maybe you're thinking you can convert me, convince me my cynicism is unfounded? Or you could humour me, appealing that I have a right to disagree but that I shouldn't spoil it for everyone else?"

I'm aware that my voice is getting louder, maybe too loud?

"Groups often take care of their own problem child, but I think everyone is a little scared of what might happen if they try and intervene right now."

I gesture to Barney, my easiest example. He just blushes.

"And I also think everyone's a little curious about

what you're going to do? I think they'll leave Me and You to it."

I'm asked: "Sam, what is it you're trying to do or prove?"

A good question, to the heart of matter, the first non-flowery thing Training Guy's said all morning.

I answer: "I'd like you to admit that this is just one big joke."

Silence.

"Of course," I say, "you're keen for me to elaborate."

A long draw of breath, then, "OK, I'm saying this. I'm saying that what you're saying is farcical. There's no substance to any of it. It's smoke and mirrors. It's all hype, packaging and spin, all systematic thinking and regurgitated management texts."

"It's a shame you feel that way," he says.

"For you, maybe? I don't think it's a shame." I take a seconds pause, look at the faces round the table now staring at me, Dick still smirking.

I turn back to Training Guy. "Listen mate, it's not you personally." I think for a moment. "Well, actually it is you, but it's also me. I've passed my bullshit threshold. So here's a "Headline Idea" for you, and I do hope you're "Actively Listening". Your Mood Boards, your Mind Maps, and your Brain Bank: they're all a pile a SHITE. You make money from what you do, so fair-play to you, but you're not a Thought Leader. You're just a balding bloke trying to blag his way to making a couple of quid."

And then I leave the room.

I didn't know if the guy was going to cry or swing at me, but I wasn't interested enough to find out.

Time: 10:42am. I will not return to the office today.

A Bolder Me

Whistling as I walk, I take the path along the south shore to Bankside Power Station, the site of the nearly completed Tate Modern. Yep, turns out they're doing a bang-up job. A Spring opening looks well on the cards.

The weather is still grizzly, but suddenly I'm enjoying the morning air. Whatever I do, it's a considerably more productive use of my time than listening to Training Guy. While digging out my phone, I look through the falling drizzle and across the river at St Paul's.

"Hi… Ariel?"

"Yes?"

My God, I really wasn't expecting her to pick up. I'd resolved that I'd leave One More Message, then that would be it, I would never again attempt for our lives on this rock to intersect.

"Hi, it's Sam, Sam Grant."

"Hi Sam! As the line goes, I've been meaning to call you back."

"Of course you have."

"No *really*. I *have*," she laughs. "I've been hectic busy, up in Manchester virtually all of last week, but now I'm back. I wanted to catch up with you; tell you all about the focus group findings."

"Okay," I say. "Sounds riveting. How 'bout over supper?"

"Sorry?"

"Supper: Me, you, food. I'm asking you on a date."

Fresh Air and my dealings with Training Guy have left me emboldened.

The drizzle becomes fully-fledged rain and I wonder, is it safe to use my phone in these conditions? Is there an outside chance of electrocution?

"I think there's a professional line we're in danger of crossing here?," she says.

"Does that mean you don't want to?"

"No."

"Oh."

Bold or not bold, Ariel's No comes as a bit of a blow. I'd gambled on her saying yes.

"No, I mean I would like to," she clarifies.

"Oh." Much better. I'm feeling more Back on Track.

"Hell, when?"

"How about tomorrow night?," I suggest. "Say, dinner at the Oxo tower?"

Vice Squad

This morning, The Blue paid an impromptu visit to the Allegedly Revered offices of Shark, Delaney & Boyd. Although a matter of business, SDB was not pitching to work on any up-coming Police campaign.

CEO Duncan Boyd was not on site to greet these plain clothed officers of the law. He was said to be in a meeting in Surrey. Charlotte later admitted to me that the specific location of Duncan's dawn meeting was a golf course. Although very much my personal hope, Vice Squad had not come to pay Duncan a personal visit.

Turns out fat-n-friendly Stuart (who up until today ran the post room) has a double life. When not delivering the mail, Stu moonlights as a pretty major league East London drug dealer. Stu the Post Room Man is, within some circles, known more fondly as Stu "The Supplier".

The police (5 of them) announced themselves at reception

and very politely asked if they could speak with the fat-n-friendly fella we all call Stu.

Stu did not incline to make himself available. He got wind and bolted down the fire-escape, pegged it across the car park and let the city streets swallow him up. For the city to swallow him, it would've been quite a meal, but from my window seat on the 3rd floor, I saw Stu as he cut across the street and I can testify, he moves pretty fast for a fat bloke. Just very occasionally, a desk is not the worst place from which to view the world.

Stu's weekday wardrobe was always Levis, Reeboks and a very substantial looking Cartier Tank watch which I'm now guessing wasn't so fake after all. It is little more than 24 hours until the agency Christmas party and I wonder whether Stu did the agency rounds in time? Otherwise, how is everyone going to get hold of their Class A's?

Afternoon Events

Duncan, having finished 10 Over is now back in work and has roped me into an afternoon meeting with a new client. He has also called Tracey in. Last time I saw Dunc, he was…

I shake the Bestial Image from my mind.

The New Client is European Marketing Director for a Scandinavian car manufacturer. His name is Lars and his colouring is much like Holly's new boyfriend, Jorgen. Lars is from Stockholm and is as Scando as they come.

"The old modul," explains Lars in reference to some upcoming car launch, "it wosh like a girlfriend who did the cooking and the ironing. Now with the nuw modul, she shtill does the cooking and ironing, but sheesh got longer legs and wears a mini shkirt."

The Nodding Dog's stopped nodding.

"Tracey," I ask, "are you taking notes, or shall I?"

Duncan looks amused. Lars is talking His Language. He starts account handling the shit out of ole Lars, asking all about this new model, talking about what an auto enthusiast he is and how he loves his Maserati. I've seen the routine before. Whether Lars finds Duncan's Charm Offensive transparent or not, I'm not sure, but I fear Lars is falling for it. Duncan is Old School, so much the Bullet Proof account handler who can slip and side-wind his way out of trouble. I once over heard him explain, "I treat my wife like a client. I buy her gifts before she wants them, I anticipate and pre-empt her dissatisfactions. It's up to me to shape the world according to how I want her to view it. That way, everything runs smoothly."

I marvel, Duncan's such a piece of work, such a scumbag. I wonder just when it must have been that he sold his soul. Was it for more or less than the price of his Maserati?

Duncan keeps me back after Lars has left feeling a Happy & Satisfied client.

Going for the icebreaker, he starts off by trying to diss my footwear. "Sam, are those suede shoes you're wearing?"

I look down at my brown suede loafers.

"No one who's ever worn suede shoes has ever become a someone," he jibes.

"What about Elvis ?," I ask.

Duncan grins but doesn't answer.

"I don't know whether to let you or Tracey handle Lars' business," he suddenly confides. I don't offer any response.

"Ordinarily, I would have said you, and I've recently had excellent feedback from Marvin Matheson…"

He trails off, inviting me to say "but," but my lips remain locked.

"I've had reports back on your performance yesterday. Quite a performance. I understand you didn't see eye-to-eye with your training facilitator?"

"We had a clash of personality and opinion," I say. "It was my opinion that he was an idiot. He naturally saw it differently."

"You know you're one of a number of candidates in line for promotion to the Board?"

"So I'd heard."

"But your recent profile around the agency has been low. Certainly I haven't heard much of you putting in many long nights hard at it."

I can't help the slight chuckle that escapes.

"Friday," I say, "I was here late last Friday… and like I said, my hearing is very good. As for performances…"

Date Night

"Wow, the view's amazing!"

I play it down, like this is much the same view I have every night from my bedroom window.

"Yeah, it's… pretty good," I say, recalling a Carnal Conversation I once had with Sarah.

The rule is always the same. You have to be on the wrong side of the river if you want to be afforded the right kind of view.

I don't resent being south-side on a night this clear, the city like a jewel box, every facet twinkling but just out of reach. Ariel tells me this is her first visit to the Oxo tower. She's being suitably appreciative, and if it's just an act, I'm at least grateful for her effort.

So far too, the food has not upset. I started on king prawn tortellini with lime and chervil. She went with sweet seared scallops and rich-braised oxtail. Mine was good-to-very-good. She offered me a taste of hers, which I took and which revealed that she'd ordered better. Although tempted, I didn't snatch away her plate and insist instead that she eat mine, proving I can be magnanimous about these things. We each drank a glass of Tuscan chardonnay: flowery, with a hint of citrus, and a thoughtful compliment to the delicate starters.

★

"Tell me something interesting about yourself?," she asks.

I ponder a moment, determined to make an effort and be good value.

"Last year I was crowned the quickest-drawing snowball fighter in Alaska."

"Is that so?," she asks, running an index finger along the edge of her empty wine glass while locking me with her large blue eyes.

Round two arrives. I've chosen braised hare with Savoy cabbage for main, Ariel's opted for lamb cutlets filled with Parma ham, rosemary and sage. I pour the wine, a Chianti, a '97 Reserve that Jamie speaks very highly of.

"My snowballs have a velocity of 70 miles an hour," I continue.

"Impressive."

"In more southerly latitudes I breed prize winning gerbils. I've also patented my own line of crushed velour and am regrettably wanted for Crimes against the State… in Guatemala."

"That's quite remarkable," she says.

"Thank you," I smile. "You wanted interesting, you got interesting: I'm a Freedom Fighter, Style Leader, marine biologist, expert snowball maker, and my most beloved gerbil is called Harold. Oh, and less interestingly, I work in Advertising.

"The advertising bit, I knew already."

*

I'm always too full for pudding but Ariel, Being a Girl, has ordered some monstrous chunk of many-textured chocolate.

By the time my coffee is cool enough to corner, Ariel's chocolate cake has vanished and her espresso drained. All this is to me just further proof that girls are made differently. No girl can say No to chocolate, every girl can find room for pudding, and every girl can drink coffee at a temperature just fractionally cooler than the surface of the sun. Girls: sweet-toothed, big-bellied, with mouths lined in asbestos.

"What do we do now?," I ask.

She mulls, then flashes me a very naughty little smile.

"I think…," she begins, then hesitates.

"Yes?"

"I think… you've done well with the cocksure and charming patter, I've played okay at dismissive while offering flashes of encouraging flirtation - it's always good to keep a man on his toes."

"Agreed," I agree.

"Now, as the sexual fission mounts, there's little need for further rounds of teasing verbal banter?"

"Reasonable."

"But we should keep on with the smouldering eye-contact."

"Like now?," I ask.

"Yes, like now," she confirms. "So now, I think now you're feeling utterly compelled to put your tongue down my throat…"

I don't know whether she's psychic but it's as close an approximation of what I'd been thinking as anything.

"… and I'm thinking… I'm thinking that I might just let you," she smiles devilishly.

"You're very sure of yourself," I tell her, my pulse and fly rising.

"I think it's probably time you ask for the bill," she suggests, and at this point, any thoughts I had of her mouth being made of asbestos have disappeared as quickly as chocolate cake.

On the Jetty

Outside, she links her arm through mine and we stroll in the cool night west along the riverbank. A series of jetties point out into the oily night. She takes me by the hand and leads me along the nearest. There is a gentle breeze that says being alive can be okay and I feel rather drunk, which is little revelation seeing as I've drunk a lot of Italian wine.

The Thames is high tonight. Every light in the city seems competing with the stars in a rarely clear sky. We are alone, as far out on the jetty as we can go. She looks up into my eyes. That naughty smile of hers again. I don't move, just look back impassively. On her toes, she leans in and bites me lightly on the lower lip, then looks over my shoulder before reaching down to my fly and going to her knees.

I don't move, just keep taking in the view of the north shore, the dome of St.Paul's, and all the lights.

I think of Woody Allen's line in his movie *Manhattan*: "It was his city, and it always would be…"

Then I think: I thought I was going to put my tongue down her throat? Then I think: Christ, you have to admire any girl who has got the better of her gag reflex.

This will not take long. It's a see-saw of inevitable consequence: demonstrated technique (a sure-fire accelerant) countered by a rather strong bottle of Chianti (alcohol affording the classic delay).

But… MYGODSHE'SGOOD. At the going, very enthusiastic rate, I figure I'll last 2 minutes tops.

I hear voices behind me, turn my head and see a couple moving down the jetty towards us, but I don't pull back, I don't care, and she doesn't stop. The couple step a little closer, but then suspecting, or more likely seeing what's going down, they turn on their heel. It's not a very dark night, all these stars. I start to work my hips, then place my hand on her shoulder, my thumb starting to dig in just below her blade, letting her know what's about come. She pulls her mouth away, takes me firmly by the hand and…

Without hearing the splash, I know that in some small way I've contributed to the water line.

A Weak Analogy

I must confess, there's definitely a Spring in My Step this morning. Think Positive and Positive Stuff happens, that's how it works. In life, you make your own Blow Jobs happen.

I even play tough and sneak a peek at the *Evening Standard* morning edition: *LA Hosts World's Largest Gun Show*. See, that's not even so bad. If Americans want to shoot fellow Americans, who am I to deny them their constitutional right?

Whatever happens or doesn't happen with Ariel, I'm going to play it cool and play it slow and play it One Girl at a time. From The Sarah Debacle, I assure myself, I have learned more than one Valuable Lesson. Don't be going out with someone, and giving it the Don Juan. It's not fair and it messes with your head, both the big and the small. Window shop by all means, but don't go trying girls on if you're already wearing one. Like sports cars, enjoy them one ride at a time. If you like German, enjoy German, but don't go driving German while at every other opportunity test-driving Italian, thinking Italian could be more your racing flavour. Do that, and you could end up taking the bus.

Despite suspecting my Sports Car Analogy doesn't really work, I do momentarily feel proud of myself, believing that I might have grown as a Human Being.

The Christmas Party

The X-only chromosome contingent of SDB appears in a heightened state of excitement. There have been women flurrying in and out of the Ladies toilets since about 5 this afternoon. Champagne trolleys have been doing the rounds for the last 2 hours ensuring the general mood is highly jolly. A bubbles-only diet is always a good start, ensuring The Boys walk tall in Black tie and the Girls wear Slinky & Sexy with self-belief.

7:20pm. I visit the Gents to change and consult a mirror for my bowtie. Yep, I can tie my own. I consider it an important Life Skill, like being able to swap scuba masks at 20 metres under, ski off a mountain, speak conversational French. The Life Skill List, I'm forever developing. Latest additions include:

1. strip and re-assemble an automatic weapon,

2. pull a wheelie on a motor bike,

3. share (in appropriate company) true tales of wild sexual adventures with Japanese twins.

As you may have guessed, I'm expanding my Life Skill List into territory that's considerably more To Do.

Outside, there's a fleet of white limo's blocking the street. They will be taking us East to The Venue, out by the Dome. As I slide into the first stretch available, I can't help but sneer. White limos for christssake! It's so B&T Hen Night, so 80's-Movie-Prom-Night, but it's not like I'm going to get a bus.

I don't know why, but Tracey steps in after me, like hers is a Conscious Desire to torture me with her presence? Tracey's taken the Little Black Dress route, and to her credit, it goes in and out in all the right places.

Tracey stepped in after me, Richard after her. Dick I discover, can also tie his own bowtie (which aggrieves me), and I wonder how au fait he is with automatic weaponry and whether he can pull wheelies on a Kawasaki?

Three minutes into the journey, Dick asks the driver, "Drives, what's your position on recreational drug taking?"

Boy, it doesn't take long before the Class A's come out to play. Stu The Supplier may be gone but he's not forgotten.

"Listen mate, I just don't want no trouble."

No one flags the double-negative and Dick advises that he should punch up the dividing glass and keep his eyes pointing forwards. Drives sighs, accepts his world, and the dividing glass begins to rise.

Besides Me, Dick, and The Nodding Dog, one of the party photographers has bummed a lift with us. Tracey turns to Photo Fella while pulling out a small cellophane bag.

"You do so much as adjust your lens cap, and I'll shove that camera so far up your arse you'll have to learn how to take pictures farting."

Pretty inelegant Trace, I think, but no one present questions the sincerity of her threat.

Photo Fella just raises his palms, wanting no more trouble than Drives.

Tracey adds with her finest Client-Facing Smile: "Of course, your absolute discretion earns you a line."

"Very hospitable," Photo Fella smiles back, watching as Tracey cuts and Dick rolls a fifty.

★

I don't know how much cash they've thrown at this, but it's got to have been a lot. Of course, I'm not complaining, so long as the cost of all this razzmatazz is in no way linked to my Christmas bonus.

The venue is a massive industrial warehouse with views straight on to the Millennium Dome. There are three bars and what seems like one drink-laden waitress to every two guests. A nice ratio.

The theme is very much Big Top, which I have to say I find a little creepy. Ask me, fairgrounds always bring to mind images of gypos with evil smiles, poisoned toffee apples and Missing Kid posters. Tonight's interpretation is, however, considerably more up-scale, more Vegas than Travelling Caravans of Kiddie Fiddlers. We have jugglers, dancers, contortionists, midgets, body-painted girls wearing snakes, fire-eating, fire-walking, sword-swallowing… and this all at ground level.

The whole Cirque de Soleil thing goes on over-head, trapeze acts defying gravity and women dangling from ribbons, spinning like bottle tops and equalling the strength of Olympic gymnasts. There are lots of Ohhhhs! and Ahhhhs!

and as time passes, everyone's behaviour becomes more booze-fuelled, the dancing more suggestive, the talk bolder, the flirtations more careless.

I drink steadily, avoid dancing, try my best to avoid talking to too many people, happy to just watch the anthropology on display.

9:25pm. Barney ambles over and tries to spark up a conversation about how he really feels he's settling in, and isn't SDB such a Great Agency to work at, and aren't we all Such Great People and isn't this a Great Party. I let Barney rabbit on while I finish my latest drink, then excuse myself saying I need to find Tracey and hit her for a few lines. I may be harsh when it comes to Barney but he is such a Boredom Grenade, I'll be damned if I'm going to be one of his casualties.

★

I lean into the bar and say Hi.

Charley turns and smiles and asks, Am I having a good time?

The fact that I'm careful not to slur a reply is sure-fire indication that I have already over-imbibed.

"Two double vodka and Red Bulls, please," I shout across the bar.

In for a penny.

It's odd seeing Charley in a gown, out of her short skirts and knee high boots. Her silver frock is backless, showing the smoothest swatch of milky skin I've seen in quite some time.

"Charley," I ask, "what's the secret to happiness?"

"That's easy," she says. "Love like you've never been hurt, dance like nobody's watching and shag like you're always on camera."

"In which case, I'd really like to watch some of your home movies."

She grins.

"Though preferably the one's that pre-date Duncan," I add.

Her smile falls, her features turning suddenly very hard.

What am I doing? I tell myself: stop this, don't be cruel, and it's none of your damned business, but because of whatever muddled feelings I have for both Charley and Duncan, I can't help myself. Possibly the thought of that Silver Fox pawing her silver frock makes me jealous?

"Fuck off Sam"; coming almost at a whisper.

"If your current night shifts aren't part of your original job description, I'd demand a new contract with better pay."

"Why are you doing this?," she asks.

"Because Charley, I don't know why you're doing him?"

"I like him," she says flatly, "and it's really nothing to do with you."

Like him? It's almost too ridiculous, but Charley doesn't allow for debate, instead turning on her high heels as two vodka Red Bulls are placed in front of me.

★

"Man, look at his eyes! He's fucking gone, Man!"

Maybe true. Maybe I was, for a short while. Though gone where?, I'm less clear, just someplace else. My eyes are in fact working fine and I doubt this little fella's any kind of optometrist.

The little runt, short haircut, short-arse in a rented dinner suit, jacket clearly shortcut, had half-bundled into my toilet cubicle. I'd forgotten to lock it after Tracey left. I'd been sitting with the seat down, just trying to escape the alien nation of the party, get a little pause.

I'd also been feeling Slightly Heady; in the way I know Champagne, Red Bull, Vodka, and Cocaine can be too-crazy party company. You put the wrong people in the room, and hey, you've only got yourself to blame.

I had crossed paths with the Nodding Dog and we had visited the communal restrooms. We did a few lines (Yes, Stu had supplied) and amused that someone in the next cubicle was, without question, getting blown. At agency parties, no one ever goes into a cubicle alone. Tracey had then left first and I'd decided to take a two second time out.

My lungs feel like I must have smoked about a million cigarettes, but I can't remember if I've been smoking this evening? Irrespective, my heart's racing like a bastard. Just as my cubicle had been invaded, I'd been concentrating on making my heart race faster. I'd wondered how crazy I could crank it before my whole chest exploded, exiting this mortal coil like The King himself, dead on the crapper.

The Short Arse who isn't an optometrist just stands there with his chump-chum.

I rise from my throne, eye-ball them both, ignore the dizziness and growl a nicely audible "Fuck off".

Hence: "Man, look at his eyes!. He's fucking gone, Man!"

Neither Short-Arse, nor Short Arse's Buddy wants the aggro. Buddy pulls at Short-Arse's arm and the two of them, nameless faceless members of the SDB family move on to cubicles less zany.

I leave my cubicle and move over to the row of washbasins, cup handfuls of water to my face, then drag down hard on the flesh at my face with wet, numb fingers. Mirror image: hardly beautiful.

Gone? Yeah, that's me. Solid gone, even perhaps jello gone, with eyes like I've just taken a peek at the inside of hell, and feel okay with what I've seen. Maybe more red than my personal taste, but not bad digs.

★

The party's still swinging. I skirt the edge of the dance floor, zig-zag my way between performing dwarves and fire-blowers and tuck myself into a darkened corner.

I look out a window, considering the Dome and all the hoopla that's surrounded it.

Charley is suddenly beside me, sharing this private party patch. She looks angry.

"Why do you care anyway?"

"Because I do," I say calmly. "Because it's a fucking abuse, because he's using you and because you're letting him."

"I know exactly what I'm doing."

"Maybe that's what I find hardest of all."

She looks like she wants to hit me. I'd like to kiss her but before the mind clip is half formed, she kisses me. Her lips are very full and warm and I'm just taken on the joyride. This is her call; she's the one at the wheel.

Charley pulls back, and I start to say something but she puts an index finger to my lips.

"A girl always likes to know somebody cares," she says.

★

"Sam, enjoying yourself?"

"I'm feeling very seasonal Richard. You?"

"Very jolly."

"I like your dinner suit by the way. Prada?"

"Yes it is," he downplays, while secretly loving that I've asked.

"Must have cost a small fortune?"

"A small one."

A beat passes.

"I've been talking to Duncan."

I have no interest in the bait.

He continues: "Jolly as I feel, I can't get a read on him, on who he's most likely to promote."

"I wouldn't worry Richard. Smart money's on you: you're a guy who gets the job done," I mug.

"Funny. That's what Duncan just said about you."

"Is that what I look like to you, Richard?"

Dick steps a touch closer, invading at the fringes of my personal space.

"I think you're a crafty one, Sam," he says. "Tell me, do you see me as a threat?"

I sense my mouth curling up at one side. I've had enough of this shit, this pointless posturing and second-guessing and politicking.

"I'll tell you what I see, Dick. I see a highly strung, hugely neurotic political beast… clawing his way up the corporate ladder, wondering when the hell he'll be found out… but nonetheless holding on ever tighter… salivating with every rung ascended, but each new rung doing nothing to silence the little voice on his shoulder whispering insecurities that he suspects may be brutal truths."

Dick has a good poker face and he keeps it together.

"That's very vivid," he says.

I lean in very close now, almost intimate, my nose no more than two inches from his, feeling the many toxins racing through my system. "I see the whites of your eyes. I see the feral in you. I see you for what little you are..."

One beat, two beats.

I step back, start laughing, pat Dick on the shoulder like we're war heroes swapping tall tales over good brandy.

"Mate, I'm joking."

Dick doesn't look like he found any of what just happened very hilarious.

"Richard, seriously, as far as this freak show's concerned," I say, gesturing an arm at all around us, "you're welcome to it."

★

Another cliché: Christmas Snogging in the back of a black cab. However, the cliché doesn't seem to be a problem for her, maybe even adds to her enthusiasm, the way she's clamping her lips against mine, one hand round the back of my neck messing my hair, the other massaging my member.

I pull away.

"Listen," I tell her. "I'm not 100% convinced this is such a remarkably good idea."

"Okay," she says, trying to look Foxy & Frisky but not quite managing it.

Then I start kissing her again, and I can't help but think: for one, that's my Sports Car Analogy blown to pieces.

★

Morning light and a foreign body in bed beside me, with me showing my back to the middle of the bed. I look at my watch. 8:10am. With Total Recall, I gingerly open my eyes and roll over to confront my slumber buddy.

She's awake, smiling back at me.

"Who'd have thought it?," she grins, looking more comfortable than I feel.

"Who indeed?," I say, then, "Tracey, would you like some coffee?"

She nods.

Going to Miami

"I was wondering whether you might like to meet up?"

"A Second Date?"

"I enjoyed the first one so much, I thought Hell, why not ask her out again?"

"You were hoping for maybe a repeat performance?," she asks.

"Yes, more sparkling conversation and that winning smile of yours."

"In that case, ordinarily I would say, Great, and what are you doing tonight?"

"Ordinarily?"

"I'm afraid Date 2 will have to be in the New Year."

"Oh?"

"I fly out to Miami this afternoon."

"A little random?"

"My parents have a summer home – well actually it's more of a winter home – in Florida. We go every year for Christmas."

"You're Jewish, you don't celebrate Christmas."

"That's why we go to Miami and I spend a lot of time well-oiled and sun-baking on South Beach."

"I'm guessing that mental image was for my benefit?"

"It was."

I look around the flat, phone still to my ear, wondering, is there anything more to say?

"So Sam, have a lovely Christmas and New Year and let's get together in Jan?"

I work hard at sounding Up and think I just about manage it as I wish her a Bon Voyage and a holiday free of melanomas.

★

I take stock. It is all encouraging.

Events have moved on. I no longer think about Sarah constantly, no longer torture myself with the *What If's?* and recollections of My Past Conduct. I have started "Dating" again. It would very much appear that *I* have Moved On. I tell myself, I have made Monumental Progress. When I think of Hans, I no longer fantasize about slowly torturing him, no longer entertain strapping the euro fuck-wad naked to a giant bull's eye and taking tactical shots at him with a BB-Gun. Yes, I am much improved.

The Letter

In Pursuit of Closure, I know I have to do this. I have to put pen to paper and write Sarah a letter. From memory, that November morning when Sarah paid me a visit, I don't recall being particularly congratulatory. In fact, I remember saying she was nuts and calling her fiancée a Teutonic Fuck. Yes, possibly a good thing that I never joined the Diplomatic Service.

Dear Sarah,

In the tradition of always starting with the strongest point, here it is:

I should have told you that I loved you.

I should have told you I loved you when I fell in love with you, which was in the beginning. But I didn't.

Maybe guys don't tend to be emotional? At least this one isn't. Maybe it's to do with being brought up on an Image-Diet of Mavericks and Top Guns, Six Guns and Geezers on One-Man-Missions? At no point in High Noon does Gary Cooper tell Grace Kelly he loves her. Gary just shoots people, then he and Grace ride off into the Sunset. Patrick Swayze could only manage "ditto" at the start of Ghost, and only found his emotional range once he was part of the afterlife.

Tough Guys don't dance, Real Men stay well away from quiche, and James Bond only said "I love you" once, and look where it got Diana Rigg. She caught a bullet.

None of the above is an excuse, but maybe some kinda lame-ass explanation? What I no longer need explaining is this:

I now know we don't have a future together.

We had what we had, good and bad. I think Destiny was always going to have us meet, we'd be attracted to each other, go out… then fall apart.

*But know this truly, you are a girl that I did love, but I
realised it late. Too late.*

*Sarah Macbeth, I shall miss you and a part of my
heart will always love you – I've marked out a patch
in my left atrium.*

*I wish you the very best of futures and I hope, unlike
Bono, that with Hans you find what you're looking for.*

Sam.

Marvin's Good Word

The eve of Christmas, I used to get so giddy about it, back
before I put away my childish things. The magic, the smiles,
the speculation of snow, the certainty of presents, all the fairy
tale stuff; Christmas is just great when you're a kid. Now it's
an excuse to drink champagne before 10 in the morning, and
what's so fairy tale about that?

Of course, if you have kids, come December 25th you get
to regress – but then there's the other 364 days when they're
just Heavy Sacrifice.

As it tallies, I'm not grumbling. I'm hopping a plane to
Barbados in less than 5 hours' time, so it's not all bad. First
though, there's the bad: Duncan's final speech to The Troops
before he rings the bell and tells everyone they can go home. In
Said Speech there's also the matter of Announcing Promotions.

Dick swung by my desk earlier to wish me luck, as too
did Tracey. The Consummate Professional, Tracey is behaving
like Nothing Happened, as am I. She has however e-mailed

me, saying we Should Talk and How about a drink? The very prospect fills me With Dread. I have yet to and might indeed never reply to her e-mail.

Time: 11:25am. Five minutes before the whole agency's to assemble in main reception and watch Duncan pomp it up on his podium, big screen behind him, looking like some sort of Big Brother.

I visit the Gents.

"Sam!"

Marvin: zipping up at a urinal.

"Hi Marvin... Merry Christmas."

"To you too," Marketing's Number One Clown beams back.

I notice his tie, the colours just lunatic.

"My Marvin, that's a bright tie. We don't need the sunshine for that do we?"

I'm hoping it's sufficient social interaction for Marvin to leave, but he stays to watch me wee, telling me how he's catching an afternoon train to Edinburgh, and how it looks like it's going to be a White Christmas up there, but hopefully a quiet one where he can also get some work done so he's ahead of the pace come January.

I finish my business, go to the washbasin and watch Marvin in the mirror, not giving a splash of piss for his stream of consciousness. I notice, one of his shoe laces is undone.

"Marvin, you want to tie that," I offer, gesturing to his feet. "Bad things can happen to people who don't tie their laces."

He looks down at his feet, but just leaves it and looks back at me.

"Congratulations on the promotion," he says.

I look up from drying my hands.

"Pardon?"

"It's okay, I know. Great news! Duncan and I discussed

your possible promotion to the Board. Duncan told me he's always much admired your professionalism and your discretion but he asked me whether I thought you were ready? I gave you my full endorsement. "

"Thank you," I say oddly.

"I've always thought you and I think alike."

While I have no immediate response for Marvin, I manage to raise my eyebrows.

"You and I, we're both Brand Purists," Marvin finishes.

I swear, it's not until this precise moment that I realise what I'm going to do next.

I've never bog-washed someone before, and all I can say is, if the mask of sanity was going to fall sometime, it was going to be because of someone like Marvin.

It took till my 28th year on this green globe to pop my cherry in the bog-washing department, but I can declare with some pleasure, Marvin was the ideal candidate (though I think events took him a little by surprise).

Duncan's Announcement

As I exit the Gents, Marvin dazed and confused and wet, lying on the grey tiled floor half in and half out of a cubicle with one shoe lace still undone, I realise I don't feel in the slightest bit guilty or ashamed. I should have tried flushing Marvin away long ago.

In reception, everyone is gathered and as Duncan takes to his podium, the room is quiet but excitable, most minds elsewhere, ready to hot foot it home and begin their Yule.

"… it has been an excellent year for SDB… I am very proud of what we've achieved and how far we've come… I am very proud to be able to work with all of you and I am very excited when I think of the greatness we can achieve in the next Millennium…"

I stand at the back of the assembly, look out onto the street as present-laden pedestrians totter past and cars hoot and stagger. I only half listen to Duncan as I dry my once more wet hands on my wool trousers.

"…I wish you all a very restful Christmas but before we race away I would like to single out a few folk particularly for their outstanding performances this year. These are the Young Blood of tomorrow, who will help represent SDB and lead our industry with award-winning work for our many and growing clients… Kristen McCoy is being promoted to… Geoff Wilcox promoted to… Martin Applewood to… and finally, the youngest ever appointment to the Board… Sam Grant. I would like each of you to join me up here and I'd ask the rest of you to applaud mightily."

Although I hear the applause, it grows quickly faint as I make my way from the back of the room, the sliding doors parting as I step on to the street, never once looking back.

The Gift of Giving

Airports are odd environs at the most normal of times, what with all the buzz of departure and the anticipation of arrival. On Christmas Eve, airports are odder still.

Heathrow's terminal 1 is full of commotion, travellers buying last minute Duty Free while trying not to dwell that before too long, they'll be more than a mile off the ground. I'm sure a few are thinking that no one deserves to be part of an air disaster on Christmas Eve. I myself am not the happiest camper at 39 thousand feet. I can explain to you the physics of jet flight, but still I don't understand how those steel birds don't just drop from the heavens.

It dawns on me as I enter the Duty Free Lounge; I haven't bought any bloody presents. The task expands or contracts to the time available, I remind myself. I also want to grab a few drinks before I take to the friendly skies.

My retail dilemmas are resolved inside of twenty-five minutes. In that time, I've spent over £500, which I tell myself is reckless. A litre bottle of Jack Daniels and a couple of Hackett shirts for my Old Man, a Hermès scarf and gloves for my Mum, various biscuits, chocolates, shortbreads and jams from Fortnum & Mason for Granny. Task complete, I head to the oyster bar where I treat myself to a bottle of champagne.

"No, just the one glass," I explain to the girl tending bar.

I'm going to Barbados, I'm going to Barbados, I hum away like a goon, my single piece of carry-on luggage and my shopping bags at my feet, feeling of booze-fuelled good cheer, thinking what a peculiar few months it's been, thinking about Sarah The Girl I Once Knew, thinking about Ariel bronzing herself on South Beach in a Burberry two-piece, thinking about Marvin and my Career Suicide, wondering what I'll do with The Rest of My Life. All this thinking, I start feeling tired. I check my watch. 5:25pm. I was supposed to be airborne five minutes ago, but the plane's been delayed an hour.

The bar girl comes over to remove my ice bucket and empty bottle.

"Y'know, I think I'll have a second," I tell her with a smile

Saturday December 25th, 1999

Christmas Day Part 1.

2am GMT.

"Hi… Mum?"

"Darling, are you allowed to call from the plane?"

"Er… no."

"Then don't. You're supposed to be landing in an hour and a half."

"The plane was delayed an hour and a half."

"Oh, so you're landing in three hours?"

"If I was on the plane, then odds on I would be…"

"What was that?," asks Mum.

"… but I missed the plane," I explain.

"Are you alright?" Bless, she sounds worried.

"Yeah, I'm okay, I'm fine, I'm just a fuck-wit, that's all."

Really, I'd just closed my eyes for a minute.

I'd finished my champagne (okay, bottle Number Two), I'd hauled myself, hand luggage and gifts towards my gate, heard that there'd be a further thirty minute delay before boarding, taken a seat, thinking the shortest power nap would do me good.

I slept nearly seven hours.

I have no idea how either. I just know that a member of airport staff nudged me awake about 20 minutes ago. How is it I was left to sleep upright for seven hours without interruption, I do not know, but I'm very tempted to complain to someone.

On the phone I hear Dad's voice in the background, then hear Mum telling him I missed the flight.

I hear him chuckle. "Tell him he's a prat!," I hear Dad say.

"Tell Dad he's right," I say. "I'm sorry Mum that I'm not going to be with you three for Christmas."

"What about a later flight?," she asks.

"I'm on standby but it looks pretty hopeless."

"Really?"

"Yeah, I'm sorry. And tell Granny sorry too. Of course, I'll see you guys in just over a week. It was always a bit of a whirlwind trip anyway, me flying out to Barbados for Christmas, then back to London for New Years."

"What will you do?"

"I'll be fine, I might grab a Turkey sandwich here at the airport," I kid.

"Sam!," she warns.

"I'll give Jamie a call. I'll definitely be able to crash his place for lunch."

I pocket my phone thinking ho-bloody-ho and what shall I do now? I yawn, knowing full well that for bog-washing Marvin I'm back at the Karma Hotel, but wondering whether I can still get a room at the airport Ibis.

Christmas Day Part 2.

"Jamie, Sam."

"It's 7 o'clock Sam."

"Merry Christmas, mate."

'Yeah, you too – but why are you calling me?"

"I was wondering whether I could come over to your Mum's for lunch?"

I can hear the cogs in Jamie's head starting to turn.

"Sam, why aren't you in Barbados?"

"I missed the plane. "

On the end of the phone that isn't mine, the groggy sleep voice breaks into laughter.

I check out of the Ibis in Heathrow at 7:45am. Feeling pity for the pimply teenager on reception who's working Christmas Day, I thank her for my 5-hour stay and give her a large jar of Fortnum & Mason raspberry conserve.

I'd offered to take a taxi but Jamie said he was happy to take his Porsche for an early morning spin. I will give Jamie the bottle of Jack Daniels (though I have had a couple of snifters) and his Mum can have my Mum's Hermès scarf.

Absently, I flick shortbread crumbs from my shirt-front. Breathing cold December air and looking at a low pale sky, I find it easy to feel sorry for myself and I can't help but think: this is all a bit weird.

Death by Frisbee

I return to my Always Quiet flat after spending 3 days in Guildford with Jamie and his clan. The experience was considerably more enjoyable than I'd probably deserved – a blur of constant food and drink, charades, two rounds of golf and lots of sleep. Jamie's Mother Angela is a total homemaker and puts on quite a spread for Jamie and his three older sisters. Jamie's Mothers partner Keith (a real Colonel Blimp type) also helps out, making sure everyone's glass is at the very least half-full. Jamie's Dad has been dead twenty years, which is obviously very sad. Of some comedy is that even to this day, Jamie feels that he killed his Dad.

Like Jamie, Colin (Jamie's Dad) also worked in the City. He racked up the hours, raking in as many pennies as possible to provide for his family, and although not home as much as he wanted, when he was on the homestead he did all he could to be The Loving Father. No catch: Jamie's Dad was one of the good guys.

One very ordinary Summer evening, Jamie's Dad returns home from a high blood pressure day of money raking and before he can swing off his jacket, Jamie's at him to play Frisbee. Jamie's been practicing with his Frisbee all day, endless energy, his mother, his sisters, the nanny, all exhausted.

Seeing his kids face, Jamie's Dad relents and right off, Jamie's launching this round piece of red plastic to all four corners of the lawn, making his Dad stretch left, then right, making him run backwards and lurch forward. Jamie's really showing off, keen to impress his Dad, but at the same time impressed that his Dad's no mug with a Frisbee either.

Colin finally calls it a day, saying he wants to wash up before everyone gathers for supper. He ruffles his kid's sweaty hair and goes indoors.

When Angela calls Supper, everyone gathers, except for Colin (and of course Colonel Blimp, who wasn't at this time in the picture).

Angela serves up and asks Jamie, "Run upstairs and get your father."

Jamie darts up to his parent's room and there's Dad lying on the bed, his shirt part unbuttoned but otherwise still in his double cuff. He jumps on his Dad, but his Dad isn't moving;

Colin's sleeping The Big Sleep. Jamie can't tell, but his Dad's aorta is critically no longer plumbed as it should.

To this day, Jamie is convinced that if he'd only thrown his Frisbee straight, rather than making his Old Man stretch so much, then it would be Colin and not Keith on drinks duties.

To torture himself further, Jamie still has the Frisbee and he gets it out every Christmas.

Doomsday Angst

"So how's the tan?," asks Tam. "I can't believe how clear the line is!"

"Where are you?," I say.

"Back up in town."

"In that case, the line's clear because you're about 4 miles away."

"You're back already?"

"I never left. I missed my plane, spent Christmas with Jamie at his Mum's."

"Whoops," she says with more than a chuckle.

"You can say that again."

"Listen," says Tam, all business. "Reason for the call, I need to confirm New Year's numbers. As you know, plan is to meet at David's offices between 9 and 10. I need to know, does Jamie want to bring that pole dancer he's seeing?"

"I'll let you know," I say, suddenly feeling a might glum as I look in the mirror, checking the Barbadian tan I don't have.

"Hey, don't be down. At least you can read my latest effort and last article of the century, out today."

"Whoopee," I manage.

I wander down to Notting Hill Gate. The sky is quarry

grey, with same-colour clouds scudding by and a chill more than sufficient to require hat and scarf. Not having either, I nip quickly into GAP, their sale already on, and buy some wool-knit accessories. I imagine my Granny sipping rum and Dad playing golf, no winter rules necessary. Have I learned anything from this latest chapter of fuck-wittery?

More suitably togged, I buy a copy of *London Lights* from the newsstand, along with a copy of *Le Monde*, which I will only be able to half-decipher, and a copy of *USA Today*. I make these purchases purely because I can, because if I lived in The Painful Provinces, I like to imagine I'd be lucky to buy yesterday's news.

★

A Girl's Eye View

December 1999

> *It's been a year of Doomsday Angst, suggests Tamsin Baron-Flint, but now at last we can party like its 1999.*

The countdown is reaching the Zero Hour.

How do you feel?

Of course, there's always been a clock ticking somewhere, but right now, the digits have never looked more apocalyptic.

How do you feel?

I woke the other morning, in the final death throes of our concluding millennium to Chris Evans blending Breakfast radio with some light-hearted Doomsday schtick. Back in

March, with Oscar in each grip, Director James Cameron eulogized how he'd not only made the Biggest Movie Ever, but had illuminated society in microcosm. Metaphors were at work, we were told. *Nothing* is unsinkable.

Indeed, 1999 has been a year of much prophecy; a year when the crazies started sounding quite sane, when more folk than most have had more-than-usual diets of Fire & Brimstone.

We've watched the docs with the catchy titles like *"Apocalypse When?"* discuss Y2K bugs, read column inches asking, *"Are the Nukes Safe?"* Everyone seems to have enjoyed getting edgy, spinning out speculations like a demented gyroscope, getting in on the "End-of-the-World" routine, talking the stuff of cataclysmic prophecies. *From the sky belched great fires and into the rivers of the world, ran the blood of all Mankind…* yardy yardy yar.

Bertrand Russell, philosopher and author of *The Tightrope Men* remarked, "You may reasonably expect a man to walk a tightrope safely for ten minutes; it would be unreasonable to do so without accident for 200 years."

Yes, I do think it's reasonable to wonder what all those countdown clocks are counting down to and yes, feelings always turn jittery at a decade's end, never mind a Millennium's

Personally, I'd like to blame The 90's, the Decade That Wasn't.

If the 90's had been more defining, had stood for something, then we might not all now feel like we're blowing in the proverbial.

The last ten years had moments, *but it wasn't enough.* Brothers Oasis enjoyed a good chunk of fame, pub rock prospered along with manufactured pop, football came home, video game-geeking became cool, everyone read Bridget Jones' Diary, and the boy Williams entertained. Girl Power entered the Zeitgeist, the one that left joined the UN. We mourned the fairy tale death of a fairy tale Princess, blamed the media, then bought the commemorative supplements and for a week couldn't take our eyes from the TV. We started off with war in the Middle East, and will end wondering whether we'll bookend the decade in similar maybe grander fashion? Not much coherence, eh? The 90's: a decade with nothing clear to say; a decade probably more for worse than better?

But then I wonder: Maybe I'm being a little harsh on the 90's? With the US itching to put Star Wars satellites in the sky and trying to bankrupt the Ruskies through nuclear stockpiling, was the 80's any safer? Thing is, the Bi-polar world did at least make for a level field of play. Like Yin and Yang, each tribe *needed* the other, each ideology countered the other. Cold War allowed some fun game-play for the puppet masters but peace enough for the masses to sleep at night and plan for warm summer holidays.

The 90's haven't had the same luxury of balance. In a One Super Power World, there's a misguided sense that there can be winners and losers, with One no longer all you can score.

Now we have US Fighter pilots in the Persian Gulf just starving for their Top Gun moment, *"Of course we want to get in the action. This is our Super Bowl, Man!"* Just how smart are the people firing those Smart Bombs? We have an ailing Yeltsin warning of "mighty conflagrations," and Netanyahu just itching to make a contribution. There's all this sabre-rattling and diplomatic fencing, full of 11th hour resolutions and last minute stand-downs. Powder-keg geopolitics is getting to be a bore. A Big Showdown feels like it's coming.

I read somewhere once, that for managing the Cuba crisis and bringing the world back from the brink, the very least John F. Kennedy deserved was an affair with Marilyn Monroe.

I'll go along with that. And I haven't got much of a problem with the Leader of the Free World indulging in a little extra-marital ejaculation. What shits me up is that every time Slick-Willy starts feeling the prickly heat of impeachment, the missiles start flying. I'm not for plotting graphs - say "opinion polls" against "bloody casualties" - but Bill's timing is hardly discrete.

The *Evening Standard* ran with a headline last week, *"So, do we have a psychopath living in the White House?"* Should we be flabbergasted by what's going on in our world, just rather anxious, or both? It all feels *So Very 90's*.

Of course, it has always been easy to find things that merit worry. There will always be a Schmorgusbord of Shit & Derision. Kosova, Super-States, Fundamentalists, Chemical Terrorists, Melting Ice Caps, Melting Skies, Melting Currencies: maybe Doomsday Angst is just the latest addition to the buffet?

I will leave you with this:

I can't believe, won't believe, *refuse* to believe that the clock only counts down. I don't believe the writings on the wall, irrespective of the authors. Nostradamus can go fly, right along with his "Red Seas," and his "grey drizzled earth". Have you read that guys stuff? Don't.

We are the authors of *our* Time. We define whether we succeed or fail, whether we keep going or end, all at once. We build our own hope. We can have the bright, shiny future if we want it. We can live like Buck Rogers or Blade Runners, or we can all hold hands and swan dive into the abyss together.

The Millennium clocks are nearly spent, the countdown nearing its end. Before we make all we can of The Naughties, listen to Bon Jovi, and keep the faith and listen to Prince. I'll see you at the party.

Forever, 2 Fast 4 U,

Tam x

Another Yesterday Girl

I pick up the phone, dial Jamie's mobile.

"Jamie, I've just heard from Tam. She needs numbers for New Years. Do you want to bring Chloe, or are you flying solo?"

"Chloe's history," he says flatly.

"Oh?"

A pause, where I presume he's thinking how to frame it.

"She's taken to screwing one of her lecturers."

"But that's such a cliché!"

"I know, it's probably how she got the idea."

"Who?," I ask.

"A lipstick lesbian who teaches Feminism on her course. Chloe confessed it all to me last night, said they just clicked after this dyke read her first essay.

"I said: *I* wrote the fucking thing, not you. Chloe said that wasn't the point and because I have a dick, I can never understand. Hell, I understand more about her course than she does."

"Are you okay?"

"Fine. I asked for all the explicit details, asked what was it like when they started touching; were they very physical together?"

"And?"

"She said she didn't want to torture me with the details. I begged her to torture all she wanted, and that in fact I could be open minded if she wanted to involve another woman in our relationship."

"How very progressive of you."

"She said she was a one woman girl and that we were over. It's a warning to us all: sexually adventurous birds can too easily turn sexually androgynous."

"How do you feel?"

"Used... dirty."

"So not too bad then?"

"Like I said, really, I'm fine, and I don't need a plus one."

Friday, December 31st, 1999

Nearing the Zero Hour

So this is supposed to be It, The Big Party, with everyone out to witness the end of the world as we know it. Do I feel fine? I just feel oiled, doing my best to Act Charming & Focus as the three of us arrive riverside.

Time: 10:01pm.

Bringing three bottles of vintage bubbly (Dom Perignon, the 1990), Jamie came over to my flat at midday, Sean soon after that (bringing lager and of all things, absinthe). The three of us together, it was like The Old Days. The Dom Perignon proved to me, that contrary to Tam's opinion, the 90's haven't been a completely wasted decade.

After several drinks, Jamie announced he had something to tell us... but then he didn't. Sean said he too had something to say... then said it could wait till later. Tam phoned to confirm a meeting time of between 9 and 10pm, and that she had something Very Important to tell me. Then she hung up. I have nothing of anything much to tell anyone, though randomly I was very tempted late afternoon to call Sarah on her mobile. I resisted the temptation and instead deleted her number from the SIM card.

★

David's law firm is located on the river, north shore, and all three floors have been turned into a party venue. The views are remarkable, a Vast Sea of People on the streets, millions teeming and whooping and drinking and waiting as the minutes peel away. Serving as backdrop: the familiar Oxo tower stands on the opposing bank, with Blackfriars bridge arching across the Thames and there for everyone to see, the *Express's* Countdown Clock reading a single solitary 1.

"Hey gorgeous!"

I find Tam by a window on the third floor, savouring the view. David stands beside her.

"I haven't seen your Father in ages," I say, turning to David. "How long has it been?"

"Always nice to see you too Sam," he says. "How's Sarah?"

Harsh dart, but well-flighted by the Old Bastard.

I offer, "I was just going the bar. Say David, can I get you a mineral water?"

Tam cuts in: "Alpha Boys, that's quite enough. Now play nicely."

There is a brief pause. I grab from a passing tray of drinks.

"Your article, I liked it," I say, changing the subject and showing I can be a grown-up. "Though your One Woman Crusade has definitely assumed a heavier tone?"

"Maybe there's a reason for that."

"Oh yes? Is this the something Very Important you eluded to earlier?"

"Now's as good a time," she says, stealing a quick sideways glance at David.

"Proceed," I tell her, feeling suddenly uncomfortable, like

a spectre has taken residence on my shoulder.

"Sam," she says, smiling with a ton of teeth, "I'm pregnant."

Like one of those Loony Tune characters, my mouth drops to somewhere just beyond my suede slip-ons. David just stands there, sipping his Evian, looking ten feet tall.

★

"Jamie, what were you going to say earlier?"

"Ah yes, my news. Bad news…"

"Of course, just what I need."

"…and some okay news."

"Hit me with the bad," I sigh.

"Put it this way," he says. "I'm considering early retirement on a small balmy island many miles from a balance sheet."

"How's that bad?"

"I have little choice. As predicted: I'm out of a job. I got canned…"

"Oh. Shit. I'm sorry to hear it. When?"

"Yesterday."

"Jamie, that's really rough."

"But I did get my Christmas bonus and my pay-off wasn't too shabby."

I take a half full bottle of Moët from the side and top up his glass, then mine.

"To a New Year and a lot of golf," I toast.

We drain our full flutes and then look out onto a London I've never seen before. So so many people.

"What?," he asks. "You don't want to hear my okay news?"

"I thought your bonus and pay-off was the good news."

"Remember mentioning that summer home in the Caymans? Well, here's the deposit."

From his jeans back-pocket, he pulls out and hands me a cheque.

"This is *your* good news," he tells me. "I traded all our shares this morning, closed the account. There's your five grand investment back, plus dividend."

"Jamie, you're joking, right?"

"In the final reckoning, we did awfully well."

"This cheque is real?," I say, my head swimming.

"Yes mate," he says, grinning from ear to ear, chinking my glass with his. "We did awfully fucking well."

★

"Not long now," says Sean.

I just stare at my cheque. Why? I know I don't deserve this.

"Sam," adds Sean, "everything okay?"

"He's fine," assures Jamie.

"I've just heard Jamie's news," I say, looking at Sean. "What's yours?"

Sean grins, takes a breath, grins again. "*Working Title*. Fucking. *Working. Title!*," he says categorically, like he just cracked the Enigma code.

"What about them? They passed on your script."

"Yes, they did," he says, "but then I get a call from them, go in to talk to them, and..."

"And...?," asks Jamie.

"They've optioned it."

"Bloody hell!," I say.

"I need to re-work it."

Jamie asks, "Sean, how many re-drafts has Blood Cops gone through?"

"Well it's going to require a few more, but *Working Title*

have bought into the premise… though they see it as a Rom Com."

"They've bought into the premise," repeats Jamie, "but see Blood Cops… a story about Soulless Demon killers and End of World omens as… a Romantic Comedy?"

"Hey, I never said the next draft wasn't going to require some fancy footwork."

I look at Jamie, Jamie looks at me, together we both look at Sean.

"Sean, it's fucking tremendous news," I say. "I'm delighted for you, really."

★

My phone rings. Time: 11:00pm. The caller ID doesn't recognise the number.

"Hello?"

"Hi… it's me."

A girl's voice, but the line isn't great.

"Me, who?," I ask.

"Me, Sarah."

And even with all the booze running through them, my veins turn to ice.

"Hello? Sam?"

"Hi," I manage finally, without a stammer.

"I just wanted to wish you a Happy New Year."

"Thanks. "

"And to thank you for your letter."

"Right."

"I'm glad you agree with me."

"Agree?"

"That you now know I'm not The One."

"Oh, yeah, I know. I don't suppose you know who is?"

She laughs. "No. I just know I'm not her."

"Happy New Year Sarah."

"Good bye then Sam. And take care of yourself."

★

We drink and toast and drink, tell each other how great we are. Well done for being us. Congratulations, We Rock! This is all getting Very Heady. Jamie keeps topping up everyone's glass. Sean, having spilt his news, is now the Living Breathing Embodiment of Euphoria. Recognition: everything that he's been waiting for.

My mind is a slur; latest details move at a pace beyond my catch-up. Tam: with David's unborn child. Sarah: moved on, with Hans. Holly: with Jorgen. Sean: a recognised scriptwriter. Jamie: still Jamie, but now unemployed but brandishing a cheque, my cheque. My Life, all these people, these familiar souls in my orbit, and I can hardly fathom any of it.

★

"Pregnant!"

I confront Tam as she sips a mineral water. David is socialising elsewhere, these days drinking mineral water too.

"Amazing, isn't it?," says Tam.

"I can't believe it," I agree. I feel an anger bubbling. "That's it then. Your life's over, and your figure's going to be shot to pieces."

Tam looks like she hasn't heard right. "These are hardly the kind tender words I was hoping from you."

"Well congratulations. Welcome to a lifetime wiping runny noses and clearing up empty vodka bottles from behind the cornflakes. Kids, school fees, and a pot-belly. A clothes allowance, a litany of flirty aupairs you'll have to keep your eye on and a mistress or two you'll have to pretend doesn't exist. Congratulations for opting to be like everybody else, like every other sucker. A life where every day you want out but everyday traps and takes you deeper and where all you want is anything else."

"My, that was quite a speech!"

She stares back at me, eyes hurt.

Then I kiss her, forcibly on the lips. She doesn't flinch, but there's nothing there, the kiss a Dead Thing, and I can almost hear myself wail inside. We pull apart and her look is all sympathy and worldly emotion.

"Never was a kiss more out of date," I say.

"Sam," she sighs. "About eight years too late."

★

"Where are you going?"

"I'm leaving," I say.

"You're drunk," says Jamie, "you're not leaving."

He takes a firm hold of my arm.

"Yes, I am."

I pull free of his grip and bolt down the stairs, out of the building and onto the street, at once becoming part of a swirling storm of people. Everything is a speeding carousel, so many faces, features morphing as faces change, so much noise, so many shouts and cries, here, there, everywhere, the Petri Dish that is Planet Earth. I elbow and push and thrust my way through the crowds, moving towards Blackfriars bridge. I don't know how long it takes, but I get to where I want to go.

The Bridge

I'm at the railing edge, looking out over this edge of reason, looking down into the dark murky waters, staring into the Infinite Abyss. They say the Thames is one of the cleanest urban rivers in the world, allegedly containing more than a hundred different species of fish.

What am I doing? I try to breathe, but can't. How often lately, I've tried to breathe. When was I last really able to fill my lungs? For months now, I've been living without breathing.

What the fuck am I thinking?

"It's the only way," I hear myself say. "Something baptismal."

Many a toxin to blame for the lack of reason or rhyme, my mind races in no sane direction. You have to face The Monster, if possible take him down; everyone finally eye-balls destiny, has to confront the Abyss.

I think of Holmes and Moriarty, meeting their maker, plunging together over the Reichenbach Falls. Yes, Holmes faced his Monster. He went out in style.

The Final Countdown has begun. I hear people yell and scream and wail and whoop, *so much* Human Energy.

Ten… Nine… Eight… Seven…

I jump up onto the railing, an audience of millions around me, feeling connected to everyone. Me: the Grand Conductor of the Great Tumult.

Six… Five… Four…

I lift my arms out to the side, giving it drama, like that statue of Christ enjoying the view over all Rio de Janeiro.

Three… Two…

Then: a moment of clarity. I get sane, tell myself: Get the fuck down. What are you doing, you loser freak? I do the best thing I could do. I listen to The Sensible Voice, bending down to grab the rail and hop back to safety.

One!

A New Millennium and...

...even easier than falling down the gap, I slip.

Oh my, these goddamn loafers that I love. From nowhere, I think of Duncan, that people who wear suede shoes never make a success of themselves. Then, as my slip becomes a slide, I think of my Dad's voice down a phone line, "Tell him he's a prat!" Yes Yoda, right again.

I couldn't quite say what happens next, but I know...

I'm falling.

Oh shit, I'm *falling*, honest to God, and although I know I won't be falling for long, I just have time to think, *Yes, what a prat! I can't believe you just did that?*, and then I hit the water, and straight away, of course, I'm under.

For whatever reason, I don't panic and I don't fight it. It's cold and quite obviously rather wet, and I at once feel the cruel embrace of the current pulling me down and spinning me, like a gator taking me in a death roll, but still I don't fight it.

I don't for a while do anything.

Am I upside down or right ways up? When I open my eyes everything is the purest black, absolutely no evidence of fish so far as I can make out, and even my eye balls can feel that the water is so cold, impossibly cold, who would have guessed it so cold.

Black and silent, that's what there is down here. Lots of Nothing, here in the abyss.

Then, I feel myself rising and in the following moment, I break the surface of the Thames, and I can see all the lights, an explosion of fireworks and all the people, all that Life. Such remarkably different worlds: one above the waterline and a whole different deal below it.

Deciding which world to be a part of is at once very very easy.

And now I'm making like a tri-athlete on speed, cutting through the brown silty water, kicking like the Reaper himself is nipping at my heels. I'm swallowing water, but for the first time in a long time, really sucking in air too, and the river wall is only getting closer. Thank Christ!

And then I'm at the bank, and people are stretching over the side of the wall, offering their hands, grabbing my clothes, pulling me from the drink, pulling me back, saving me from myself, saving me from my date with the never-ending abyss. The water line is mercifully high tonight. How many people, I wonder, fall into the abyss, then get pulled out?

I lean against the concrete wall of the riverbank, breathing heavily.

"Fucksake mate, are you alright?"

I'm shivering, numb with cold, feeling at a distance from what's just happened to me.

"Yeah, I'm cool," I say, still gulping air. "Thanks for the hand."

"This bloke was the muscle."

I look first at the guy, this Ordinary Joe, then at the Man Mountain next to him.

"I don't believe it!," I blurt. "Eric?"

Neck Tendons beams at me with that Big Beaming Grin of his.

"You're not a hallucination are you Eric?"

"No," confirms Eric, "but you're a lucky bastard, Sam. I thought I recognised you up there on the bridge. I saw you fall. I was half-tempted to leave you to it."

"I'm glad you didn't," I say, then at a tangent, "Did you know Sarah's getting married?"

"Hans."

"That's right."

"Sarah and I keep in touch."

I stand there, dripping wet, Eric looking me up and down.

"First thing I'd think about is a change of clothes". He turns to go.

"Eric," I quickly ask, "How much for the champagne?"

"What?"

"Your champagne?"

"Sam, you're mad."

"I have just jumped in the Thames, so yes, probably."

"Sam, get your own champagne."

"Listen. I'm alive, and I want to celebrate, so what say I trade you my watch for your bottle of Veuve? This watch," I explain forcing my teeth not to chatter, springing the strap and holding it up to Eric's face "is an antique Rolex Submariner, 1965… like the one Sean Connery wore in *Thunderball*, released that same year. I'm not so mad to assure you you're getting a *very* good deal."

Eric considers a moment, looks away at the tall red head I've just twigged he's with.

He gives me the bottle, and I hand him my watch.

"Dry clothes and maybe a jab," he suggests, before disappearing into the crowd.

Coincidence, Man, life is built on coincidence. I consider the bottle for a moment, then pop the cork, watching it arc out into the middle of the Thames. I take a swig from the bottle, some revellers still eyeing me with great suspicion.

"You utter twat!"

Jamie stands in front of me, marvelling, not looking even slightly concerned for my well-being. Behind him comes Tam, then Sean.

"Happy New Year!," I announce with great theatre, arms outstretched. I smirk at the three of them, like a toddler who's just learned a new naughty word. From nowhere, Tam slaps me across the face, then throws her arms round me, hugging tight.

"You really are one daft prick!," agrees Sean.

"Here," I say, handing him the bottle of bubbly, then, "I know – I always have been."

Happier, Ever After...

Now I'm one of Them; a *Profiteer* amongst the dot.com crusaders and web warriors. I'm one of the Early Doors Internet victors. I got in on the thing that my generation was invited to get in on. In cyberspace, turns out I was riding a gravy train. By no more than fluke and Matey advice, I've made a fist full of cashola, the easy way. By pitching it blindly, randomly, into what it turns out was The Next Big Thing. I gave Jamie 5 grand, I pretty much forgot about it, and two years and one month later, he gave me 106 grand back. Now that's an okay deal. That's 101k profit. 101 - Not such a cheerful number for Winston Smith, but pretty darned okay for Samuel Grant. £101k should keep me in Smarties for a while

So it's lucky ol' me, for all sorts of reasons.

And now I'm more confused than ever.

I get caught in a lucky-son-of-a-bitch windfall, and I have to think, *Why?* Just like everyone else, I'm asking questions and trying to get by without them. I should find *getting by* easier, 101 thousand times easier, and while I can't go out shopping for desert islands, things could be worse, but this wasn't the Happy Ending I had in mind.

EPILOGUE

JANUARY

Monday, January 3rd, 2000

Just Another New Year

Well, we made it. All of us, pretty much. In a gathering of nearly 3 million people, celebrating the biggest non-fatal fire-in-the-sky in history, I read in the paper that only 2 revellers didn't make it home. One heart attack, one Thames drowning. I shiver, knowing I could have easily added to the stats.

I remember it all. Big Ben struck Midnight and I took a bath, but everything else went swimmingly. The Countdown Clocks fused, the night sky erupted in great Technicolor blossoms of light, and the Bug didn't bite. The Russian nukes weren't triggered, Boeings didn't fall from the heavens and ET didn't rock up in the Mother Ship.

A New Year; a New Century. There were hugs, kisses, cheers, craned necks and plenty of smiles. People were living the moment. A relief, a joy, a fleeting optimism; maybe there was a case for hope after all, maybe people would now stop using the word "Millennium" quite so much?

January 3, 2000. Only a Monday, but it rings in the ear like a Starship Captain's Star-date. *"Captain's log, Entry One…"* Pause, for effect. (Like T.J. Hooker used to, back when he was lost in space.) Then: *"Millennial moment gave way to the usual traumas, hangover, melancholy, realisation. A New Dawn perhaps but in a still-so-familiar world. The old ways still much in evidence. The old wants the same as ever. A tube ride, a grey sky, the daily trek… toil… grind. The need to escape; an obligation not to."*

I have to ask the question: What's changed? I scan my fellow journeymen. Everyone just looks that bit fatter or slacker. Tube faces show little joy. They internalise The Woe. Back to it. Must. Keep. Going.

I can hear their thoughts. Just how tricky is embezzlement? How much would a tropical island really cost? Some say, spending a lifetime on a beach would become quickly dull. I'm not convinced. The first thing I'm guessing a good many do when they get into work, ask for their holiday form.

Of course, I am not returning to SDB. I've parted ways with that Good Time Gang. Marvin and Duncan had a chat, and then Duncan put in a call to me. All very discreet, I get two months gross pay and I don't grace the office ever again.

This, a New Millennium, but as Bob Geldof once asked, *"Is that it?"*

Kosova is still a powder keg craving a flame, the Middle Eastern Problem is no less problematic, and the Russians are kicking three bells of shit out of Chechnya. No one's quite sure where Chechnya is, and it looks like soon there won't be any of it left to not know about. *USA Today* headlined yesterday with "A New Millennium, a New Russia, an Old Threat". The editorial was not upbeat. *The Daily Mail* some days earlier covered the stepping down of World Leader & Vodka Lush Boris Yeltsin and reported that New Guy Vladimir Putin had received hand-over notes that were mostly illegible. Conservative, detached home-owning Middle Englanders read that Putin was something of a "grey hawk," wearer of grey suits, believer in bureaucracy, a Russian John Major almost, but also ex-KGB with gimlet eyes and a poker face. A relief, Middle England was getting its steady propaganda fix.

What time is it? I look at my wrist. No wristwatch. I think that little trade with Eric could have been a little rash, but what's done is done.

I exit at Blackfriars station, taking the steps two at a time, racing past commuters who can't help but drag their feet. Topside, the station exit is still decorated with New Years Eve detritus, swept absently into lonely corners, broken bottles, some lager, some Boli, more than a few well torn party hats. Overhead, London is wrapped. The air: a damp blanket of mist and a light rain.

The skeleton of the Countdown Clock still stands. No more numbers and four days obsolete, it appears like a broken toy ready for donation. Job done, party over.

I miss that clock already.

Good Advice

We meet at Gabriel's Wharf, at a coffee stop with views of the river. The river, I know it so well.

"How are you feeling?"

"I should be asking you," I tell her.

"I'm okay. Morning sickness, nausea that passes when I eat – which is slightly bizarre – otherwise, I think I'm going to be a good breeder."

"That's good. You know, I think it's the most remarkable thing a human being can do – create life, make another human being."

"And virtually everyone has what it takes to do it," she says simply.

A steady flow of folk pass along Southbank; joggers, pushchairs, tourists, everyone looking Really Quite Happy, wrapped up against the January chill, their breath making plumes.

"Funny," I say. "All I ever wanted to do was something remarkable, have a more interesting life story, lead a life less ordinary... but that's maybe what everyone ordinary wants?"

"Sam, you're far from ordinary," Tam assures me. "I wouldn't worry, your life story is far from a cliché."

I smile. Vladimir Propp, only 31 naratemes? Hell, what did he know?

She smiles, holds her small bucket of coffee with both hands, warming her palms.

"You know, I think I'll be okay now," I say.

"You know what Sam, I believe you will be." Then after a beat, "Just remember to breathe."

★

APPENDIX

The LoveFilm Movie Collection:

While Samuel Grant isn't strictly real, that hardly stops him loving movies or having his nostalgic favourites.

For the cinematic best of 1998 and 1999, go to *www.lovefilm.com/samuelgrant,* or scan the QR Code with your smartphone, to automatically access *Samuel Grant's Movie Collection*.

And if you're not currently a LOVEFiLM member, the following code: **AMAP1** entitles you to a 30-day free trial and a £15 Amazon voucher (redeemable after the first payment). Enjoy.

The Spotify Playlist:

If you're going to party like it's 1999, you need a backing track.

Go to *http://spoti.fi/samuelgrant*, or scan the QR Code with your smartphone, for *Samuel Grant's Playlist* to automatically open in your Spotify player.

And if you don't yet have Spotify, go visit **www.spotify.com**.